The Ancients and The Call

Books by Cheryl Lafferty Eckl

Personal Growth & Transformation

A Beautiful Death:
Keeping the Promise of Love

A Beautiful Grief:
Reflections on Letting Go

The LIGHT Process:
Living on the Razor's Edge of Change

Wise Inner Counselor Books
Reflections on Being Your True Self in Any Situation
Reflections on Doing Your Great Work in Any Occupation
Reflections on Ineffable Love: from loss through grief to joy

Poetry for Inspiration & Beauty

Poetics of Soul & Fire

Bridge to the Otherworld

Idylls from the Garden of Spiritual Delights & Healing

Sparks of Celtic Mystery:
soul poems from Éire

A Beautiful Joy: Reunion with the Beloved
Through Transfiguring Love

Twin Flames Romance Novels

The Weaving:
A Novel of Twin Flames Through Time

Twin Flames of Éire Trilogy
The Ancients and The Call
The Water and The Flame
The Mystics and The Mystery

The Ancients and The Call

Twin Flames of Éire Trilogy - Book One

Cheryl Lafferty Eckl

FLYING CRANE PRESS

To our Francis,
with gratitude for the call

Beckoning from the Unknown,
we feel it—
a future from the past,
a glimmering sense of purpose,
oneness forever sealed
in the heart of our ancient calling.

Dear Reader,

One of the fascinating aspects of being a *seanchaí*—that's the Irish word for storyteller—is the way that characters reveal themselves when the author listens to what they have to say.

That happened to me recently. Sarah and Kevin have lived in my imagination for several years, but when I paid them renewed attention, they let me know that their story was not complete.

Although they reached a point of profound insight and reconciliation in *The Weaving: A Novel of Twin Flames Through Time*, that experience of unity was only the beginning of a grand adventure that continues here in *The Ancients and The Call*.

As these twin flames (two souls created as one in the beginning) are drawn into the group known as the Friends of Ancient Wisdom, they grapple with age-old questions asked by all who walk the pilgrim's path to eternity: *Who was I in a past life? Who am I now? Who or what am I meant to become? What is my life's purpose, and how am I to accomplish it?*

For Kevin and Sarah, those questions are vital because they remember their past embodiment as the first-century Irish druids, Ah-Lahn and Alana, who, in those days, had mystical powers.

Now, in the twenty-first century, they are called by the Ascended Master Saint Germain—who clearly desired a major voice in the *Twin Flames of Éire Trilogy*—to merge their present awareness with their past attainment on behalf of an enlightened future for themselves and for other twin souls who are depending on them for help in achieving their own reunion.

Will Sarah and Kevin succeed? Will they overcome the forces that oppose the unity of twin flames? This is the story they wish to share.

Come sit with me a while, and I will tell you what I learned from these characters when I listened with a *seanchaí's* ear.

Beannachtaí duit (blessings to you),
Cheryl Lafferty Eckl

P.S. You will find a glossary and Irish language pronunciation guide at the back of the book, plus a few notes about the Ancients.

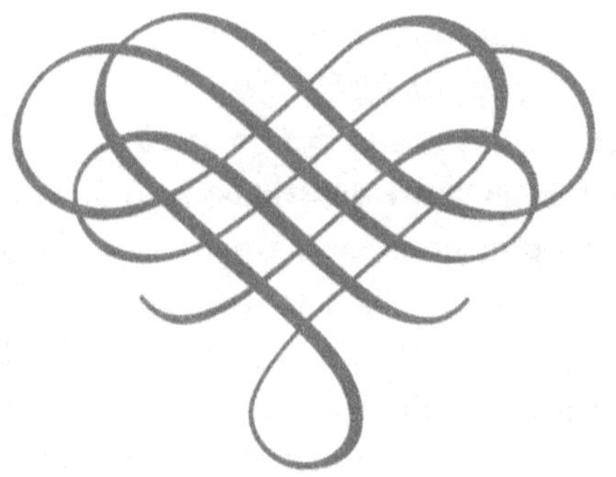

Prologue

Dark, dank clouds heavy with rain hung over Kevin's head as he dragged his body through a forbidding forest. A rank, moldy smell filled the atmosphere as if the air itself were decaying.

The path twisted and narrowed as each desperate step carried him further into an ominous swamp.

Slippery vines wound around his ankles.

Sharp tree branches grabbed at his arms in a savage attempt to slow his pace.

His feet were molasses-bound, bogging him down in the sticky goo of a future that would suck him under if he yielded to its deadly pull.

At the same time, an invigorating inner force was steadily urging him toward a rendezvous, a promise as yet unfulfilled.

Ahead lay an alternate future that could draw him out of this dark morass into a hopeful, light-filled unknown that, though it guaranteed no certainty, did offer escape.

Here was a risk he had to take—but how?

Exhaustion threatened to overwhelm him. His legs ached and his lungs burned.

Then—miraculously—through half-closed eyes, he spied an abandoned truck up ahead. If he could start it, perhaps he could reach the rendezvous on time.

Willing himself forward, Kevin wrenched open the driver's side door and slid behind the wheel.

Oddly, the engine was already running. All he had to do was put the truck in DRIVE and gun it. He'd be free in an instant.

But where was the gear shift? Why was there no gas pedal? And why wouldn't the steering wheel turn?

Panic gripped the man's robust, thirty-five-year-old body as the engine's vibration grew stronger, louder, and more insistent that he move. Now!

One

Ugh! Sprite! Stop!" grunted Kevin, waking to the intensity of two bright emerald eyes peering into his face. His wife's black mini-panther kitten was sitting on his chest, purring vigorously, and licking him with her raspy little pink tongue.

At Kevin's exclamation, Hero, the wire-haired pup who was still growing into his enormous grey and white feet, jumped up on the bed, whining and dancing on the covers. He nosed Sprite out of the way and began slurping his owner's face and hands.

"Okay! Okay! I'm awake!" Kevin groaned, pushing back fifty pounds of bouncy canine so he could sit up. Rubbing his blue-green eyes, he looked at the bedside clock. 6:00 a.m. He'd been asleep for only a couple of hours. However, his four-legged housemates held tenaciously to their own schedule. Even on a Saturday, they insisted that 6:00 a.m. meant doggie business in the backyard for Hero and breakfast for everybody.

Clearly, no rest for a sleepless man. That was weird because his wife was the one who sometimes had insomnia. Where was Sarah? Her side of the bed was empty.

Oh, right, he remembered as he shuffled into the kitchen, let the dog out, put on a pot of strong coffee, and fed the cat. His wife had taken a morning flight to Boston yesterday to visit her family in Braintree, narrowly missing the early November snowstorm that had howled like a banshee across New York on its way to Massachusetts.

Good thing Sarah was going to be away for a few days, Kevin said to himself. He needed to get his head straight.

Hero did his doggie duty faster than usual and bounded back into the house with a happy "Woof!"—all wagging tail and clumsy feet that sent his empty metal food dish clattering across the tile floor.

Sprite, who was enjoying her fancy canned tuna on the counter, looked up disdainfully and rolled her eyes at Kevin as he filled the dog's dish and set it down on the floor before the eager hound.

"Yeah, I know. Hero's a goofball. But you don't fool me. I know you two snuggle at night when the wind is up."

Talking to his animals nudged further back in Kevin's mind the troubling images that had kept him awake until 3:00 a.m. and then given him nightmares. But as soon as he sat at the kitchen table to drink his black coffee and eat a bowl of cold cereal, the memory of his experience in the swamp of mediocrity came rushing back.

He tried reading the sports page in the morning paper, but his mind was too full of "what ifs."

"I need a plan," he said to Sprite and Hero as he took a large swallow of coffee. "At least I've got a few days to come up with something before Sarah gets home."

He had declined his wife's invitation to accompany her to Braintree. He liked her family, but they could be a noisy bunch, and right now he needed quiet. Only a few months earlier, Sarah would have pushed him to go with her, even though she knew he didn't always enjoy the Callahan family's exuberance.

When she hadn't insisted this time, he'd been a bit surprised. Could she tell he needed a break? Or did she need one, too?

Although they'd reconciled after their big blowup last summer, now, in early November, signs of strain were once more troubling the harmony they had promised each other after returning from Ireland.

Kevin grimaced at the memory of July's emotional separation. After nearly a year of frequent misunderstandings and arguments, Sarah had angrily packed herself off to a writer's retreat near Dublin—with no promise of returning home to her husband.

One night, while caught up in the Emerald Isle's liminal atmosphere, she had dreamed of past lives that she and Kevin had shared— in first-century Ireland as the druids Ah-Lahn and Alana, on the continent of Atlantis before the flood, in Egypt at the time of the pharaohs, and in ancient Greece during the fifth century BC.

The magic had not been confined to Sarah's dream. While she was in Ireland, Kevin was experiencing similar recollections in their home on Long Island. Vivid memories of the same past embodiments had kindled in his mind when he'd slipped into a state of lucid dreaming.

He had never encountered phenomena like these life reviews. He didn't know what to do with them until he was shown a prophecy that he and his wife could permanently lose their opportunity to stay together if they did not do the deep, personal, inner work necessary to resolve the antagonisms that had separated them in many former lives.

Spurred by this dire possibility, he had rushed to Ireland where he poured out his heart to Sarah—the woman he couldn't live without.

They were twin flames, he had passionately reminded her—souls created together in the beginning as two halves of the same whole. They belonged to each other as they could belong to no one else.

Fortunately, his fervor had sparked Sarah's waking memory of all she had dreamed, and the truth of their shared destiny had moved her to reconcile with him.

He had stayed with her through the end of her writing retreat, and they had come back home to Long Island where they once more relished their time as a couple—walking on the beach, laughing at their animals' antics, finding renewed affection in one another's arms.

Throughout most of the summer, these reembodied druids had held each other even more fervently than in the first days of their marriage. Because now they knew that love could be lost. The full horror of that possibility had left its imprint on them, lest either man or woman should stumble again.

Unfortunately, in recent weeks, an obstacle to their oneness had resurfaced.

When they'd returned from Ireland, they had agreed that Sarah would resign from her position as a marketing writer for prominent Manhattan politician A. B. Ryan so she could work full time on the novel she was inspired to write about their past embodiments.

That meant Kevin would be their only wage earner. A small price to pay for getting her away from A. B.'s negative influence, he thought as he put aside the newspaper and set his bowl of half-eaten cereal in the sink.

At the time, the arrangement had seemed like a good idea. But now Kevin was beginning to wonder if they'd made the right decision—not for Sarah, but for him.

She was thriving in her work as a novelist. "The chapters are just pouring out of me," she often exclaimed. "I'm amazed at how much I'm remembering about our past lives." And when she couldn't recall certain details of the lifetimes they had shared, Kevin often did.

He was glad to help her fulfill her dream of being a novelist—that is, as long as he didn't compare her enthusiasm for her work to his boredom with his.

He used to enjoy his job as manager of accounting at Nordemann Financial Services, the successful mid-size firm he had joined ten years ago. But now, after all he'd learned about who he used to be as the druid Ah-Lahn, his life was beginning to feel like the nightmare of life-sucking mediocrity whose image still lingered in his mind.

Exploring his lifetime as a powerful druid had been a revelation. In that embodiment he'd been a skilled master healer, a wise arbiter of the law, an inspired poet. In many ways, Ah-Lahn had out-pictured the inner genius of Kevin's True Self that nowadays he only occasionally tapped into.

"If I was so advanced in ages past, why am I still embodying?" he asked Sprite and Hero. "Did I commit some terrible error that caused me to backslide? Did I totally miss the mark in other lifetimes? Why am I so much *less* today than I was centuries ago?"

The animals offered their full attention, but no ready answer.

"A decline like that would keep anybody awake at night," Kevin grumbled as he padded into the bathroom and stood at the sink. He looked in the mirror and winced. The image that stared back at him was not a pretty one.

His dark brown hair needed a trim—a chore he'd been putting off along with several others that were just too much effort right now.

Yesterday's whiskers grizzled his chin, tempting him to let his beard grow for a couple of days.

Dark circles under his blue-green eyes told the story of last night's sleeplessness and of the gathering emotional storm he could feel near to breaking on the shores of his domestic life.

Kevin stood staring in the mirror for several seconds, wondering if he could live in his sweats until Sarah got home. Then Hero bumped open the bathroom door and Sprite jumped up on the sink with an inquisitive, "Meow?" that snapped him into action.

"Come on, MacCauley, you can do better than this," he admonished himself and stripped down for a shower. Once under the steamy hot spray, he automatically lathered up, shaved, and washed his hair. Finally feeling less like a fairytale troll, he toweled off and pulled on a clean pair of jeans and royal blue turtleneck sweater.

With a clearer head, Kevin decided to meditate—something he hadn't done for a while. He'd let his practice slip. Another behavior that wasn't like him.

He had always said that when he meditated, he knew who he was. Without that clarity, he'd been avoiding the conversation with Sarah that was becoming absolutely crucial to his own survival.

No more procrastination, he vowed. When she returned home from Braintree, they would talk about their future.

Kevin poured himself a second cup of coffee and carried it into the living room. If he could meditate anywhere in his house it would be here in this room that he and Sarah had redecorated to look like a quaint Irish cottage—ironically, he observed, a full year before their adventures on the Emerald Isle.

In the past, the coziness of this space had put him in touch with a wise inner part of himself. He hoped it would again. If he was going to avoid the stifling mediocrity that he felt closing in on him like a nightmare, he needed that internal stability.

Two

Kevin switched on the gas fireplace and yawned as he sank into his favorite leather chair. He stretched out his long legs and rested his slippered feet on the matching ottoman.

He could feel last night's lack of sleep trying to catch up with him, but he was determined not to doze off. On the other hand, Sprite and Hero were already curled up together on the cozy, oversized dog bed they shared by the fire.

Kevin sipped his coffee and gazed at the bright, gas-fed flames. He appreciated not having to chop logs or clean ashes from the grate, but he missed the earthy aroma of Ireland's turf fires that had warmed him body and soul last summer.

"The healing fires of home," Sarah had called them. Kevin agreed.

After several minutes he began to slip into a contemplative state. However, just as his mind was going deeper, he heard his voice of inner wisdom speak:

Open the Shakespeare. The big one.

"That's odd," he said aloud. But, glad for any clear direction, he got up from his chair and walked to the tall bookcase where he kept the hardbound volumes he rarely used. The annotated Shakespeare held pride of place on the top shelf with the other literary treasures Sarah had dubbed his "tomes."

As soon as Kevin pulled down the book, it fell open in his hands. His heart leapt at what he saw. Tucked inside the gold-tipped pages were many of the cards and notes that Sarah had given him in the early days of their relationship. He hadn't seen them for years. In fact, he didn't remember saving them.

Now he was curious to read what Sarah had written when their love was new. Before the burdens of workaday life had intervened. Before the heart-wrenching loss of two miscarriages had worn a hole in their togetherness. Before fear and doubt had precipitated their separation last summer.

A lump formed in Kevin's throat as he sat with the book on his lap and absorbed each expression of his wife's affection.

Here was the birthday card where she'd called their marriage her life's most precious gift. And the anniversary poem that had assured him they would stay in love forever:

> My heart sings when I am with you,
> when I feel the oneness of our souls
> and the purpose of our union.
> I love you from the very core of my being.
> I am honored by our life together.
> —For eternity, *Sarah*

As Kevin leafed through more pages, he discovered a picture he had taken of her beaming at him several days after their serendipitous meeting at a party neither had wanted to attend.

That's how she looks when she really sees me, he thought.

They'd been strolling through Central Park, their hearts rivaling October's shimmering golden leaves glow for glow. As they gleefully crunched along a leaf-strewn path that glistened with autumn's brightest crimsons, golds, and oranges, Sarah had turned to him and exclaimed, "I will love you forever, Kevin. I promise!"

"I promise you, Sarah!" he'd answered with new love's confidence.

Would they be able to keep those promises? Kevin wondered as he stared at the photo he tenderly held in his hand. And what about the vow he'd made to himself, before they'd met, to fulfill his potential in this lifetime? Had Sarah made a similar pledge to herself? How would these vows work together? Or would they?

Kevin gently returned his mementos to Shakespeare's safekeeping and instantly felt a rush of love for his wife spiral in and around him like a whirlwind. He wanted her there with him. His whole being longed to embrace her, to reinforce their spiritual oneness with the tenderness of human touch.

Sarah was his one true love. His soul's twin. The other half of his being, before whom all other human loves were as wisps of smoke—incapable of completing him as only she could do.

During their brief time together in Ireland they had rekindled the intimacy he now longed for, although she had demurred during the days she thought she might become pregnant. They didn't speak of it, but he understood and did not pressure her.

He was just grateful she was letting him touch her again. After her second miscarriage they had slept apart many nights. A double grief for both of them. An abyss neither would cross. He would not force, and she would not invite.

Now Kevin wondered—Did Sarah still feel the same depth of love she had expressed in their early days of marriage? He was certain she believed she did. Yet as soon as she'd immersed herself in writing her novel, a familiar wall had gone up. Not a thick one. Not one so dense as most people would notice.

But Kevin noticed.

Nowadays, Sarah was becoming secretive about the writing process. As if the book were her story alone and not theirs. If he asked questions, she pulled back. If he made too many suggestions or contradicted her recollection about a specific event, she got defensive.

Once again, it seemed that hers was a heart closed off. But closed off to what? he wondered.

Perhaps she was afraid of being hurt or abandoned. Countless scenes from the life reviews had painted their separations in devastating detail. Sometimes one of them was older and passed away sooner. But, more often, one of them had died young.

A sick feeling rippled through Kevin's gut at the memory of these sudden departures from this world. That kind of traumatic soul memory could certainly discourage a heart from opening all the way, he admitted. Even when your twin flame's face is the first one you see each morning.

And what am I afraid of? he asked himself.

Fear slithered around in his belly, looking for a place to hide. He spotted the movement and named the culprit. He wasn't afraid of being hurt, but of hurting. Of wounding the one he loved beyond words. He couldn't bear to think that in this life he might inflict more pain upon his darling Sarah.

What a pair they were, he mused. Dancing around love and fear, trying to avoid hurt and causing it just the same. Despite being eternally joined soul to soul, they couldn't seem to break the pattern of losing each other. Still, Sarah's anniversary poem affirmed there was purpose in their union.

"But what is that purpose? Have we ever really known? If not, how do we find it?" Kevin wondered aloud, as he settled back into his leather chair.

"What is our purpose? What is our purpose? What is our purpose?"

He repeated the words like a mantra and closed his eyes as a welcome warmth gathered in the center of his chest. His breathing slowed naturally. He could feel his heartbeat pulsing throughout his entire body—gently at first, then growing in intensity.

As his concentration deepened, the interior glow began to expand. His heart chakra was spinning like a wheel. The sensation became so strong that he couldn't move. Riveted to his chair, he felt the whirling within him accelerating faster and faster, until his form could no longer contain it.

His eyes flew open. Where moments before only blue and yellow flames had been ablaze in the living room fireplace, now dozens of lustrous, jewel-toned orbs were spiraling around each other like animated Christmas tree ornaments.

For an instant Kevin sat motionless, staring at the brilliantly lit globes. Then he heard it—the powerful inner voice that had guided his life reviews last summer.

Be alert, the voice commanded. *Pick an orb and step in.*

Kevin did not hesitate. While his physical form remained at peace, in his soul body he stood up from his chair and entered a luminous, crystal-pink sphere.

In an instant, a bridge that looked like a Milky Way made of clear crystals appeared before him, arcing from one side of a small lake to the other. Here was a gateway to the Otherworld. Its unspoken invitation that he should cross over was familiar and clear. He had sojourned here before.

Kevin made his way to the middle of the bridge and stopped to look over the side. He was not entirely surprised by what he saw mirrored back in the perfectly still water.

Here was an image of himself as the druid Ah-Lahn. He was dressed in a white linen robe woven with arcane symbols. The golden medallion that hung around his neck signified his office as *ceann-druí*, the chief druid he had been in those days of long ago.

Then he understood: *An Síoraí*, the Eternal One, was calling him to some purpose. A powerful inner knowing vibrated within him, even as Ah-Lahn's figure disappeared in the slight breeze that ruffled the lake's surface.

Eager to learn more, Kevin crossed the starry span.

As he stepped off the far side of the bridge, his heart quickened in anticipation of meeting Lady Master Nada, the powerful ascended being who had been coming to his soul's aid since the time of Atlantis some twelve thousand years earlier, when she was known as Nhada-lihn.

In those days he had served as a priest with his twin flame in the lady's Temple of the One Light. The fair-haired master had taught him many secrets of ancient wisdom that had elevated his own occult powers, though neither those abilities nor her intercession had been able to preserve his life from the treachery of an evil high priest.

Kevin had felt the Lady Master's goddess-like presence of the Divine Feminine many times in the ensuing thousands of years, and he looked forward to renewing that special relationship. But in this moment, it was not Lady Nada's ruby-cloaked form he saw before him.

Here, instead, was a resplendent male figure clad in the shimmering white robe, gold torc, and jeweled medallion that identified him as an exalted master druid—one who had ascended to *Tír na n'Óg*, Land of the Ever-Living.

Kevin stood, awe-struck by the presence of this masterful being. The brilliance of his aura was like the sun itself. His light brown hair glistened with golden highlights. His immaculately trimmed mustache and beard gave him a youthful appearance. Indeed, everything about his elegant, arrow-straight figure spoke of vitality and a sublime power that radiated mercy, grace, and generosity.

"Greetings, my son," said the Master with a gesture that Kevin recognized as one the ancient druids had used when greeting those of their community. His voice was warm and musical. His violet eyes sparkled. His sunbeam smile transmitted a radiance that flooded Kevin's entire being with joy.

"You may call me Saint Germain," he said in answer to the younger man's unspoken question. "I speak on behalf of *An Síoraí*, the Eternal One, as the voice of All-Consuming Love. Indeed, I tend that flame, which is in your heart, as it is in mine."

Kevin's eyes grew wide as the Master indicated his own chest. Three gleaming plumes of rose, sapphire, and sun-lit gold shimmered into view. They were in constant motion, intertwining and throwing off tiny sparks of light that seemed alive with an inner intelligence.

Saint Germain gracefully circled his wrists and the flames dissolved into an iridescent mist that lingered briefly, then vanished. A sense memory quickened in Kevin's own hands. He knew that move.

The Master read his thought and smiled, and then made a broad, sweeping gesture with his right arm.

Immediately, a million tiny rainbows flickered into view and began weaving around each other, creating strands of light that quickly coalesced into a spiral staircase of translucent, diamond-like substance that was even more beautiful than the one Kevin had just traversed.

He felt his soul drawn to join Saint Germain on the stairway. Anyone observing them might have thought they were druid brothers, so comfortable did they appear in each other's company.

Side by side, they rose up to realms of enlightened consciousness known only to the most advanced adepts, such as Ah-Lahn had been and which Kevin might yet become—again.

Three

Kevin had no idea how long or how far he traveled with Master Saint Germain. The instant he placed his feet on the spiral staircase, time ceased to be. Now all was light in a brilliance that was neither blinding nor hot. He was aware of movement, but only as one is aware of a vast ocean urging its waves to shore.

Questions that had troubled his mind evaporated in the aura of generous hospitality that emanated from Saint Germain's being. The Master's solicitude reminded him of the *céad míle fáilte*, the hundred thousand welcomes he had experienced during his visit to Ireland months earlier, multiplied another thousand-fold.

As the luminous staircase carried them higher, the Master began to speak, his voice exuding tones of such ethereal beauty as to set the very ethers to humming. Truly, thought Kevin, here is the spokesman for *An Síoraí*, the Eternal One.

I am Love.
Essence of the Divine.
Listen for my voices:
I am Lover and Beloved.
I speak as persons and distant forces.

May all who cherish connection
learn to understand the wisdom
of a graceful finish.

I am Love.
I will not leave you comfortless.

Saint Germain and Kevin stepped off the iridescent spiral onto a plateau whose soft, emerald-green grasses shimmered in the noonday sun under cloudless azure skies.

The two immediately proceeded toward what appeared to be an impregnable mountain of dark green and grey granite that rose straight up from the plateau about fifty yards ahead. They soon halted directly in front of a smooth rock face that Kevin observed was shot through with multicolored veins of crystal that glistened in the sun.

He instinctively stepped to the Master's right to make room for whatever might happen next. Immediately, Saint Germain cupped his upturned hands on arms slightly out-stretched at his sides—his intense focus now building a forcefield of scintillating energy around them both.

As they stood motionless, Kevin detected a sound like a single note held by a dozen bass violins. Or perhaps the deepest register in a choir. For now, hundreds of voices were intoning an OM within the mountain's farthest reaches.

The volume increased and more voices were added. Tone upon tone, they ascended the musical scale, filling in every harmonic, finally reaching the highest octaves with a crystal-pure clarity Kevin knew could come only from angelic choirs.

The earth itself—if some etheric earth this was—sang out. Rocks and trees and the grass beneath his feet resounded with the OM. Distant oceans and waterfalls joined in the chorus as all of cosmos resonated with the primal sound of creation.

Kevin shifted his gaze to observe his companion. Clearly visible through Saint Germain's garments were the tripartite plumes of fiery energy glimmering as they spiraled in the center of his form. The flames began to spin faster around each other, growing in size and accelerating until the Master's body was subsumed in a milky white radiance that reached out to the mountain.

A pinpoint of intense violet light appeared on the rock face. It quickly took on the form of an exquisite rosebud that began to rotate slowly, unfolding petal by petal as it turned, blooming within the stone. The expanding blossom grew brighter, taking on a deep purple color as it spun faster, melting away the surrounding granite.

The euphony of angelic voices reached an immense crescendo until they held a final ecstatic chord that shook the very firmament.

Suddenly, a portal flashed open in a shower of amethyst crystals. A pathway lined with violet-colored rose petals invited entry. Kevin and Saint Germain were drawn inside as if by some magnetic power, and the portal closed behind them.

The milky white radiance that had surrounded the Master's body dissolved. The visible plumes of spirit-fire resumed their normal size, then disappeared from Kevin's view. His own heart was still spinning and burning with a heat he thought might consume him on the spot.

He could have remained transfixed where he stood. However, Saint Germain turned away from where the portal had been and motioned for Kevin to follow him deeper into the interior. The entire structure was filled with a soft light and the fragrance of violets and roses.

What had first appeared as a pathway became a tunnel lined with faceted gemstones that led further into the mountain. On each facet was carved a unique, arcane symbol. Some Kevin recognized as Egyptian hieroglyphs. Others were the same Celtic designs he had seen on ancient ruins in Ireland and that were woven into Ah-Lahn's druid robe. Still others were strange to him.

As his eyes lingered on these foreign signs, the word *alchemy* came to him as a soundless sound. But what type of alchemy? he wondered.

The Master smiled at his companion and spoke cheerfully.

"Greater mysteries await us, my son. Place your full attention on your heart and follow the inner voice. Still your mind, put aside all questions, and trust that Love knows the best way forward in any situation."

Kevin did as the Master bade him and instantly felt his being pervaded by a calm he had never experienced. As he basked in that peace, the multifaceted tunnel opened out into an enormous spherical space filled with a glistening, rain-kissed garden.

Glorious sprays of flowers in every possible variety and color spilled out of intricately woven baskets suspended in mid-air or arranged on pedestals positioned on the edge of reflecting pools.

Exotic trees and plants grew around a jewel-encrusted fountain that splashed in a courtyard outside the entrance to a magnificent temple unlike any Kevin had seen in his life reviews.

Guarding the entrance and supporting the structure's roof were two enormous pillars that appeared to have been carved from starlight, so brilliantly did they glisten. Though equal in height and breadth, each one bore a dramatically unique design.

The pillar on the left was fashioned with strong, vertical columns between which were carved intricate floral patterns that rose straight up from base to apex. The pillar on the right contained dozens of thin vertical columns that were swirled about with delicate floral garlands that seemed to be in constant motion.

As Kevin gazed at these two magnificent pillars, he felt his awareness vibrating as if a living being were looking back at him. As he stood meditating, he observed that the pillar on his left was the being's right hand, or masculine side. The pillar on his right was the being's left or feminine side.

What had appeared to him as opposites, in fact, were complements. A unity of being carved in ethereal substance that sparkled with the refracted rainbow light of a million tiny diamonds.

As Saint Germain guided Kevin forward, again he heard the word *alchemy* and wondered at its significance.

Passing a niche that held a burnished gold disc fashioned to look like the sun, the young man caught sight of his reflection. Once more he saw himself clothed in the white robe and intricately inscribed medallion of the druid Ah-Lahn. He wanted to study the image, but it melted away before he could detect the meaning of this apparition.

"Let us proceed," said the Master, leading down a softly illumined hallway. "I believe you will remember what we are about here."

Indeed, as a deeper mind in him recollected, Kevin recognized a series of individual chambers that were decorated in jewel tones so luminous as to set one's heart aflame.

In each room he could see that benches or chairs were positioned before a large screen. These were the chambers where individuals were shown scenes from their past lives.

These reviews usually took place during the instruction all souls receive between embodiments. Occasionally, when an individual's progress warranted the revelation, that one could be gifted with insights in a dream or vision, as he and Sarah had both experienced.

The purpose of these life reviews was always for the liberation of souls from past errors—the great mercy that Kevin detected in the presence of Master Saint Germain, who soon halted before a door the color of golden topaz. He ushered Kevin into an elegant, though simply furnished chamber.

Their feet sank into luxurious, dark-green carpet. The walls were covered in violet silk with gold threads woven into familiar Celtic spiral patterns. Several straight-backed chairs, upholstered in rich shades of purple and gold, were arranged in a semi-circle in front of a projection screen.

At Saint Germain's invitation, Kevin took a seat directly opposite the screen. He gratefully accepted a silver goblet that appeared in his hand, filled with the effervescent elixir he remembered from previous life reviews. He quickly drank the beverage and the goblet vanished. He closed his eyes and gathered his attention into his heart.

Moments later, revived and at peace, he looked up at Saint Germain. The Master stood before him, his aura ablaze, flooding the room with brilliant rays of violet, gold, and white. Without a word, he activated the screen and images began to appear. Kevin focused his full attention on the scenes before him and allowed his consciousness to merge with the events they portrayed.

Once again, he was the druid Ah-Lahn, although Alana was not with him. In this scene he was watching his beloved twin flame from the Otherworld—the place to which his soul had flown after an untimely death at the hands of his mortal enemy, the druid Arán Bán.

Four

The soft soles of Ah-Lahn's tall suede boots made hardly a sound as he walked along a perfectly groomed path through the luminous garden of the Otherworld that, due to the treachery of Arán Bán, had suddenly become his habitation.

Nevertheless, his heart swelled in gratitude for the joy that suffused his daily existence. For life and consciousness continued here in this ethereal plane of perfect goodness, truth, and beauty—beyond the murder that had ripped him from his beloved Alana a month ago, as earth counts time.

"O, Alana, how I long to share with you the wonders I have seen."

Ah-Lahn spoke as he stepped into the vast garden that stretched beyond the horizon in a mosaic of rainbow hues. Here he hoped to commune with his soul's twin—she who yet lived on Éire's emerald isle.

How he yearned to sit with her, to hold her safely in his arms. To protect her from the evils of her world. To defend her from those who might bring her harm. To shield her from those who did not understand her soul as he had come to know her in the short months they had shared in this life as druids.

Alana was not really alone. The druid community had gathered her to its collective bosom. Ah-Lahn's mentor—the master druid affectionately known as Uncle Óengus—had placed her under his protection as grandmaster of his school where she was studying to fulfill her destiny as a druidess, known as a *bandruí*.

However, the days when she could not seem to hold the thread of contact with Ah-Lahn's consciousness were filled with the desolation of loneliness. The fact that he could not reach her until she made the connection herself was a sword in his heart.

Few persons in embodiment would believe the dead could grieve in the blissful garden of the Otherworld. Ah-Lahn knew differently. He experienced regret for not fighting harder to stay alive this time.

Could he have been wiser, more aware of how virulently his love for Alana would be opposed by the dark forces working through Arán Bán? Could he have been more mindful of his own vulnerabilities?

All lessons for another life. And, of course, there would be many others. Not until the trials of earth were satisfied would his soul and Alana's bask in the reunion that was their divine destiny. The bliss of permanent union would not be theirs until all bridges had been crossed, all errors forgiven, all wounds healed, all promises fulfilled.

The signs were written in the stars. Ah-Lahn had many miles to travel before *Tír na n'Óg,* Land of the Ever-Living, would call him to its heavenly spires and parapets.

"I will not go without Alana," he had vowed to the cosmos before this lifetime. "We ascend together or not at all. Though it may take us ten thousand years, I'll not abandon her to find her way home alone. May it please *An Síoraí,* the Eternal One, that I stay with her—as close as breath, as familiar as the beat of her own heart."

As if to encourage his resolve, vivid jewel-toned flowers of endless variety bloomed up around him in a symphony of color and heavenly scent. Rose trees as tall as a man leaned in to convey their understanding that longing could exist here in Spirit's garden.

Buoyed by their fragrant compassion, Ah-Lahn sat on the edge of the healing fountain whose crystal-clear waters splashed and danced in fanciful sprays. He found special comfort here in communion with Alana when they could connect soul to soul—in a vibration more concentrated and somehow even more profound than the ineffable gladness that permeated this garden of spiritual delights and healing.

He knew he could have reembodied soon after his most recent passing. The Great Law would have allowed him to try again to bring healing to earth. To be born anew amidst the druid community that yet survived. To help his cherished friends and family hold the line against a tyranny of ignorance in church and state that he and his fellow druids had foreseen would likely come upon them in a future fraught with sorrow.

But he had chosen to remain in the Otherworld until Alana passed from mortal life to the garden where he waited for her. If she continued listening to him with her whole being, there were keener insights to share with her, deeper mysteries to reveal. If she could let go her fear and unreal sense of separation, he felt certain she would have a clearer vision of what could be for both of them.

Otherwise, they might not reunite until many centuries had passed.

Ah-Lahn moved to a seat within an arbor of violet climbing roses and focused his attention on his beloved's heart. Waves of ecstasy then flooded his being, filling his aura with a crystal-pink mist that bloomed out across the garden, kissing all it touched with the shimmering glow of love's pure radiance.

He beamed his love to Alana and felt her tentative answer. "I know she hears me," he said to the attentive rosy faces who nodded in the delicate breeze that wafted through the garden.

All agreed that Ah-Lahn was right to sustain his communion with Alana across the veil between their two worlds. The more light and love she could absorb from her twin flame, the stronger would be the bond between them, the more resilient their soul connection. And the less likely they would be to repeatedly slide past one another in lifetimes too brief or relationships too weak to complete the work that only their united hearts could accomplish in the world of time.

As if in response to a distant sound, Ah-Lahn turned and stood outside the arbor. He brought his right hand to his heart and gazed into the distance. In his reverie he imagined a future self who might succeed in the things of earth that had eluded him and Alana in this embodiment. He felt a flicker of recognition that such a self might one day answer his call, and prayed it would be so.

The screen went dark. Kevin was once more conscious of sitting in the life review chamber. He closed his eyes, allowing all of his senses to absorb the fullness of his experience as Ah-Lahn in the Otherworld.

His entire being reverberated with the druid's determination that his soul and Alana's should continue to develop in future embodiments. His former self had clearly been projecting to him—Ah-Lahn's future self—his desire that the knowledge of their connection not be lost to other pairs of twin flames.

But how was that possible? Druids did not record their wisdom, lest it fall to those who would distort or misuse it through ignorance or malice.

Their concern had been well-founded. However, the lack of written records meant that outpourings such as Ah-Lahn's had disappeared. His legacy had evaporated when Alana's days on earth were done.

Kevin opened his eyes. He stood and addressed Saint Germain. "Is it possible to bring Ah-Lahn's words to life, here in this century, for those souls I can feel him trying to reach?"

"If you and Sarah keep the vows you made before this life, even greater wonders are possible," answered the Master. His deep violet eyes took on a faraway look as he spoke from the very depths of *An Síoraí*, the Eternal One.

Love is a promise to be faithful to a holy vow,
to live in integrity, to right all wrongs,
to fix the broken, mend the torn,
heal the wounded;
to smooth out jagged edges,
repair what has been damaged.

To fill up empty hearts,
all with Love, for the sake of Love,
for the future of Love,
in order that Love
may continue unfettered.

Accept now Love's transforming action
as it penetrates, expands,
pierces, and emanates—

glowing and growing,
enveloping and consuming all unlike itself.

Love cannot be separated into parts.
Wherever its exists, a unity is found;
for Love is never partial,
being eternally aware only of wholeness.

Each act of Love is a promise fulfilled
and a promise to act again for Love.
That is how Love works. I promise.

Saying no more, Saint Germain removed from his left hand a heavy gold ring set with an enormous amethyst circled with diamonds and rubies that flashed as he pressed it firmly to the center of the young man's chest before returning it to his own person a full minute later.

Kevin's heart quickened as he felt the commission to secure Ah-Lahn's desire for the union of twin flames settle upon him like a cape.

"Because you are capable," the Master remarked with a touch of humor that flickered behind his more serious demeanor.

Kevin started to express his thanks. However, something in Saint Germain's expression told him that his gratitude was already understood and accepted.

Making the druid's sign of blessing, the Master turned and vanished in a shower of tiny amethyst crystals.

For a moment Kevin stood alone in the empty chamber, inhaling the fragrance of roses that remained. Then he, too, disappeared from the temple he now recognized as the Master's Cave of Symbols.

Hero stretched and yawned, fixing his big, chocolate-brown eyes expectantly on Kevin, who was snoring lightly in his leather chair.

What to do? Sometimes the man was hard to wake up, and this was one of those times. Sprite was no help. She had wandered off to lounge in the ray of sunshine that streamed in through a south window.

"Woof!" said Hero. No response. "Woof, woof!" Kevin stirred, though not enough. Hero had to act. He'd get in trouble if he peed in the house. He was still a puppy and he had to go outside. Really bad!

The man's hand dangled off his chair. Perfect. Hero began licking and whining and scooping his nose under that hand until Kevin opened his eyes, automatically scratching his pup's head. The man ran his fingers through his own hair and cautiously sat up. Life review visions always left him a bit disoriented.

"Hey, Buddy, what is it? You gotta go? Okay, come on. We need to build you a doggie door, don't we?"

Kevin stood up slowly as Hero dashed to the back door, dancing anxiously until he could run outside. Sprite padded in from the living room and jumped up on the counter with an expectant, "Meow?"

"What do we do now, Sprite?" Kevin said, distractedly stroking her silky head.

The felt sense of himself as Ah-Lahn reverberated throughout his body, mind, and soul. His future emanated from his past. His past held the key to his future. Both were now, in this time, where past and present-future must be connected in his being and in Sarah's.

Was this the purpose of their souls that he had been trying so hard to fathom? Were these mysterious experiences all part of a grand design that had led Sarah to rush off to Ireland, sparking her dreams and his visions that would prompt him to follow?

Somehow, he could sense Saint Germain's hand in all of this. The Master's blessing and admonition that they must keep their vows rang true. Kevin could only hope that the Great Druid would show them how to proceed with so profound a commission as facilitating their own reunion and that of other twin flames.

"Should I call Sarah?" Kevin wondered aloud to Sprite. The kitty's only answer was to purr and lick his hand, signaling that his continuing to pet her for the next hour would be more than acceptable.

No, he realized as he opened the door to let Hero bound back inside, his body one big wiggle. When Sarah called last night, she said she'd be busy with her family all weekend. Probably better not to involve her quite yet. Not until he understood more about his connection with Ah-Lahn.

How strange to think of his former self in the third person, almost as a separate self. But that wasn't right either. Kevin could feel the druidic presence as a different aspect of his being.

He had briefly connected with that masterful essence in Ireland when he was pouring out his heart to Sarah. In that moment she had recognized him as Ah-Lahn. He could see it in her eyes. That awakened experience had convinced her to return home with him.

Now he would have to wait and see how she responded when he told her about this morning's visions. In the meantime, he could write down what he sensed Ah-Lahn was trying to convey.

Sprite walked to her food dish and let Kevin know she was ready for a snack. Hero had the same idea. He flipped his metal food dish over with a big paw and began nosing it across the floor.

"Yeah, I'm ready for a bite myself," Kevin said as he got out treats for the fur kids and made himself a sandwich. "Then we'll see what we can do about tapping into our former greatness."

Five

Safe. Cozy. Protected. That's how Sarah felt in her parents' home in the Boston suburb of Braintree. Even with an icy wind whistling against the double-pane windows and thick grey clouds blocking the sun from warming her childhood bedroom, she could relax here.

She hadn't bothered to change out of the sweats that served as her wintertime pajamas. After a late breakfast, she had returned to the room that held many comforting memories. Here, in the peace of her personal sanctuary, she was talking out loud to her favorite stuffed animal.

"I know I'm pushing Kevin away, but I can't seem to stop myself," she confessed to the plush toy panther she had saved from countless neighborhood garage sales. She'd given away most of her stuffed animals years ago, but she had never been able to part with this one.

The toy had remained safe in this room that still reflected Sarah's girlhood preferences for big floral prints and rich colors.

"Her garden room," she'd called it. And smiled now to remember how as a five-year-old she had insisted on sunny yellow walls. The curtains and matching bedspread were made of polished cotton fabric scattered with vibrant blue forget-me-nots, golden sunflowers, deep purple violets, whisper-pink peonies, and crimson roses. New England winters were long and dark. In Sarah's bedroom, summer never faded.

"I don't mean to be distant or cruel to Kevin. It just happens," she continued, sitting cross-legged on the field of bedspread flowers, cradling the stuffed panther that was so much more than a toy.

She had named the panther "Ba" years before stumbling upon a past-life connection to that name. It was only last summer that she had discovered the presence of a liminal panther spirit guide that nudged her into her Irish journey of self-discovery. The panther had appeared in many of her past lives, including Egypt, where she'd named her feline "Mau Ba."

Since she and Kevin had returned from Ireland, her animal spirit guide had not appeared, except on the pages of her novel. Sarah hugged Ba closer and pretended the toy was warm as well as soft.

She turned her head and let her gaze drift out the window, through bare tree limbs to the big backyard where she and her brother, Brian, and the neighborhood kids used to play. Their mother had enforced strict rules about TV time, so they'd spent hours outside inventing games and pretending they were famous historical people.

Sometimes those "pretend" settings had felt so real that Sarah had had trouble pulling herself out of her imagined Ireland or Greece or Egypt. After last summer's life reviews, she knew why. She had lived in those places in ancient times.

So had Kevin, although their relationship in those embodiments had not always been harmonious. And now they seemed to be at another crossroads. Her heart twinged when she stopped to think about the possibility of them drifting apart again.

How could that happen when they had been so determined to love each other unconditionally? She remembered the joy of lying in his arms, of homing to the shelter of his embrace. But they hadn't snuggled like that in weeks.

She was glad he hadn't wanted to come with her this weekend. They both needed some alone time. Not that she'd get it with Brian, his wife Ivy, and four-year-old twins Kerry and Kaitlyn, arriving later today. That is, if they could get through the blizzard that hovered over New England.

Road conditions were getting worse in Braintree. Were they already icy in and around New Bedford where Brian lived with his family? He had called this morning to say they were keeping an eye on the storm and might stay home if conditions didn't improve.

"Maybe it will be quiet here after all," Sarah said to Ba, arranging the panther on the bed next to her. She stretched out and tried to focus her attention on her marriage.

Why *was* she pulling away from Kevin?

He had been so powerful last summer in Ireland. His fervor had helped her gain the profound insights into her own behavior that had led to their reconciliation. Their relationship as twin flames had been so clear to her then. She had overcome some deep psychological issues in the magic of Ireland's numinous atmosphere. But the magic she found there proved ephemeral.

She had hoped their renewed affection would miraculously resolve all issues between them. Perpetual honeymoon. That's what she wanted —though, of course, Hollywood endings weren't realistic.

There was something going on with Kevin that he wasn't confiding in her. Probably because she barely spoke to him these days. And that wasn't fair. He was being helpful by filling in events from their past that she couldn't remember—although she had dreamed more about those events than he'd been shown.

Sometimes details flooded back to her in waves, which meant she needed less of Kevin's input. And, she admitted with a touch of guilt, that suited her just fine.

In order to remember the specifics she'd re-lived in her dream state during the writer's retreat, she'd had to completely immerse herself in the story of Alana and Ah-Lahn. The deeper she got into writing her novel, the more she wanted to stay in the narrative and not come out to take care of mundane chores like grocery shopping, cleaning house, or cooking dinner.

Having to pull herself out of the stories that were saturating her imagination was physically painful. Sometimes she felt like she was being wrenched back and forth through a time warp. The experience made her cranky and irritable.

Why couldn't Kevin be more understanding—more like Ah-Lahn?

The thought astonished her. That was part of the problem, wasn't it? He'd been so masterful in Ireland—almost luminous. So masculine, confident, insightful, able to reach into her soul in a way he hadn't done since the first night she'd met him in this life over seven years ago.

The more she wrote about Ah-Lahn, the more she compared Kevin to the person he had been.

"How are the mighty fallen," she said aloud to Ba, and groaned that she should say such a thing. She hated to think of her husband that way.

But there it was. And he probably thought the same about her.

Alana had been an accomplished druidess in her own right. Both she and Ah-Lahn had been able to access the spirit realm at will. Now Sarah and Kevin were but shadows of their former selves. How depressing.

"Sarah, I'm going to the grocery store. Do you want to come with me?" her mother called up from the hallway downstairs.

Eileen Callahan was a petite, energetic, fifty-eight-year-old woman whose hair still flamed red, framing sparkling green eyes. She was sixth generation Irish from Connemara and proud of it. "My Celtic Warrior Wife," her husband, Patrick, called her. And he was right. Nobody put anything over on Eileen, including her six-foot-tall husband and her two children, whom she loved with the ferocity of a mother bear.

Though Sarah could be as volatile as her mother, even as a child she'd been glad not to deal with the inevitable comments about red hair. Brian had inherited that problem and the fiery temperament to go with it. No wonder Kevin had wanted to stay home.

Sarah's own curly auburn hair and hazel eyes came from her father's side of the family that originally hailed from County Clare in the West of Ireland. At a physically-fit age sixty, Patrick was still the peaceful rock of this active bunch, though you didn't want to provoke him.

His temper boiled slow, but was just as slow to cool if you got him going. Especially about the Red Sox. Patrick's blood ran true red for his team and he'd take on anybody who said they weren't the best. Kevin, being an equally loyal Yankees' fan, enjoyed those tussles. And showed impressive restraint in letting his father-in-law have the final word.

"No, Ma, you go ahead," Sarah called back down the stairs. "I'm still tired. And I'm not dressed to go out."

"That's fine, darlin'. I won't be long. You rest up. We'll have a nice family dinner. I'm making my Irish stew in case Brian and Ivy can get here after all."

"Thanks, Ma. I'll see you when you get back."

Sarah knew she would have plenty of time before her mother

returned. Eileen inevitably ran into friends from church or the neighbor-hood, and no one enjoyed a spontaneous conversation more than Mrs. Callahan.

Suddenly weary of thinking about her personal problems with no obvious solution in sight, Sarah pulled up the down comforter that lay at the foot of her bed and wrapped her arms around Ba.

Sleep came quickly as she fell into the otherworldly atmosphere her storytelling immersion easily evoked these days. Once more she landed in first-century Ireland where the druidess Alana contemplated her earthly life without her beloved Ah-Lahn.

Six

Alana was no longer shocked by Ah-Lahn's absence. She knew he was dead. She had held him in her arms as he took leave of this world. She had felt his spirit lift off to invisible realms.

What shocked her now was how much of her own soul he had taken with him. Somehow, she'd always known he would go first. But she was not prepared for this absence—as if her heart had been amputated.

There was a hole in Alana's being and she did not know how to mend it. She prayed, she meditated, she beat her bodhrán drum as if its rhythm might convince her desolate heart to come back to life. But nothing filled the void that now defined her.

She was wandering across a vast wilderness, desperate to regain her identity in the midst of this one great loss, in the memories of countless other losses that rushed through her like a torrent. She stood at the threshold between this world and the next, yet she dared not step across—not to end her life, but to find surcease in deep communion between her soul and Ah-Lahn's.

Panic raced through her. This connection with the soul she knew to be her twin was very different from the shape-shifting she'd been doing since childhood. Here was an unknown she had not explored.

She was accustomed to changing her human form. Her father, the druid Carwyn, had taught her the techniques and boundaries to ensure her safety. But this step was too fearful, too final.

With so much of her heart and soul already absent from her being, what if she lost herself while trying to connect with Ah-Lahn in the Otherworld?

Does the snowflake remember its unique pattern when it falls to earth? Does a drop of seawater contain the whole of the ocean? Or does the ocean simply swallow up a billion drops in its unfathomable depths?

Alana sat paralyzed at the edge of the abyss. Fear gripped her in its claws as if she were a field mouse caught in the talons of a bird of prey. This winged thing was not one of the companionable hawks or eagles that often bid her fly with them toward the sun. Here was a beast that had imprisoned her for centuries under its powerful wing.

She knew she'd reached a turning point. In brief moments of clarity, she had seen Ah-Lahn's blue-green eyes fixed intently on her own, urging her to break through the veil between worlds that kept their souls apart. But she could not, or would not—until now.

She fell to her knees and cried out to the spirit of Ah-Lahn to show her the way to their reunion. Soon, she heard his voice, offering guidance and encouragement from the Otherworld. She was stunned at his message and wondered how to accomplish what he asked.

Your fear desires your love. All those disowned elements of your human self want to be gathered into your heart like prodigal sons and daughters who long for their parents' acceptance.

You are father, mother, daughter, son—worthy in all aspects. Embrace yourself as does An Síoraí, the Eternal One, and learn that wisdom emanates rays of hope.

Be that Light and fear will not trouble you, for you will have welcomed it home for healing. Follow your heart and uncover the truth you have resisted.

Alana sat in silence as her soul's deep longing for reunion with the soul of Ah-Lahn washed through her mind and body. She willed herself to accept the fullness of the sensation, and as she did, her natural gift for shifting shapes awakened in a scene she could not have anticipated.

Without further thought, she and her spirit animal, Sprid—both of them now silky black panthers—embarked on a new task. Stealthily, they prowled through a primeval forest. Their huge, feline paws carried them silently through the underbrush to the edge of a clearing that glimmered, as if touched by fairy magic.

Alana started to bound forward, to romp and play in the green grass that sparkled with dew. But Sprid's rumbled warning held her in check. Danger lurked in the shadows beyond the glen, so she remained in place.

Then she saw them—two startling yellow eyes, round as golden orbs, peering out from a tree limb at the edge of the glen, scanning the open space. Whatever owns those eyes is hungry and cruel, she told herself, and shuddered.

She watched the orbs flash with what she took to be jealousy, resentment, aggression, ignorance, arrogance. Alana had seen them before, set in human faces of those who had opposed her and Ah-Lahn. And she had seen them in her dreams, cloaked in guilt and regret.

These were the eyes of the winged thing she believed to be her jailer, the beast she had allowed into her consciousness, the creature that only she could slay.

Alana's sinewy feline body shivered in the cool dark safety of her hiding place. Sprid was with her and would not leave her side—at least not yet. Though how long they could remain hidden, her guide would not reveal. Until that moment of confrontation made itself known, the two panthers waited.

Sprid's quiet purring comforted Alana, reminding her that panthers are creatures of Nature's wisdom. Born of the Unknown, they instinctively know the potential of the void. They can see through its night-time. They know the way to the light that lives beyond its depths.

For, in Nature's way of seeing, day and night are not enemies. What had Ah-Lahn said? "Dark nights come to those who love enough to bring their light to the darkness. Love cherishes the fertile darkness as the place of creation's beginning."

Sprid's purring deepened as she did her best to infuse Alana with her own fearlessness. Both knew the time had come. Only the one called was allowed to face this initiation. Alana must step into the glen while Sprid remained hidden, watching.

To encourage herself, Alana tried to purr but could not. For she was no longer a panther who could defend herself with claws and teeth.

Taking a deep breath, she stepped to the center of the clearing—out of the shadows, into the open unprotected territory, defenseless and visible to whatever might attack her human form.

From deep within the bracken, she heard the wail of harsh regret, the groan of guilt, self-pity's whine. The snarl of vengeance pierced her ears, the haughty laugh of arrogance taunted her to react. Ignorance whispered audaciously, and jealousy slithered within her.

Alana looked around, confused. Were those sounds emanating from the foliage or from her own throat?

"Surely, you know those sounds are lies," declared the stately snowy owl that fluttered silently into the clearing on gold-tipped white wings. She perched on a large boulder and folded her five-foot wingspan around her downy form.

"I thought you were a dark, angry bird," said Alana, peering into the owl's deep golden eyes.

"Even a ray of truth can be a frightful thing when your mind is beset with fear," said the owl matter-of-factly.

"If I am hearing lies in my own head, then where is truth?" Alana ventured. Was this bird friend or foe? She could not tell, and one look at the owl's sharp beak and powerful talons made her tremble at the thought of her human vulnerability.

"Truth is often subtle and slips in on quiet wings," said the owl fluffing her feathers. "Panther can guide you to this place of encounter. However, only you can bring your own discernment to the lies that block the truth. And that block you from knowing your True Self."

Although the owl's voice was soft and low, Alana quaked inside.

"Fear not the truth, Alana," said the owl, opening her golden eyes as if she meant to beam the light of illumination into her listener.

"To discover your True Self today, you must forgive the false self you have been in the past. Fear will not dissolve entirely until you discover the origin of its lies. Then you must forgive fear's many disguises—some of your own creation and others that clever minds have convinced you to believe."

"How do I know which is which?" asked Alana. "Such discernment is not an easy task."

The great bird nodded slightly and softened her expression. "No, it is not. Yet I would teach you the way to wisdom.

"Catch yourself in fear and ask what it would teach you. Listen carefully and do not be surprised at what event or misunderstanding may have spawned it, far back in time. Then, and only then, will you offer fear its rightful place as guide and guardian against actual danger.

"Allow fear to tell you the truth of its origin and you will have made of it a powerful ally. However, to hear the truth of fear, you must be willing to look at all the lies you have believed, especially the ones you have told yourself. And you must do so every day."

Alana was suddenly full of questions and would have asked them had the snowy owl not abruptly spread her magnificent wings and lifted off, disappearing as quickly and as silently as she had appeared.

Sometime later, as Alana and her panther neared their cottage, something white caught the eye of the druidess.

She stooped and picked up a delicately gold-tipped feather that had fallen from the snowy owl now soaring silently overhead. As she watched, the majestic bird rode a rising breeze into an ever-widening spiral until it vanished into clouds brushed with sunset's gold and ruby fire.

In that moment, Alana believed she would never fear again—if only she could remember who she really was.

Seven

Sarah, are you awake?" Eileen knocked gently and opened her daughter's bedroom door. "Sarah?" she repeated and stepped in.

She moved to the side of the bed where for nearly two decades she had nurtured this young woman who had left home at eighteen years of age, yet would always be her child.

The mother sat, automatically holding her hand on the smooth, feminine forehead, checking for signs of a fever. "Are you all right? I called from downstairs, but you didn't answer."

"Oh, hi, Ma," Sarah sat up slowly and rubbed her eyes. "I was in a dream. Part of the book I'm working on. A new part. An event I'd never seen before. Don't worry, I'm fine."

"Well, you don't look fine. Come to the kitchen and I'll fix you some tea. And get dressed, Sarah. It's the middle of the afternoon. Pull yourself together before your father gets home."

"Where is he?"

"He went to a retirement party for one of his work buddies. You remember Clancy Howard from Distribution?"

"The one who played Santa every year at the family Christmas party? I loved him. I remember he and Dad always got along like old war buddies."

"I think that's why Clancy decided the company's early retirement package was too good to turn down. He followed your father right out the door. Now they're planning all sorts of adventures. Fair play to both of them."

She stood and walked to the bedroom door. "Hurry along now and I'll fix your tea, *a iníon mo chroí.*"

Sarah loved to hear herself called "my darling daughter" in Gaelic—

one of many terms her mother had picked up when she stayed with Irish relatives when she as a teenager. She smiled to herself and did as her mother told her.

Life was easier that way. Besides, she knew Eileen's perfect cup of tea would lift her brain fog so she could consider the dream that had swept her back into Alana's life—in a very strange way.

Should she call Kevin? she wondered as she brushed her hair and put on navy cords and a bright green sweater. After all, they had shared many profound experiences as Alana and Ah-Lahn. And, despite her current inclination to keep the novel to herself, her husband remained a part of the project. Yet something held her back.

"What should I do?" She closed her eyes and listened—something she realized she hadn't been doing nearly enough of lately. Her mind had been busy with the stories that deluged her imagination. For weeks her emotions had been clouding the insights that could come to her only when she was quiet.

She inhaled deeply, settled herself, and breathed a grateful sigh as the voice of inner wisdom spoke:

This dream is about Sarah in the present, as well as Alana in the past. Give yourself time to absorb the message that may benefit you and Kevin. Other matters are at hand. Pay attention.

Comforted by any direction from her wise inner guidance—even when as mysterious as this message—she decided not to worry about the dream of Alana and the owl, and went downstairs into the warmth of her mother's kitchen.

As soon as Sarah finished her tea, her mother put her to work cutting up chunks of lamb and vegetables for tonight's stew while she made her famous scones. Another perk of being home.

"Nobody makes scones like you, Ma," Sarah declared as she relished the homey scent of her mother's baking. "Mine turn out like doorstops."

"You have to keep your hands cold and don't fuss with the dough," Eileen laughed as she popped a batch of perfect rounds into the oven.

A gust of icy wind and snow blew into the kitchen with Patrick, back from his retirement party. "Any word from Brian and Ivy? The roads are getting worse. I hope they don't try to get here."

"They haven't called," said Eileen, kissing her husband of thirty years on the cheek. "I'd hoped they would have by now. Would you try Brian's cell? I'm starting to worry something may have happened."

"I will, in one quick minute," agreed Patrick, returning her kiss with the spontaneous affection Sarah had always admired in her parents. As her father had done for three decades, he poured himself a cup of tea from the pot his wife had steeping and popped a hot scone on a plate. He took his seat at the kitchen table where butter and strawberry jam were ready for spreading.

He devoured the hot pastry with relish, reached for a second, then reconsidered and pulled out his cell phone. He dialed, listened.

"Went right to voice mail." He frowned, then made a conscious effort to brighten. "But you know how busy they get with the twins."

Eileen knew he didn't feel as positive as he was trying to sound. Nevertheless, she followed his lead and blew out a slow breath. "You're probably right. Finish your tea now and go catch up with Sarah. Dinner's at six-thirty."

"Come with me, Dad," said Sarah, ushering him into the living room before he could start on another scone. "Tell me what's new with the man of leisure."

Patrick carefully observed his daughter as they automatically took their seats on the comfortable, tapestry-upholstered side chairs where they had shared their deepest, most important conversations ever since either of them could remember.

They chatted about his retirement, the state of the economy, off-season baseball, which players were healing, who wouldn't make it to spring training.

But something was going on with the lass. Her father could always tell when she tried to play her cards close to the vest. Her face was far too expressive to hide the cloud hanging over those soft hazel eyes.

He knew that she and Kevin had had a serious argument last summer. However, he assumed all was well now. Especially since they'd adopted a puppy for Kevin and a kitten for Sarah, and talked about their pets as if they were babies.

"You okay, Sarah?" he asked at last. "You seem distracted."

"Oh, sorry, Dad. My head's at least half-way in my book right now. The story is running in the background all the time. Do you think that's weird?"

"Not for you, my Fairy Queen." They both laughed at his nickname for her. "You've always had a grand imagination. I'm glad you're putting it to use instead of working for that crook of a New York politician."

"Oh, now, I'm not sure A. B. Ryan is really a crook," Sarah began. Then chuckled, "Yes, he probably is. Anyway, I'm glad to be out of that job. Kevin definitely helped me see the light."

"Kevin okay, too? You haven't said much about him." Another reason her father was watching her.

"Oh, he's fine. A bit tired is all. He's been working extra hours to make up for my not earning a paycheck. He just needed to take it easy this weekend. You know how we can be."

Patrick nodded and put his arm around his daughter as they both rose and she guided him to the dining room.

"Come on, Dad. Let's set the table and help Ma finish dinner."

Eileen's stew was fantastic. As usual, she had made enough food for a battalion. She liked having plenty of leftovers and her family never complained. The three of them chatted about this and that, but their apparent ease was strained. Brian hadn't called, and he still wasn't answering his cell phone.

At seven-thirty Patrick's phone rang. Everybody tensed at the sound. He grabbed the phone and stood to answer. Mother and daughter held their breath amidst the staccato of his conversation.

"Yes, this is Patrick Callahan. . . . What? . . .Who was in the car? . . . How bad? . . . And the twins? . . . Where are they? . . . Who's with them? . . . Yes, we'll come. . . . No sir, not tonight. . . . Not if the roads are that slick. . . . Thank you."

Eileen and Sarah were on their feet. "What's happened?"

"That was the State Patrol," said Patrick. "There's been a big pile-up on I-195. Cars and trucks hit a patch of black ice, and the kids were caught in it. They'd barely left New Bedford, so the ambulance was taking them back to St. Luke's."

"Are they hurt? What about the twins?" Eileen demanded.

"The patrolman didn't have all the details. He thought the twins were okay. They were in their car seats in the back. Most of the impact was on the front. Brian's was the last car in line. That's lucky. But he and Ivy were definitely injured. That was all the officer could tell me."

"We have to get to them," Eileen declared, instantly moving into action. She was already clearing food from the table and making lists in her head of what they would need to pack.

"Absolutely," agreed Patrick, "but we can't go tonight. The patrolman said the main highways are closed until they can clear the wrecks and get the roads plowed and sanded. The storm was worse than Mass-DOT expected, so they're behind. That's one reason for the black ice.

"I'll try to reach Millie and Jack. They live there in New Bedford. Maybe they can go to the hospital."

Before he could dial, Patrick's cell phone rang again.

"Millie. . . . Hi. . . . We were about to call you. . . . Yes, we've heard. . . . No, we can't get there tonight. State Patrol said not to try. . . . You can? . . . Great. . . . Thanks a million. . . . Okay. . . . Call when you know anything. . . . You, too. . . . Bye."

"Millie and Jack are on their way to St. Luke's. They should be there in less than half an hour. They'll stay at the hospital tonight. We can rely on them. Don't worry, *a ghrá*." Sarah smiled at her father's Irish endearment for his wife. They all took a deep breath.

"Aunt-Meewee" and "Unkka-Mack," as Brian's twins called them, had raised four children of their own and always brought a reassuring presence to the rest of the family. Especially to Eileen, whose fiery temperament Millie seemed able to calm with little effort.

She was Patrick's older sister and even more a rock than he in times of crisis. They had lost their mother when Millie was twelve years old, Patrick was eight, and another brother, Colm, was ten.

Millie had become the boys' surrogate mother while their father, a dedicated family man, worked as an auto mechanic and provided as stable a home as he could manage through very difficult times.

Colm had taken the loss of their mother especially hard. He ran away several times and finally, at age fifteen, convinced a Navy recruiter he was old enough to join the service. The family didn't hear from him until two years later when they learned he'd been lost at sea in an accident that felt to them suspiciously like suicide.

Patrick folded his arms around his wife and daughter, holding them close. The thought of losing another member of his family was too much to bear.

Eileen could sense what was going through her husband's mind and hugged him fiercely. When he took a deep breath, she leaned back and looked up into his misty hazel eyes.

"Are you sure we can't go tonight? I need to see my son—my family."

"Ma, you know we can't drive on black ice." Sarah put her hand on Eileen's arm and guided her toward the kitchen.

"Millie and Jack will take care of everything that can be done tonight. Let's figure out what we need to take so we can leave as soon as the roads are clear in the morning. I'll help you get ready. We'll all go."

By 10:00 p.m. enough clothes for two weeks were packed in suitcases. Eileen's many quarts of stew, nearly two dozen scones, and all perishable items were prepped to pop into coolers first thing in the morning.

Sarah doubted that any of them would sleep much that night, but she was going to try.

First, she had to call Kevin.

Eight

Kevin answered his cell on the first ring. "Sarah? I was getting ready to call you, but I thought it might be too late. I had a feeling something was going on. Is everybody okay?"

"No, they're not." She quickly told him what she knew. Talking to him helped push away the fear that was rippling through her.

"Aunt Millie and Uncle Jack said the hospital was swamped from this accident and several others. No fatalities that they know of, but some fairly serious injuries for people in little cars that got squashed between big trucks.

"Brian was driving their SUV, so they were more protected. Still, he has a bad concussion, and Ivy has slightly bruised ribs and a broken arm. The little ones were mostly scared, but the docs are keeping them overnight to be sure that's all. Millie and Jack are staying in their room tonight and will be checking on Brian and Ivy as necessary."

"That's a relief," said Kevin. "What about you? You sound really tired."

"I am, and it looks like I won't be coming home for a while. We're leaving in the morning for New Bedford. I'll call you when we get there."

"Okay, good. Is your dad taking his four-wheel drive?"

"Uh-huh." Sarah paused. She really wanted to tell Kevin about her dream, but she was desperate for bed.

"What else is going on, Hon?" He sensed something in her voice that sparked his attention. "Are you sure you're okay?"

She hesitated. "I'm fine. It's just that I had the strangest dream about Alana in a scene I hadn't remembered, from after Ah-Lahn had died. I want to tell you about it, but I honestly don't have the energy tonight."

"That's interesting," said Kevin. "I just had a vision about Ah-Lahn, perhaps from the same time period."

"Really?" Sarah was alert now. "In my dream, Alana is afraid she'll lose herself if she steps through the veil and crosses the crystal bridge to connect with him."

"And Ah-Lahn is afraid they'll both be lost if she doesn't," said Kevin. "We definitely need to compare notes, don't we? But you should rest for tomorrow. We'll talk soon."

"Thanks, Hon. I love you."

"Love you too, Sarah. Be safe, okay?"

"We will. Good night."

The next day was Sunday. Kevin kept vigil all day, cell phone in hand. Hero and Sprite felt his distress and stayed by his side.

Sarah called with frequent updates on road conditions, expected travel time to New Bedford, their arrival at the hospital. Ivy's broken arm had not required surgery, so she and the twins could go home today. The docs would keep Brian in the hospital for another twenty-four hours to monitor his concussion.

She looked on with admiration as Eileen and Patrick worked like soldiers on campaign: Sending Millie and Jack home for some well-earned sleep. Talking to doctors and the State Patrol. Monitoring Brian's status. Getting Ivy and the twins released and back to their own home.

The parents were in charge. She would have to remember this scene if she and Kevin ever had children.

That old pang of jealousy twinged in her gut—one reason she and her sister-in-law rarely spoke. Ivy had popped out two perfect babies on her first attempt at getting pregnant. Sarah had miscarried twice and didn't know if she could face trying again. Adorable as Kerry and Kaitlyn were, it was going to be hard for her to be around them.

By the time Sarah called New York to report that the twins and their mother were home, fed, and tucked up in their own beds for an afternoon nap, Kevin felt like he needed one, too.

Hero and Sprite were happy to join him on his bed, under a cozy comforter, where he drifted off with Ah-Lahn's image in mind—and dreamed of master druids training him to remember vast oral histories and occult mysteries long lost in the veils of time.

In this dream Kevin saw himself as a young druid. He was spending hours memorizing, reciting, going into deep meditation—sometimes in dark isolation to open his inner sight.

He was mastering the Brehon laws, composing songs and poems. Even more importantly, he was learning ancient healing practices and powerful prayers and invocations for overcoming dark forces.

He was being shown the long years of study required for Ah-Lahn to become the chief druid, known as *ceann-druí*, which meant he wasn't fully asleep. This was lucid dreaming, and he was meant to remember everything he witnessed.

The scene changed. Once more Ah-Lahn was sitting by the healing fountain in the garden of the Otherworld. He appeared happier than he had been during yesterday's vision. He was composing new lines of poetry and memorizing them as they came to him.

As Kevin watched, Ah-Lahn looked off to his right. Walking on the familiar crystalline bridge was Alana. When she reached not quite halfway across, she stopped and gazed longingly toward the far side.

Kevin felt emotion well up in his throat as Ah-Lahn stood and began moving toward his beloved. There were no words for the ineffable luminescence flooding in, through, and around the druid's form. His aura expanded to at least nine feet around him in a translucent sphere that shimmered with rays of pink, gold, and white.

Ah-Lahn approached the gateway between worlds. When he reached the bridge's edge, he stopped and began reciting the poem he had been composing for his beloved Alana.

> Step to the edge, wise heart.
> Dare to push the boundary
> of what has felt safe till now;

great battles are fought
on the threshold of mind and feeling.

What are you willing to sacrifice?
A mask, a shield, a safety net—
none of which was ever true,
though useful as you found your way.

Fire up, wise heart.
Feel the energy of exhilaration
and determination
to leave the past where it lies.

New dimensions call to the wise heart
who longs to bring all to one last push
for the task at hand.

Come up higher, wise heart.
The summit can be won,
and greater heights will beckon in time.

Then, as today, your radiant heart
will be the portal and the beacon
toward which to aim enthusiastic steps
that only wise hearts take,
because others see mere walls.

Rise up, wise heart!
Fear has no power here
when courage comes alive
more fervently with every passing day.

Now is the time.
This is the work you were made for.

Ah-Lahn's words reverberated in the ethers as he lovingly regarded Alana. Then, to Kevin's amazement, he turned and looked directly into the eyes of his future self and held his gaze for a full minute.

This message is also for you. Remember what you are about to witness.

The druid conveyed this meaning to his future self in clear telepathy. Then he turned back and walked most of the way across the bridge where he stopped and centered his attention on Alana.

Kevin could see a transparent, gossamer-like curtain coming into view, suspended in the middle of the span. Ah-Lahn and Alana stood on opposite sides of that wispy veil, each completely focused on the other.

A delicate silver thread made of multiple filaments as fine as a human hair intertwined like exquisite embroidery fiber to create a single strand. The thread passed through the gossamer—connecting the two figures heart to heart, soul to soul, and gently wafted up and down in the soft breeze that swirled around the couple.

As Kevin watched, the glow in Ah-Lahn's aura intensified and a small disc of rosy light began to turn on the outside of his chest. It spun there for just a moment until the druid inhaled deeply, drawing the disc into his own heart. On his exhale the disc arced over to where Alana was standing and anchored in the center of her bosom.

At that moment Ah-Lahn spoke with quiet authority, "I am here." As the vision began to fade, Alana answered, "And I."

Kevin bolted up in bed, scattering comforter, dog, and cat. He grabbed the journal and pen he kept on his bedside table and began to write.

He could almost feel his hand being guided across the paper as he transcribed Ah-Lahn's words. Typing on his laptop would have been faster, but he knew that using electronics could interfere with the delicate energy of the vision.

He was ecstatic. Ah-Lahn, that aspect of his being that was profoundly masterful, had communicated to him—directly.

They had connected! Ah-Lahn had shared not only his intention of preserving the legacy of his communion with Alana, he had demonstrated how they did it. Moreover, thought Kevin, using this technique might allow him and Sarah to assist other twin flames, as Saint Germain said was part of their commission.

Over and over, Kevin read the druid's poem and his own description of this dream that was clearly not a dream. He was amazed and grateful, his mind was full of questions. He quickly wrote them down.

Will I be able to repeat the process Ah-Lahn showed me?

Can I be as attuned again as I was just now?

What about Sarah?

Will she be willing to play her part?

Or is she already playing her part?

Wasn't her dream about Alana's fears the same time period as my vision of Ah-Lahn?

Are Sarah and I being shown the same events from different perspectives?

When will I be able to share these experiences with her?

How long will her family need her to remain in New Bedford?

Around nine o'clock Kevin willed his mind to rest. Monday was a work day and he needed his wits about him.

Nine

Peace at last descended at Brian and Ivy's home where, soft and silent, new-fallen snow blanketed the old whaling town of New Bedford as it had done for hundreds of winters. The home's exterior and tall trees reflected its rich history. Inside, every room gleamed with the latest decorating trends.

Although Sarah did not share her sister-in-law's preference for modern grey walls and metallic finishes, she was grateful that Brian and Ivy had purchased a house with three upstairs bedrooms plus an attic guest room and a downstairs office. With the entire family staying together for an undetermined length of time, they needed the space.

The past twenty-four hours had been a whirlwind of emotions for all of them. Only the twins appeared sanguine now that they were snug in their own room. The adults had finally worn themselves out with mutual concern and gone to bed.

Sarah was dreaming again and she recognized the setting. Traveling in her soul's light body, she arrived at the shimmering marble colonnade of the Temple of the One Light where she had served as an Atlantean priestess. Her companion was the serene, goddess-like figure who had appeared so powerfully in the life reviews she'd dreamed about while in Ireland—though she was now called Nada.

The Lady Master looked as radiant as ever in her ruby-colored gown and jeweled diadem that she wore as a circlet across her brow, highlighting the beauty of her flaxen blonde hair. The difference in this scene was in Sarah's own appearance. On her last visit to the temple she had been there as Alana. Now she was here as herself.

She and Lady Master Nada were walking across a tiled courtyard, chatting like old friends, admiring the profusion of flowers, clear reflecting pools, and gaily splashing fountains. When they entered the interior and stepped onto the spiral walkway that circled into the temple's center, Sarah fell silent. The atmosphere of holiness was breathtaking. She had not remembered being enfolded in such deep feelings of unconditional acceptance and tender mercy.

They had ascended only a few turns of the spiral walkway when Lady Master Nada said in her angel-song voice, "Here we are." She opened a doorway the color and texture of a pearl and gestured for her companion to step into a small, yet exquisite chamber.

"Oh!" exclaimed Sarah, holding her hands to her heart. "It's like walking into a rose."

The floor was carpeted in lush green pile the color of summer leaves. The walls and upholstered benches were covered in myriad shades of dark pink, magenta, and burgundy silk. They glistened in the soft light that filled the room. On a far wall the screen used for life reviews appeared like a large dewdrop with images floating within its crystal-clear interior.

Sarah instinctively took her seat on a bench facing the screen. As if on cue, she raised her hand to receive the goblet of clear elixir that appeared. She drank the beverage and settled in to observe the images that began to come into focus on the screen.

She expected to observe Alana or possibly one of her other embodiments. Instead, she saw her own image standing with Kevin before a panel of a dozen exalted masters.

All were dressed in robes of dark purple. Each wore a gold medallion on which unique symbols were carved. Some were bare-headed. Others wore turbans. Still others wore circlets like that of Lady Master Nada, who had joined the twelve.

"Do you promise?" the presiding master was asking Kevin and Sarah. He was barely visible in the white light that emanated from his form. His voice was warm and kind, and filled with a majesty that spoke of unfathomable wisdom.

"We do," the couple responded in unison.

"Then give your vows to each other as we wish you Godspeed."

Exactly what she and Kevin were promising, Sarah did not know. There seemed to have been some kind of instruction given before the images came to life on the screen. Whatever was being asked of them was obviously very serious.

As she watched and listened, she and Kevin stood facing each other, clasping hands, gazing solemnly into one another's eyes. Her husband of many centuries began.

My beloved, I pledge to you my loyalty, my protection, and my dedication to our union. This time, we must succeed.

May we find each other in the flowering of our hearts and the promise to *An Síoraí*, the Eternal One, of what two souls united in Love can accomplish for all of life.

Once again, I feel the stream of our souls' oneness flowing between us. I will always be a part of you, as you are a part of me. Fire for fire, forever and forever.

They briefly released hands, then took them again. Sarah felt her heart catch in her throat and watched Kevin's eyes grow misty as she pledged her constancy to him in a poem.

My beloved, come what may,
I will harvest what we sowed.
Though life take us from each other
Or give us leave to never part,
What began in eons distant
I will bring back to the start.

Through raging storms or gentler weather
I'll not falter, I'll not wane.
I will keep my pledge of loyalty
All for you, I will be strong.

Do not forsake me, my beloved,
Though dark ones threaten our resolve,

I'll not abandon what we came for—
To prove the wisdom of pure Love.

Though life may send me through a desert
Or a dimly lighted path,
I'll come home to you, my darling
My love for you is all I have—

That, and faith in *An Síoraí's* direction
To bring us back as one together
Held in an orb of radiance;
By a silver thread we're tethered.

Dawn was breaking when Sarah awoke in the attic bedroom where she was sleeping on a day bed. She pulled the curtains open to watch clouds brushed pink, purple, and gold, like fingers of fire, blazing across the horizon to the east where the small, dormer window faced.

She stared as the sun rose over the neighborhood rooftops, casting a luminous glow that reminded her of scenes she had seen in her dreams.

"Oh, my God!" she exclaimed aloud. "My dreams! I have to record them before they evaporate!"

She rushed to her briefcase, being careful not to bump her head on the attic's steeply sloped ceiling. She pulled out pen and paper and began scribbling the words she prayed she would remember. She transcribed Kevin's first as they were quickly fading from memory. Hers were emblazoned in her mind.

Her hand shook and tears welled in her eyes as she wrote the promise she'd made not quite thirty years earlier. Before taking the plunge once again to enter a baby's body and grow up on Planet Earth.

Disturbing thoughts flooded her mind. How many times had she made similar vows and not been able to keep them?

How many times had she slipped away into her own death—guilty of not holding firmly enough to the life she lived or to the man she loved—the man who was her other half. They were together again. But could she, would she, hold on this time?

Kevin had said this time they must succeed. What exactly did that mean? They had overcome the prophecy of separation that had sent him rushing to her in Ireland. There must be something else.

She had promised she would do better in this embodiment. That much she knew. She would love her husband as she had not loved him in many a lifetime. She had shut herself off from him in ages past. No more, she had vowed anew.

Sarah felt an enormous longing for her beloved gather in her breast. She missed him terribly and needed the comfort of his embrace. Her heart burned for him. This time she would not fail.

"Kevin, I love you!" she cried aloud. She reached for her cell phone to call him, then remembered it was Monday morning. He would already be on his way to work and too busy for an important conversation.

She would connect with him tonight. They had already agreed to discuss their dreams and visions. Now she had even more reason to confide in Kevin and share with him the vow she had made in Lady Master Nada's etheric temple—the commitment she was determined to honor once and for all in this life. She would not waste one more opportunity to prove her loyalty to her soul's other half.

"Sarah, are you up?" Her mother's voice broke into her reverie.

"Everyone's had breakfast but you. I've told Ivy to stay in bed. She doesn't need to be fussing around the house so soon after being injured. I need you to clean up the kitchen while I help the twins get dressed. Grampa has promised them games in the family room and they're bouncing around like rabbits while he gets ready."

"Be right there, Ma," called Sarah as she pulled on jeans and a sweatshirt. For the first time in months she was glad for an opportunity to keep her hands busy and her mind occupied with some simple domestic chores.

Ten

Kevin had gone to work earlier than usual. Partly to miss the crush of eight-to-five commuters, and partly to beat his co-workers to the office. If he was already at his desk, they would be less likely to engage him in Monday morning chatter.

Today he needed to focus on clients who had questions about their end-of-year charitable giving. And, truth be told, he was more interested in leaving his attention open for any inner wisdom that might come to him from that aspect of himself he knew as Ah-Lahn.

He could still see and feel the druid's intense gaze as it met his yesterday. He knew that his soul's awareness was not limited by time and space. Inspiration could spark at any time.

"Kevin?" He sat up straight, his attention snapped back to this world. His secretary, Jane, stood in the open doorway of his office. He noticed that she was particularly well-dressed today in a light taupe business suit and heels. Had he forgotten an office event that required more formal attire?

"Good *morning*," she said, a wry smile playing on her lips.

"Uh, yes, good morning, Jane." Kevin did not usually daydream at the office. He wondered if he was blushing. If so, his secretary pretended not to notice.

"As soon as you have a minute, Greta wants to see you."

"Okay, thanks. Tell her I'll be right there."

Kevin smiled as he walked down the well-lighted hallway to his boss's office. He appreciated that she had chosen to decorate their workplace in warm, sunny tones with live plants throughout and beautiful landscape photographs on the walls.

That's Greta Nordemann, he said to himself—always considerate of her employees and their well-being. In his case, she was especially respectful of his time.

He would have been annoyed if anyone else had interrupted him this morning, but he enjoyed conversations with Greta. And he liked to think he'd been a source of comfort to her since her husband, Karl, had died of a sudden heart attack six months earlier.

Karl had built up the financial services business from doing taxes for friends in his kitchen to a thriving firm with three regional locations and a board of directors. Kevin worked in the main office near midtown Manhattan with Greta, who had stayed on as CFO, the position she'd held while Karl was CEO.

Everyone had expected that she would become CEO. She knew the business inside and out, and was keen to build on Karl's legacy of client-centered service. Her taking the helm would probably have meant a promotion to CFO for Kevin. Although there were elements of the job that, even then, he found mundane, he had liked the idea of having more authority over daily operations.

However, the Board had decided the company needed new blood. Instead of hiring from within, they had brought in a young CEO—a hotshot named Hildy Gleason whom they'd lured away from Edward Jones.

Greta and the new CEO had clashed almost immediately. Hildy had started making changes without learning more about the company than the state of its balance sheet, ignoring Greta's input at every turn.

A showdown was inevitable.

"Come in and close the door, Kevin." Greta sat in Karl's leather chair which she had filled for the past six months with dignity and strength. Today it seemed to dwarf her.

She was hunched over, elbows on the desk, holding her forehead in her hands. She glanced up as Kevin entered and slid her fingertips over her lips as if she dared not speak.

She never closes her door, he observed as he took the chair opposite her. One look at Greta told him something was terribly wrong. Her hair, which had gone from blonde to grey almost overnight after Karl died, was pulled back severely from her face. Her red eyes said she'd been crying. Her dark navy suit gave her the appearance of someone in mourning. Kevin realized she was reeling from a fresh death.

"Greta, what's the matter?" He reached a hand across the desk, encouraging her to speak.

"It's a coup," she said plainly. Her hand went to her throat.

"What?" Kevin sat straight up in his chair.

"Over the weekend. A bloodless coup perpetrated by our high-heeled CEO."

Office gossip was that Hildy wore four-inch heels and short skirts to pull attention away from Greta's classic style and make the older woman look frumpy in comparison. The ruse hadn't worked, of course. Greta was always perfectly groomed in tasteful designer suits that fit her position and the tone of the company. Something Hildy appeared not to appreciate.

"I don't understand." Kevin couldn't believe what he was hearing.

"Hildy called me at home late yesterday and told me to be here at 7:00 a.m. Of course, I didn't sleep all night. I knew something was up.

"She was waiting for me. As soon as I walked in the door, she whisked me into her office and, standing there all smug in her bright red mini-skirt, told me I'm out. My services are no longer required. The Board met yesterday and decided I'm an expense the company can no longer afford. Apparently, my position is now redundant."

"Can they do that?"

"Technically, yes. Six months before Karl died, he resigned his position as Chairman of the Board and sold all but ten percent of his interest in the company. It's almost as if he knew he wasn't going to live long. I've had no standing other than as a minor shareholder and an employee who works at the pleasure of the CEO—who called me a dinosaur, by the way. Old processes, old ways of thinking. She said I was a fossil."

Kevin was astonished at how quickly vengeful thoughts crowded his mind. Drowning in the East River would be too good for Hildy.

"I'll get a nice severance, of course," Greta continued. "At least they're giving me that. And they'll buy out my remaining shares if I want to sell them. They can't touch my other investments. Karl made sure our portfolio was secure. But to be pushed out like last week's garbage is just too much. It's too much, Kevin."

Greta threw up her hands as she stood. "Oh, and I have to be out of here by noon. Hildy told me she'd have me arrested if I tried to take any company files with me. As if I would!" Her hand went to her heart.

"That's ridiculous." Kevin was on his feet, pacing, instantly in problem-solving mode. "Can't you petition the Board?"

"No. I have a signed letter from them saying their decision is final. All daily operations are to be immediately transferred to Hildy and the staff of her choosing."

"Well, I'm going to go talk to her." Kevin started for the door.

"You can't do that, Kevin." Greta stopped him. "You're out, too."

Stunned, he turned back to his chair.

"Hildy called you 'teacher's pet' and said she couldn't afford to have you mucking up her plans by holding on to outdated procedures."

Kevin could barely speak. "So we're both out at noon?"

"Yes." Greta shrugged. "Hildy has called a staff meeting for 11:30 this morning—which we are not allowed to attend—to announce the changes. We're supposed to be gone by the time the meeting is over."

Greta turned to Kevin. "I'm so sorry. You'll get a month's severance, COBRA benefits. And, of course, you can apply for unemployment."

"References?" Kevin's head was spinning.

"Form letter only from Hildy. But don't worry, I will personally write you a spectacular recommendation."

"I'll be glad to do the same for you."

"That's sweet, but I'm retiring. Hildy can't touch me except to fire me, so I'll be fine. I just hope you will."

Me, too, thought Kevin, being careful not to voice his concern. Finances could get tough in a hurry if neither he nor Sarah was working.

He and Greta faced each other, their eyes glistening. When she walked around her desk to see him out, he took both her hands in his.

"It has meant a lot to me to work for you and Karl."

"We've always felt the same about you, Kevin. You've been like a son to us. More than a son, really. I hope you'll stay in touch. Let me know how you're getting on."

Kevin dropped her hands before they both dissolved into puddles of emotion. "Guess I'd better start packing. I have my car if you need help getting home. I usually take the train, but this morning something told me to drive in."

"Then I'll see you in the parking garage." Greta smiled wanly. "I drove in, too. I'll ask Jason to help me with boxes. Surely Hildy won't begrudge me that."

"Let's go to lunch after we've cleared out," Kevin suggested. "We can talk about the good old days. I don't want either of us leaving here with bad memories."

Good grief, what else could happen? Kevin mused several hours later as he drove over the 59th Street Bridge to Long Island. November's grey skies had never looked so ominous.

At least Greta had been smiling by the end of lunch. She had even waved good-bye with laughter in her eyes. The shared stories of happier times with Karl had brightened their conversation, and that made Kevin feel that he had done them all a final service.

But who was going to tell him happy stories? he wondered as he stopped to pick up Hero from doggie day care. At least they wouldn't have that expense if he and Sarah were both at home.

What in the world was *he* going to do at home? Sarah had her book to finish. But one of them needed to bring in a paycheck. He had signed a non-compete agreement with Karl when he was hired, so he couldn't ask any of his clients to follow him. Some other solution would have to materialize.

And, he thought, as visions of his scary dream-time escapade in the swamp of mediocrity popped into his head, there was a big part of him that was glad to be liberated. He did, in fact, have other, more hopeful dreams—some recently sparked by druids and a cave of symbols.

Eleven

Sarah was finishing the dinner dishes when Kevin called. She had wanted to call him as soon as she thought he'd be home from work. But then she'd been swept up in the flurry of bringing Brian home from the hospital and settled into what Eileen called "Recuperation Central."

Their mother was determined that neither her son nor his wife should overexert themselves.

After being part of the Callahan family for six-plus years, Ivy had learned the futility of contradicting Eileen once she was committed to a plan of action. The woman was like a general, giving orders, keeping an eye on the terrain. Might as well relinquish command, concluded the daughter-in-law, who ceded the field, including her own kitchen.

Once resigned to the situation, Ivy found herself resting better and enjoying having some time with the twins. Kerry and Kaitlyn were fascinated by her cast and had announced yesterday that they were helping Mommy because she had a broken wing.

Last month they had watched a video about a veterinarian who had mended the wing of a red-tailed hawk. So now Ivy was their hawk and they were making sure she healed just as successfully.

They took turns brushing her long, copper-colored hair. They called the activity "smoothing her feathers" and agreed between them that she was too gentle a bird to be returned to the wild. They would keep her as their special pet and teach her to read to them. So far, they were pleased with her progress.

Sarah hurriedly dried her hands on a kitchen towel and grabbed her cell phone before the call from her husband rolled over to voicemail.

"Oh, Kevin. I meant to phone you earlier, but things have been crazy, and I've been helping where I can and . . ."

"It's okay, Hon," Kevin reassured her, "I've been kind of, uh, busy, too. How is everybody?"

"All home now and resting. Brian's concussion was severe, so he's on a reduced work schedule for at least four weeks. Ivy's injury was a clean break, but it's her right arm, so she's limited by her cast. The twins are playing nursemaid and loving every minute of it. Dad's in the garage repairing something, and Ma's got everything and everybody well under control."

"I can imagine," Kevin chuckled. "How are you?"

"Fine. Tired. Relieved. We were so worried. I'm sorry I can't come home right away. Ma says she needs me here, though I'm not sure she really does. Millie and Jack have already volunteered to lend a hand as needed. I think Ma just wants us all together in one place where she can put her arms around us."

"Can't blame her for that."

"No, I can't. But I need to talk to you and . . . well . . . I'm sorry I haven't been a good wife. I'm going to do better, I promise."

Kevin shook his head. "Where did that come from?"

"Another dream I had, early this morning. About vows we made before this lifetime. I haven't been fulfilling my promises very well, and I'm sorry."

"I don't know what to say." He really didn't.

"I know, and I . . ." Emotion welled up in Sarah's throat. The stress she'd been holding in for two days spilled over into sobs.

"Hon, what's wrong?" asked Kevin.

"I'm mostly just tired," she sighed. "But I do wish we could talk about all these dreams in person."

"Me, too. I have so much to share with you—though I'm still trying to figure out what I've been shown," Kevin offered, his own voice going soft. "I know I'll understand things better when we compare these experiences. Should I come to New Bedford? Or is the house too crowded?"

"It really is. And besides, don't you have to work?"

"Uh, that's the other reason I called." He took a deep breath. Sarah already enough stress with her family. He hated to add to her burden, but she had to know what happened. "I got laid off today."

"What? How? No warning?"

"None. Hildy fired Greta and me so she can run the company without opposition. She'll probably run it into the ground, but that's no longer my concern."

Sarah's heart sank. Would she have to go back to a regular job so soon after finding her calling as a novelist? "I knew she was whittling away at your responsibilities, but this is draconian."

"Yeah, well, I probably should have seen it coming. She'd already reduced my position from manager to more of a glorified clerk. I never thought I'd be bored at work, but I have been." And haunted by the beast of mediocrity, not to mention Hildy's willful ignoring of Greta's wisdom and experience, he thought.

Sarah was beginning to understand why he hadn't been himself of late. "Then, is this a good thing?" she asked bravely, reviving a game they used to play—reframing difficult situations into potentially positive outcomes.

"It's not great. But I've got severance and unemployment. And we have an assignment."

"We do? From whom?"

"From the Master Saint Germain and from Ah-Lahn."

"I don't understand. Aren't you Ah-Lahn?"

"Yes and no. Are you someplace where you can talk? I need to give you the whole vision, from the beginning."

"I'll go up to my attic room. Then I can tell you about my dreams."

"Sounds good. I miss you, Hon."

"I miss you, too. You have no idea how much."

After two hours, Kevin and Sarah were still talking. The other Callahans in New Bedford had gone to bed early after a very full day.

At the MacCauleys' house on Long Island, Hero and Sprite had given up on nighttime treats and taken themselves off to warm their human's bed, should he ever decide to join them.

Time had vanished as husband and wife shared their dreams, filling in one another's experiences and identifying where their perspectives fit together to create a larger picture.

They started devising a plan for understanding what was being asked of them. First, they needed to identify what they knew about Alana and Ah-Lahn's conversations between worlds.

Sarah started. "We know that the bits and pieces I've recorded in the novel are only part of the communion that Alana and Ah-Lahn maintained between his death and her eventual passing."

"That's right," agreed Kevin. "I'm fascinated by Alana's fear that she would lose her identity if she entered fully into communion with Ah-Lahn's soul."

Sarah picked up the thread. "And you said he was intent on sharing with her what he was learning in the Otherworld that would strengthen her identity as her True Self."

"Right, again. I felt him impressing on me that he wanted to help her soul's spiritual development while she was still in embodiment. I got a clear impression that we should recover who and what we were as druids and then build on that legacy in this life."

"What does that actually mean?" asked Sarah.

"I'm not entirely sure," said Kevin. "My sense is that the details of our assignment will unfold as we accomplish each step. And there are steps—as if each of us is walking a path or climbing a ladder to reach the consciousness of our True Self. At the same time, we're supposed to be working on uniting our souls more deeply before we can accomplish whatever is next."

"Good heavens!" exclaimed Sarah. "That's quite an assignment. Did Saint Germain give you any direction about how we accomplish all of that? I don't want to end up in some kind of psychic morass because our human minds aren't able for the task."

"The Master gave me a blessing, which felt like a protection against psychic intrusion. But I think we should ask for confirmation that he and Lady Nada truly want us to be tapping into the records of our past lives like this. I hope they do. I can't help being excited that Ah-Lahn showed me how he and Alana connected."

"Yes, and we did the same thing on Atlantis when we served in Lady Nada's temple, when she was Nhada-lihn. But that was twelve thousand years ago. Do you think we can repeat the process?"

"We can try." Kevin's pulse quickened. He could imagine himself and Sarah connecting their minds and hearts in deeper communion than they had ever achieved in this life.

She continued. "In my recollections of Ireland, Alana did eventually learn how to connect with Ah-Lahn in the Otherworld. I believe what we've been shown is more about how that process unfolded and what she, in particular, had to overcome to make the connection so we can do the same. Now we're both here and they're . . . where exactly are they, Kevin?"

"Good point," he agreed. "In a way, they're inside of us. We are the sum of who we were in all of our embodiments. At the same time, I have this sense that these parts of self we identify as Ah-Lahn and Alana are pieces of our souls that have been split off and that, somehow, we're supposed to pull back into our total reality. Does that make sense?"

"Wow," said Sarah softly. "Amazingly, it does. I know I was Alana, yet she does feel separate from me. I never really thought of this, but there are times that she almost feels like a child who wants her mother to rescue her."

"Exactly," agreed Kevin. "Even though I detect Ah-Lahn when he's in the Otherworld, I also pick up a vibration of him being stuck on another plane of consciousness that is not so exalted."

"Fascinating," said Sarah.

They were both silent for several minutes. Then Kevin said, "Hon, I think what we're being prompted to attempt is to access the energetic records of our past experiences. Those akashic memories must exist in our souls as well as in the ethers."

"I'm willing if you are," said Sarah.

Kevin continued. "Does your brother's house have a fireplace?"

"Uh-huh." Sarah picked up his thought. "And it's gas so I can just switch it on. If we can step into an orb of light at the same time, we might be able to meet up with our masters and maybe even with our former selves."

"Exactly. Do you want to try now while everybody is asleep? In about fifteen minutes?

"Absolutely." Sarah's fatigue was long gone. "I'd love to meet Master Saint Germain, and I'm sure you'd like to see Lady Nada again.

"I would. What time does your phone say?"

"10:00."

"Mine, too. At 10:15 let's both put our attention on the flames. If we see orbs of light, we'll each pick a crystal-pink one and step in."

"Perfect. Then afterwards, let's talk to compare experiences."

"Good idea. And Sarah?"

"Yes?"

"Don't worry about me losing my job. That may be part of what we're heading into."

"You could be right. I hope so."

"Something will work out. You're doing great, by the way, so keep it up. You know, I heard Ah-Lahn say, 'I speak because she listens.' That's you. We're both listening now, but you started this in Ireland."

"And we'll finish our assignment together. I know we will, because we promised before this life. We have to succeed this time."

Sarah gave a deep sigh, remembering the gravity she'd felt in last night's dream. "I'll see you soon, Hon—somewhere."

Twelve

At exactly 10:15 p.m. Sarah switched on the gas fireplace in Brian's living room. She wrapped a warm woolen shawl she'd bought in Ireland around her shoulders and settled onto the immaculate, white leather sofa that faced the hearth where blue and yellow flames burned brightly.

Kevin has it easy, she thought. He's home alone and he's done this before. Tonight would be her first experience of visualizing orbs of light and stepping into one of them in her soul's light body. All of her other visions and past life reviews had come to her in dreams. She was willing to give this process a try, but a sudden onset of butterflies made her wonder if she could do it.

Sitting cross-legged and pulling her shawl a bit tighter, she breathed a prayer to Archangel Michael for spiritual protection of the ritual she was about to perform.

She closed her eyes and followed her breath like she did in yoga class. In and out. Easy. Not controlling. Feel the relaxation and open your eyes when you're ready.

Gazing at the dancing flames, she tried not to push. You can't *will* a vision to happen, she reminded herself. Relax. Enjoy the flames for themselves. Forget about orbs or crystalline bridges to the Otherworld. Be Sarah, here and now.

Maybe if she closed her eyes again, she'd see something when she opened them. Alana had been able to do this. Why couldn't she?

But something was missing. Or someone. Of course—Ah-Lahn.

He had placed one hand on Alana's back and the other on her forehead to quicken her inner sight. Kevin had done exactly the same thing at Sarah's cottage in Ireland to help her remember her dreams.

She tried to recall the sensation. As she concentrated, she felt a gentle pulsing begin behind her heart. "Breathe into the feeling," she remembered Kevin saying.

As she breathed in and out, the pulsing grew stronger and began to move through her body—its rhythm increasing until she could feel her heart chakra spinning, creating a sphere of scintillating energy that surrounded her entire body.

Wonderful, glorious, indescribably delicate, like eiderdown yet translucent. She could rest here forever in this ineffable sweetness.

Ever so gently, Sarah opened her eyes. Yes, the light was there in the fireplace. She and her orb were being pulled in to join the flames now burning green and gold and purple and blue. The hearth was a Christmas tree, and she was part of the gaiety that shone in, through, and around her.

She was traveling now. Moving through space, approaching a starry bridge that looked like the Milky Way. The sensation was so exhilarating, she laughed out loud. Never had she felt such joy, such total happiness, such. . . pain!

Without warning, she stumbled and fell out of her sphere, landing back on Brian's sofa. When she came back to herself, she was looking into two small faces whose blue eyes sparkled with anticipation.

The twins, Kerry and Kaitlyn, stared at her with intense interest. Their lisping questions tumbled out as they spoke on top of each other.

"Aunt Sewah, we heard you laughing."

"We saw you in the pink bubble."

"Are you playing a game with the Rose Lady?"

"Can we play too?"

"I want a snack!" demanded Kerry.

Sarah scrubbed her hands over her face and blinked her eyes. She wanted to cry. Hurtling out of the sphere of light was completely disorienting. Her body felt like she'd been pulled through a knothole.

Yet she couldn't help laughing at the pair of redheaded four-year-olds standing expectantly before her in their matching flannel bunny rabbit jammies.

"What are you two doing out of bed?" she asked.

"We heard you laughing," repeated Kaitlyn.

"We want to play in the pink bubble with the Rose Lady," Kerry chimed in.

"How do you know the Rose Lady?" Sarah's heart was suddenly racing, though she tried to sound matter-of-fact. They must mean Lady Nada . . . but how?

"She visits us sometimes," explained Kaitlyn.

"And she takes us flying and we go to her house and she tells us stories," chimed in Kerry. "She's really pretty and she sings. Only she doesn't have snacks."

"Do you know her, Aunt Sewah?" Kaitlyn wanted to know.

"Yes, I believe I do, and I'd like to hear your stories about her. But it's very late. Don't you think I should tuck you back in bed?"

"I'm hungry," pouted Kerry.

"You're up and so are we." Kaitlyn was a confident spokesperson for the duo. They each took one of Sarah's hands and pulled her from the sofa into the kitchen.

"Okay," she acquiesced. "Let's find something to eat. How about milk and apple slices?"

"Yay! Then a story about the Rose Lady," Kerry insisted.

"We'll see," said Sarah. She was suddenly very tired and hoped that a bit of food would make the twins sleepy. Sure enough, half a glass of milk later and the little redheads began nodding.

"Come along, you two," she said, taking them each by the hand. "Aunt Sarah's tired. Let me put you to bed and tomorrow we'll talk about the Rose Lady and the pink bubble."

"Okay, but don't tell Mommy," said Kaitlyn as her eyes drooped. "She doesn't understand about the Rose Lady, so we don't try to tell her anymore."

Kevin sat before the fire in his living room, confident and excited about the prospect of meeting Sarah in the etheric temple where she had seen

Lady Master Nada. He was eager for them to confer with her and Saint Germain—hopefully both of them together.

He stilled his mind, focused his attention on his heart chakra, and gazed at the flames in his fireplace. In barely a minute, the multicolored orbs began to appear. They were incredibly alive tonight, twirling and spinning around, as if they were old friends greeting him.

In the center of the conflagration was a gorgeous, crystal-pink sphere. It beckoned to him and grew in size as if to surround him with its joyful presence. Without hesitation, he stepped out of his physical body and into the orb.

In an instant, he was running across the starry bridge toward Lady Nada's temple, which he could see up ahead. In a flash, he reached the end of the bridge. He stopped and looked around. Where was Sarah? He was certain she would be here—if not now, then soon.

He turned and looked back across the bridge. Yes! There she was. Just stepping on to the span. She was moving fast. They were doing this! His plan was working! He could hardly contain the joy he felt and the love that poured through him for his beloved who was . . .

Gone! Disappeared! Evaporated as if he hadn't just seen her entering the bridge, enfolded in a sphere of rosy light. He waited, hoping she would reappear. But she didn't.

He considered proceeding alone into the temple to ask one of the masters what had happened. Then he felt the pull. A not-so-subtle tug that had him zooming back the way he'd come.

Suddenly, he was once more in his physical body, coming awake in his living room where his cell phone was beeping. He had a message from Sarah.

Almost made it. Exquisite sphere of light.
The twins interrupted. Will call you in the morning.
Very sorry. Love, S.

Thirteen

At Brian and Ivy's house, another two inches of fresh snow had fallen overnight, adding a layer of white fluff to the backyard where Sarah's father was planning what he had dubbed "The Great Snowman Creation Project."

His grandchildren were old enough now to participate in rolling big snowballs for belly, chest, and head, and then decorating the form with stick arms, carrot nose, button eyes, hat, scarf, and stones for the mouth. It was hard to tell who was more excited—Grampa or the twins.

However, they'd hit a snag. As Patrick drew a picture and explained how they would go about building their snowman, Kaitlyn's little mouth drooped, her lower lip in a pout.

"What's the matter, sweetheart?" Patrick asked. "Don't you want to make a snowman?"

"No," she sniffled. Tears were brimming in her bright blue eyes.

"Why not? Can you tell Grampa?"

"We're not supposed to say," said Kerry, spooning up the last of his "bug cereal." That's what he called Gramma's special hot oatmeal made with cinnamon and raisins. He reached over to his sister's plate for the piece of bacon she wasn't eating.

"Brian, do you know what this is about?" Patrick asked his son, who had finished his breakfast and was heading to the den to catch up on the morning news programs. He couldn't work on the computer for a few days, so television would have to suffice.

"It's something about a fairy woman they've imagined they can see. Ivy and I don't think it's healthy for them to be obsessed with a person who's not real."

"But the Rose Lady *is* real," whimpered Kaitlyn as tears spilled down her little pink cheeks, "and we *can* see her." Despite her frustration at not being believed, she managed *not* to blurt out that they had seen the Rose Lady last night with their Aunt Sarah.

"Kaitlyn, Honey, remember what we talked about." Her father put his arm around her. "Fairy stories are exciting but they're imaginary. Okay? Kerry? You, too. Grampa is an excellent snowman builder. I'm sure you'll have lots of fun with him."

"Okay," Kerry answered softly. Kaitlyn said nothing. Her lower lip was still quivering.

"And Ma, I don't want you filling their heads with Irish nonsense." said Brian. "This 'rose lady' stuff has gone far enough. I'll be in the den if anyone needs me."

Eileen had been listening to this interchange and rolled her eyes at her husband as Brian left the kitchen. She knew they were thinking the same thing. When had their son lost his imagination? As a boy, he had told them vivid stories about fairies and elves and his own imaginary friends. Apparently, those days were long gone.

"Okay, little ones," Eileen said cheerfully to the twins. "Let's get you dressed to go outside. You don't have to build a snowman if you don't want to. Grampa has lots of snow games you can play."

"I do," he agreed, catching his wife's meaning and lifting the twins from their booster seats. "Would you like to go sledding instead?"

"Yay!" cried Kerry. "Can we have hot cocoa after?"

"Of course," said Eileen. "Now, run upstairs. I'll be right there."

"Hi, Aunt Sewah! We're going sledding with Grampa and then we get hot cocoa!" exclaimed Kerry as he ran past Sarah, who was just now coming to breakfast. She'd been on the phone with Kevin. Last night's experiences in their orbs of pink light had given them a lot to discuss.

Kaitlyn shuffled behind her brother, looking at the floor. Before Sarah could ask what was wrong, Eileen had chores for her daughter.

"Sarah, as soon as you've eaten, I need you to check on Ivy. I took her a breakfast tray earlier, but I have to get a few things from the store and I don't want her trying to carry anything or coming downstairs without help.

"Grampa is entertaining the twins this morning and Brian is watching the news on TV. He's promised not to get on his computer, but you might peek in to make sure. The doctor said he's not supposed to stress his brain or focus his eyes for too long on any one thing. His partner, Hank, is coming over later this morning to talk strategy until Brian can go back to work. That should keep him occupied until lunchtime."

"Okay, Ma," Sarah agreed, hoping her reluctance to interact with Ivy didn't show on her face. The two sisters-in-law never seemed to know what to say to each other. As close as they were in age—Sarah was twenty-eight and Ivy was twenty-six—they inhabited very different worlds.

Ivy was technically gifted like her husband and had worked with him until the twins came along. Nowadays she did some support work from home, or at least as much as keeping track of two energetic four-year-olds allowed.

Brian shared his father's ability with anything computer-related. And, like his father, he was also a skilled salesman. He and his buddy, Hank, had started their software company while still in college. After six very busy years, they were doing extremely well.

Initially, they had hired Ivy as a part-time programmer, but her skills and creative input quickly made her a valued partner in the enterprise and—much to Eileen's chagrin—in Brian's personal life.

Within six months, he had moved in with Ivy. They'd lived together in her apartment until they could buy their big house in New Bedford and had married shortly before she got pregnant. Or close enough. It was hard to tell for sure because the twins came early.

Eileen had nothing to complain about now—except, perhaps, for her son's and daughter-in-law's dislike of anything having to do with the Celtic culture and folklore that were so dear to her and Patrick.

Nevertheless, she was proud of their business success that afforded them a very comfortable life style. She wanted her children to be happy in life and was delighted that her son appeared to be perfectly content with his.

She couldn't help wondering about Sarah, though. The girl seemed moody and preoccupied. However, there was nothing a mother could do unless her daughter confided in her.

As slowly as possible, Sarah ate her poached egg and the fresh scone her mother had risen early that morning to bake. Yes, she was delaying going up to Ivy's room. But she really did need to reflect on her morning's conversation with Kevin while their exchange was fresh in her mind.

They had laughed together when she described how the twins had interrupted her meditation and claimed to know the Rose Lady. They agreed that being sent whooshing out of a sphere of light and crashing back into one's body was definitely unsettling.

After failing to create these visions separately, they decided that they needed to be in the same place at the same time to make the connection with their druid selves as well as with their masters.

"Ah-Lahn was nearly always with Alana for her life reviews," Sarah reminded Kevin. "And I needed you with me in Ireland to spark my memory of the events I had dreamed the night before."

"When do you think you can come home?" asked Kevin, urging her.

"Ten days. Maybe more. It's hard to say. Millie and Jack have offered to help out since they live a few minutes from here. My mom and dad might even take the twins home with them to Braintree for a couple of weeks until Brian and Ivy are in better shape.

"I may ask my folks if I can go back to Braintree right away and work at their house. I'm really close to finishing the novel, and I need to get it to my friend Gillian who works in publishing.

"When did that happen?" Kevin tried not to sound irritated that here, again, was an aspect of their book Sarah hadn't shared with him.

She felt his displeasure.

"Hon, I really am sorry. I totally forgot to tell you. I got an email from Gillian the day we drove to New Bedford."

"Oh, okay. I understand."

Kevin and Sarah both breathed a sigh of relief. The emotional bridge they were building to each other was still fragile. Neither of them wanted to threaten its stability.

"Gillian's found me an editor with connections to a small publisher who's taking on new authors. This could be the break I've been hoping for—if I can send them the manuscript in the next couple of weeks."

"That's great," said Kevin. "Yes, finish your book. I'll be busy with unemployment paperwork anyway. And—who knows what else. Right?"

"Right," agreed Sarah. "Call me if anything comes up. I'll call or text when I know if I can get back to Braintree."

"Will do. Bye."

Fourteen

Sarah ran her hand along the clean lines of the stairway in Brian and Ivy's house. Metallic railings and open wooden stair treads led up to the second floor where three large bedrooms lined a long, open hallway that looked out over the living room below.

A large, abstract painting in shades of pale blue, light grey, and dark purple covered most of the adjacent wall. Tall, thin lighting fixtures were hung on either side and matched three more that subtly lit the upstairs hallway. A baby gate looked out of place at the top of the stairs.

Sarah shook her head. This decor was so different from the classic, oriental carpeted stairs with quarter-sawn oak railings she had climbed at her parents' house every day of her childhood.

Those walls were covered with a family photo gallery that stretched back from more recent baby pictures of her niece and nephew to images of both sets of grandparents' weddings.

Amazingly, those couples had all lived to be very old, so Sarah had known them before they slipped into the sepia faces who lovingly gazed out from her memory.

They had been hardy folk, she mused. Descended from ancestors who fled Ireland's devastating potato famine in the mid-nineteenth century, their generations had survived and raised large families to work the land her mother's people had farmed, or to become entrepreneurs like her father's great-grandparents who had operated a mercantile shop in the small village of Braintree.

Theirs had been lives of unimaginable hardship, and the women had bravely borne their children through it all.

Sarah had never thought of herself as the Earth Mother type who could give birth in the morning and fix dinner that evening for her husband and three other small children under the age of five.

That was an exaggeration, of course, but the message of courage and perseverance was true.

No, she didn't have the temperament to handle a noisy brood, but she still wanted at least one child. Kevin's child. A son or a daughter. Perhaps one of each. Four to make a family and carry on the MacCauley name.

Her husband obviously enjoyed playing with her brother's twins. Over the past two years she had observed him gently wrestling with them as toddlers, bundling them into their fluffy snowsuits a year ago Christmas, building sandcastles at the beach late last summer, teaching them to solve puzzles or create fantastical shapes with Tinkertoys or Legos.

He preferred the old toys he'd played with as a child. He said they helped the little ones expand their imaginations rather than being distracted from their inner teacher by artificial images and noises.

That was Kevin's way. Sarah had watched and loved him for his tender playfulness. And all too frequently she'd brushed away the unbidden tears that filled her eyes—the persistent response to her failure to bear a child.

Her reverie was suddenly pierced by cries coming from the far end of the hall.

"Ow, ow, ow! Damnit! Ow!"

Sarah rushed into Ivy and Brian's spacious master bedroom to find her sister-in-law tangled up in a burgundy fleece sweatshirt that she was unsuccessfully trying to tug on over her head. She had somehow managed to pull on the matching pants, but the top was now perched like a jester's hat, sleeves flapping halfway between her shoulders and forehead.

"Ivy, what are you doing?" Sarah tried not to laugh at the young woman who sat in the middle of her bed, nearly dissolved in tears. "Here, let me help you."

"Ow! Be careful!" Ivy gritted her teeth as her sister-in-law tried to remove the pullover. They were both glad she was still wearing the camisole that served as her pajama top.

"How can two slightly bruised ribs be so painful?" moaned Ivy. "I thought I could get dressed, but everything hurts. Even more than yesterday."

"Do you have a cardigan?" asked Sarah. "That might be easier."

"In the closest. Get the mauve one. No, next to the violet one. The mauve is old and stretched out. I was going to give it away. I'm glad I didn't."

Sarah smiled at Ivy's closet. Sweaters, blouses, jeans, slacks, skirts were all arranged by color on matching hangers. Ah, yes, she thought, remembering how she intended to organize her own closet—one of these days. She and Brian's wife were very different people.

At last Ivy was dressed and lying back on the extra pillows that Sarah plumped behind her.

"Ugh, thank you." She sighed, then asked, "Where are the twins?"

"Outside with Grampa. I think they're going sledding."

Sarah avoided saying anything about them not building a snowman. She hoped to find out later why little Kaitlyn looked so unhappy.

"That's a relief. They wore me out yesterday. They're very sweet to want to take care of me. I'm their wounded hawk, you know."

"Uh-huh," Sarah nodded with a smile.

"I don't know where they get these ideas," said Ivy. "Actually, I do know where the hawk idea came from. But they have such vivid imaginations and they want so much of my attention. It's hard to tell them that Mommy's busy sometimes. At least they're getting old enough to spend half days at nursery school so I can do more work for Brian."

Sarah's heart sank. She would have given anything to have two little ones demanding her attention. And here was Ivy, wishing she had more time to herself. Would she have felt that way about her own children if she was trying to find time to write? No way of knowing.

Ivy took a deep breath. "Ow."

"Are you sure you're okay now?"

"Yes, as long as I don't try to breathe—or laugh." Ivy grimaced.

Sarah couldn't help but chuckle.

"I was wondering," said Ivy hesitantly, "could you spend some time with the twins while you're here?"

Sarah tensed.

"That is, if that's not too hard after . . . I'm sorry. I don't know how to say this. I've never been able to tell you how sorry I am about your . . . losses. I can't imagine what that's like."

No, you can't possibly imagine, thought Sarah. She pushed back the sarcasm that rose in her throat and admonished herself. Ivy was trying to be kind. Give her a break.

"That's okay, Ivy. I know you stay really busy. And it's not like we live next door."

"You're right. If we did, I'd probably be begging for help. I wanted children, but the twins came so fast and two at once. All I can say is that this has been more than I bargained for. And Brian works so many hours as the business grows, I'm on my own a lot."

Sarah was beginning to see a picture of how her very tidy sister-in-law had been overwhelmed by the need for two sets of diapers, bottles, and toys—and now the myriad requirements of two growing children.

"I know I shouldn't say this, Sarah," said Ivy, "but sometimes I envy you—working for a high-powered New York politician and now being a novelist."

"You're kidding." Sarah was genuinely stunned.

"No, I'm not," said Ivy. "And I can't believe I've just told you so."

"Well, I've envied you because you've had two babies while I've had . . ." Sarah felt her eyes prickle, her voice choked.

"I am sorry," Ivy started to reach out for Sarah's hand, then drew up short. "Ow! These damned ribs."

"Oh, Ivy." Sarah wiped her eyes and winced on her sister's behalf. "Let's get you tucked in for a nap. Do you need something else to eat or drink?" She eyed the remains of the hearty breakfast that Eileen had served earlier.

"No, I'm not hungry. Your mother sent up enough food for three people."

"I know," smiled Sarah, picking up the tray. "She equates food with love and serves up lots of both, especially when she's worried. Then she cooks like a famine's coming. I'll let you rest now."

"I'm not really tired either, just bored." Ivy drew out the sound of the word. She hesitated. This conversation was turning into a lot more personal disclosure than she was used to. She and Brian seldom talked this way.

"Before you go, I have a question."

"Okay." Sarah set the tray back on Ivy's nightstand.

"Do you know anything about the 'rose lady' the twins claim to see? Kaitlyn seems very attached to this imaginary friend. That worries me, and Brian agrees. We want our children to grow up as clear thinkers with common sense."

"They are amazingly bright," said Sarah carefully, then added, "I don't think you have a thing to worry about." Should she tell her sister-in-law about Lady Nada? She decided to take the plunge. After all, Ivy had broached the subject.

"To answer your question—yes, I am acquainted with their Rose Lady, though the twins and I haven't discussed it. Now that I know you're concerned, maybe I shouldn't talk to them about her."

"They keep wanting to tell me about their adventures with this beautiful lady who wears a ruby-colored robe and golden crown. It all sounds so . . . fantastical. I don't know what to say to them. I didn't grow up with fairytales, and Brian says they're nonsense."

"Ivy, can I tell you a story about the Rose Lady? You don't have to believe it. I'm just thinking perhaps a little bit of fantasy told by an adult will help you understand your children."

"Would you?" said Ivy, unconsciously clapping her hands like Sarah had seen her little daughter do only last night. "My mother never told me stories. She and my father were scientists. Ours was a very logical household and . . . well . . . you get the picture."

"I do," said Sarah as she pulled up a chair next to Ivy's bed and considered how to tell a fairytale to someone who had never heard one.

She took a deep breath and began with the opening line that, since ancient times, has invited listeners of all ages to settle into a story meant to carry them far beyond the restrictions of their daily lives.

Once upon a time, there was beautiful, fair-haired goddess who lived in *Tír na n'Óg,* Land of the Ever-Living. She had a great love for human beings because she once had been one herself.

She had lived in eons long past, on a continent that sank below the waves in an ancient disaster that was now only a myth, its memory lost long ago in the veils of time.

Fifteen

Sarah sighed as she leaned back on the attic day bed, grateful that the house was quiet for a while until lunchtime. Her sister-in-law had drifted off to sleep during the story about the Rose Lady. Sarah would have to find out later what she'd thought of it.

Eileen had returned from the grocery store in time to extricate Kerry and Kaitlyn from their snowsuits and settle them in the kitchen with mugs of hot cocoa and tiny marshmallows. Patrick was in Brian's office talking computers with his son and Hank.

Eileen had declined her daughter's offer to help make lunch, so Sarah was free to reflect on her surprising conversation with Ivy. Was this one of those fears that Alana had been told she must welcome home for healing? Sarah had to admit she'd been afraid to interact with Ivy. And Ivy had seemed reluctant to express her frustrations as the mother of twins.

Imagine the irony. She and Ivy envied each other. And what is envy, except fear that another person has what you want and doubt that you will ever achieve that desire? Perhaps even an unconscious belief that the other person is more worthy of reward than you. The green-eyed monster of jealousy was sure to thrive in that dark soil.

What other fears were lurking in the recesses of her mind? Sarah wondered. *Write them out,* she heard her voice of inner wisdom suggest.

Of course. Recording her thoughts on paper had always been a natural way of gaining clarity—especially when those thoughts were confusing or hard to pin down.

Sarah dug out her journal and pen from her briefcase and wrote at the top of a new page: "What am I afraid of?" She could have titled the page: "What do I worry about?" And weren't worries just fears that revolved over and over in her mind?

"Yes!" she declared out loud, planting her flag for truth. "Let's call them what they are and stop ruminating."

What Am I Afraid Of?

I'm afraid for our finances. We have house and car payments and were already economizing since I'm writing full time.

I'm afraid that I'll have to go back to work at a "regular" job because Kevin lost his.

I'm afraid we'll have to ask my parents for money—or even move in with them.

I'm afraid of being a failure as a novelist.

I'm afraid I won't be able to connect with myself as Alana in the way that Kevin can connect with himself as Ah-Lahn.

I'm afraid of my feelings of resentment toward Ivy.

I'm afraid that Kevin is unhappy and I don't know what to do about it.

I'm afraid of getting pregnant.

Whoa! Sarah stared as that last phrase. All too true. As much as she still wanted a baby, the fear of another miscarriage was all too real—despite Ivy's complaint of being overwhelmed by her children.

What can you control? asked her voice of inner wisdom.

That had always been Kevin's question to her when she'd confided her fears to him in the past. She made another list:

Things I Can Control

I can work on my feelings about Ivy. We're both here in this house and we've made a start.

I can spend time with the twins and find out more about their experiences with the Rose Lady.

I can start facing my fear of getting pregnant.

I can finish my novel, send it to Gillian, and keep breathing until I get some actual feedback from an editor.

I can call my former assistant, Debbie, and ask about part-time work at A. B. Ryan's office.

Sarah gasped at the audacity of that thought, then reassured herself. Maybe she could do some freelance writing for Gwen and Tony, the politician's senior writers. That way she wouldn't have to interact with the boss.

At any rate, she wouldn't mention any of this to Kevin until she had an actual plan.

"Lunch is ready!" called Eileen from downstairs. The sound of male voices told Sarah the computer crew were on their way to the dining room. She put away her journal and made her way to Ivy's room.

"Hey, Sis, do you want to come downstairs for lunch?"

"I do, if you don't mind helping me navigate," said Ivy who was awake now. "God, I feel like such an invalid."

And a bit of an intruder in your own kitchen, thought Sarah, as she remembered the look on Ivy's face when she came home from the hospital. Knowing that she was in pain, Eileen had shooed her up to her bedroom to wait for her meals to be delivered.

Sarah knew her mother meant well, but Ivy was clearly ready to be released from isolation to join the family for a meal.

"Yay!" cried Kerry and Kaitlyn together as their mother walked into the dining room with Sarah at her side. They had finished their hot cocoa in the kitchen and were now seated in their booster seats at the big family table—well into their turkey sandwiches. As usual, their exclamations tumbled out on top of each other.

"Mommy Hawk is walking."

"She's not well yet."

"Don't let her try to flap her wing, Aunt Sewah."

"Are you feeling better, Mommy Hawk?"

"Yes, I am." Ivy smiled into their bright blue eyes and did her best not to grimace as Sarah helped her sit at the table. "Just half a sandwich for me, please, Eileen," she said. "I'm still full after your wonderful breakfast."

Good for you, thought Sarah, as her mother accepted Ivy's request. Stake a small claim for your independence. Then her sister-in-law surprised her by taking a courageous step she had not expected.

"Kerry and Kaitlyn, I'm wondering if you would tell me about the Rose Lady. Aunt Sarah was sharing a very interesting story, but I fell asleep before she finished. Would you tell me about her after we've all had our afternoon nap?"

Everyone except Hank, who knew nothing about 'rose lady' stories, looked at Ivy in surprise. Her husband raised his eyebrows, as if to say, "Are you sure?"

"Don't worry, Brian," she answered his expression. "We're trying something new, that's all."

The twins blinked at each other and grinned. Kerry poked his sister's shoulder and looked on as Kaitlyn peeked up from under her long eyelashes. "Can Aunt Sewah come too?"

"Of course," agreed their mother. "Sarah? My room at two?"

"I'll be there."

That would give her an hour to make a phone call, or possibly two. Sarah felt a wave of fear swirl in her belly. She quelled it with a bite of her turkey sandwich, successfully overriding the subtle suggestion from her voice of inner wisdom that going back to work at A. B. Ryan's office might not be a good idea.

Rising heat from the lower floors in Ivy's house warmed Sarah's attic bedroom to a toasty comfort. Winter's midday sun sent a beam of light through the dormer window to add to the cheer. Still, she shivered and pulled her woolen shawl around her shoulders.

Despite what should have been a cozy atmosphere, she could not help feeling like Alana, stepping unprotected into an open glen where a dark and tangible fear challenged her to pluck up her courage and take a bold step.

She blew out an audible sigh, dialed her friend's number, and waited anxiously—almost hoping there would be no answer.

"Sarah, how are you?" Debbie's voice was full of affection as she picked up the call on her cell phone. "I haven't heard from you since you got back from Ireland and quit working for A. B."

"I'm good, Debbie. Sorry. I meant to call, but I went right into working on my book, and we'd just adopted the dog and cat, and . . ."

"That's fine, Sarah," Debbie interrupted with a laugh. "I knew you'd surface one of these days. I've been busy, too. Lots of changes here."

"Really? What's going on?"

"Well, it's a good thing you called my cell because I'm also no longer working for A. B."

"That *is* a change. Though I wondered how long you would put up with his shenanigans." And how crazy am I to think I'd go back to his office? thought Sarah.

"I'd wondered the same thing," said Debbie, "especially after you left. His behavior became even more erratic once his wife started divorce proceedings."

"She's finally divorcing him? That's amazing. I thought she either didn't know about Ursula or didn't care."

"Apparently she's known about A. B.'s affair with his assistant for over a year. Their adventures in the Middle East brought everything into the open. Ursula made no attempt at discretion when they were together, and the newspapers ate up the story.

"I'm surprised you haven't seen the photos in the tabloids—of Ursula leaning on A. B.'s arm, looking like a cat who'd swallowed the canary. I guess she got tired of his promises to dump his wife and took matters into her own hands."

"Wow!" said Sarah. "I'll bet that's costing A. B. a bundle."

"More than you can imagine," agreed Debbie, "which is one reason why I'm no longer working for him. He fired several of his staff, including me, Gwen, and two of the assistants. We suspected that Ursula made him get rid of all the women and retain the men she figured she could intimidate. After I got over the surprise, I was relieved to be free of the place."

"So you were going to leave anyway?"

"I was definitely thinking about it," said Debbie in a positive tone. "You remember how I've always worked with herbs and essential oils? My youngest sister, Cyndi, decided to open her own health food store. She'd asked me to work for her months ago, and I was considering her offer. Then this thing with A. B. happened and I figured it was a sign. So now I'm the herbs, oils, and teas lady while Cyndi does the supplements and food items."

"Are you earning enough?" Sarah was suddenly concerned about her friend's finances.

"Not as much as I was with A. B., but the quality of life is lots better. Fortunately, there's an apartment over the shop where I can live rent-free. My sister didn't want to move there herself. She's glad to have me on site."

"That's great, Debbie. You sound much happier than when we worked together."

"I am. And what about you, Sarah? You sound kind of stressed. I thought being a full-time novelist was what you wanted to do. Has something happened?"

"Yes," Sarah drew out the word. "Several things. Do you have time for a story?"

"Always," laughed Debbie. "I hope it has a happy ending."

"Me, too," said Sarah, "but I won't know for a while."

As succinctly as she could manage, Sarah told Debbie about Brian and Ivy's car accident, Kevin losing his job, and her fear for their finances. However, she didn't offer any details about her book or Kevin's experiences with Ah-Lahn or her own dreams about Alana.

Their tandem attempt to connect with their former selves was too nebulous to explain, even to her friend who was comfortable with matters of the occult. Although it had been Debbie who'd explained Sarah's visions of a black panther spirit guide before her trip to Ireland, these latest excursions into the spirit world needed time to develop before she felt comfortable sharing them.

"Thanks for the update," said Debbie when Sarah paused. "I have a feeling there's another reason why you called."

"Your intuition never fails," laughed her friend. "There is something else, and I hope you're not shocked."

"Go ahead. I'm not easily shocked these days."

"I haven't told Kevin this, and I probably won't, at least for a while." Sarah took a deep breath. "I've been thinking I might ask about doing some freelance writing in A. B.'s office. Maybe working directly for Tony so I wouldn't to have interact with the boss. Do you think I'm crazy to go back into the snake pit?"

"Yes, though your timing might be good. The Universe does work in mysterious ways. Late last week I got an email from Tony asking if I could help him out, sort of behind the scenes. He said he's swamped because A. B. cut so many positions. He doesn't want to ask the boss to hire anybody full-time, but he thought he could make a case for part-time help without benefits.

"I declined, of course, but I told him I'd let him know if I heard of anybody who might fit the bill—and here you are."

"This does feel like a sign, doesn't it?" said Sarah. "I'd like to contact Tony directly. Do you have his cell number? I don't think my call should go through the office switchboard or email."

"You're right about that," agreed Debbie. "He's in Manhattan, 586-4236. Tell him you talked to me and see what he says. Good luck, Sarah. Let me know what happens. Let's have lunch when you get back to New York. I don't want us to lose touch."

"Thanks, Debbie. I agree. I'll let you know if Tony has anything for me. I'm going to text him right now before I lose my nerve."

Sixteen

The atmosphere outside of Ivy's bedroom was bubbling when Sarah came downstairs a little before 2:00 p.m. She could hear the twins' clear little giggles and her sister-in-law's groans as she tried not to laugh.

"Come in, Sarah, and pull up a chair," said Ivy eagerly. She was sitting on her bed with Kerry and Kaitlyn scrunched in next to her left arm, away from Mommy Hawk's right wing. All three faces were beaming. "I guess you'd better close the door."

"This is private," Kaitlyn said very seriously.

"Now?" Kerry prompted his mother impatiently.

"Yes, you can tell her now."

"Tell me what?" asked Sarah.

"Mommy Hawk saw the Rose Lady!" exclaimed Kerry. "We were with her so we know she did!"

Sarah's eyes went wide. "Really?"

"I know." Ivy chuckled carefully. "I'm as surprised as you." She put her left hand to her lips and blushed. Sarah thought she looked like a schoolgirl sharing secrets she was embarrassed to admit.

"Did you talk to her?"

Kerry and Kaitlyn were full of excitement and jabbered all at once.

"The Rose Lady didn't talk out loud this time."

"She smiled and we all got hugs."

"Mommy Hawk's wing wasn't broken when we were there."

"Mommy was shy, but we weren't 'cause the Rose Lady is our friend."

Ivy looked up at Sarah and shrugged with an amused smile, as if to say, "What am I to do with these children?"

"That's so exciting," said Sarah to her niece and nephew. "Shall we let Mommy tell the rest of the story?"

"Tell her, Mommy Hawk," said Kaitlyn, "and we'll smooth your feathers."

Ivy turned her body toward Sarah and let her long, copper-colored hair fall down her back. Her little boy scrambled across the bed to retrieve a hair brush from the bedside table, and the twins set to work grooming their pet hawk. She breathed a gentle sigh and began telling Sarah the story that she herself could hardly believe.

"Kerry and Kaitlyn insisted on napping with me, so we all snuggled in together. We must've fallen asleep right away. I don't remember much except that I was sort of half-awake, but not really awake—if you know what I mean."

"I do," said Sarah. She had a feeling she knew where this story was going. "Tell me more."

Ivy's face brightened and she continued.

"I have no idea how we got there, but the three of us were in a sort of palace or temple. There were large columns and fountains and gorgeous flowers. Everything was glistening like sunlight on snow."

Sarah gazed at her sister-in-law in amazement. The often-taciturn woman was positively glowing as she spoke. Here was truly a new lightness of being.

Ivy accepted Sarah's offer of the glass of water she couldn't reach without disturbing her little groomers and went on with her story.

"I think I may have glimpsed the Rose Lady before when you were telling me the story about the goddess, but I figured that was simply your description. In fact, I didn't even remember that image until this afternoon. Her name is Nada, isn't it?"

"Yes, Lady Master Nada." Sarah nodded and kept nodding as Ivy revealed more of the details that were so new to her.

"Right. I didn't actually hear her say her name, but somehow I knew it. She's the most beautiful, luminous woman I've ever seen—like an angel. Or a goddess, like you said in your story. With a sweetness that absolutely melted my heart. I couldn't speak. I was totally in awe."

"We were there," chimed in Kerry. He had stopped helping his sister with feather smoothing and was once more snuggling against his mother's left arm.

"Yes, you were. That seemed to be important—for the three of us to be there together." Ivy paused and looked intently at Sarah.

"Have you ever had a dream that was far more than a dream—like the event was really happening, and not in your imagination?"

You have no idea, chuckled Sarah to herself. "I have, several times, and it's always a surprise."

"A huge surprise," agreed Ivy. "Anyway, we all sat with the Rose Lady by a fountain made of . . . pink quartz, I think. I could tell she was communicating something to the twins—telepathically, would you say? This is all so strange. Sarah, am I making any sense?"

"You are. Perfectly. Please, go on."

Ivy blew out another careful breath.

"Okay. After a while the Rose Lady turned to me with the most tender, loving expression anyone has ever sent my way. We just sat there, gazing at each other. I could feel the tears running down my face as she enfolded me in love, love, love. She didn't utter a word, though I felt her conveying that she would help me with my children."

"And Daddy!" declared Kaitlyn. She had also finished with feather smoothing and was pushing in next to her brother. "Don't forget about Daddy."

"That's right. We're all going to help Daddy believe in magic again, aren't we?"

"Yay, Daddy!" cried Kerry.

"But gently, remember. Not until he feels better, and the Rose Lady guides us. We must be respectful of Daddy's opinions." Two little redheads nodded in agreement. Ivy turned back to Sarah. "I guess that's all there is to tell."

"Wow, that's a *lot*," said Sarah. "What's next? Do you know?"

Kaitlyn was ready with the answer. "Mommy Hawk has to rest and get better and we're supposed to help Gramma and Grampa."

"That sounds like a really good idea," agreed their aunt. "Shall we go find them and see what they're doing? Maybe we can all play a game or watch a movie."

"I want a movie!" said Kerry, scooting off the bed, "and popcorn!"

"Do you want to join us, Ivy?" asked Sarah with a grin.

"No, I think I'll stay here for a while. This is a lot to process for someone who was raised on a steady diet of science and logic." Ivy laughed a little too hard. "Ow! And my ribs still hurt."

"Give yourself time," soothed Sarah. "Lady Nada is very gracious and definitely not one for interfering. I'm sure you'll hear from her when the time is right."

"That's good to know," said Ivy. She closed her eyes and began sinking dreamily back on her pillows. The twins and their aunt were nearly out the door when she called in a clear voice, "Thanks for believing me, Sarah. I'm not entirely sure I do. But knowing you don't think I'm crazy means a lot."

"Of course, Ivy. Any time. You rest now." Sarah gently closed the bedroom door and leaned back against it for a moment. She did not try to stop the tears that filled her eyes. Who would have thought it possible? Ivy and the Rose Lady. How wonderful.

"Come on, Aunt Sewah!" called Kerry from the top of the stairs.

The twins were supposed to let an adult open the baby gate for them and supervise their descent to the first floor. As Sarah knew from experience, that mandate did not stop them if they were on a mission. However, since she was within sight, they were obedient this time.

Later that evening, Sarah's cell phone rang as she was climbing the stairs to her attic room after helping with the dinner dishes—the chore that had become her norm.

Her throat clutched as she read the name on caller ID.

"Here we go," she whispered to herself and answered the phone, willing her voice to sound calm and professional.

"Hello, Tony."

"Sarah, darling? Oh, how I sang your praises when I got your text! I'm dying over here. When can you come rescue me? You know how I hate overtime."

"I do, you poor thing," said Sarah, immediately switching to her most sympathetic tone, which Tony always managed to elicit from her. He was a great one for complaining about overworking and then putting in more hours than anyone. Probably why A. B. kept him on, thought Sarah. This time, he sounded genuinely stressed.

"I'm glad to hear from you, Tony, though I didn't expect you to have a hiring budget right away."

"I don't—yet. But knowing I could get you on board should ease the skids when I talk to A. B. He always thought you had talent."

"Really?" Sarah couldn't help being flattered by the praise.

"When can you meet me in the city? I can make time tomorrow and then I'm off for a couple of days at a conference that A. B. insists I attend with him and the wicked Ursula."

"I'm sorry, Tony, I can't. Family issues far too complicated to explain landed me in New Bedford, Massachusetts. I didn't expect you to need me so soon. I have a couple weeks of work remaining to finish my novel before I submit it to my new editor. Then I could start, if that would help you at all."

"Very impressive, darling," gushed Tony. "And convenient, too. We'll be in Boston all weekend. Among other things, A. B. is meeting with an investment group. I don't know why they're not in New York, but that's the boss's business. He's diversifying his investments. Glad I'm not involved in *that* right now. I think Ursula wanted me around this weekend because she knows I'll take her shopping for slutty clothes."

Sarah remembered the woman's style. Low-cut tops and long, tight skirts slit to the thigh. Tony's description was apt.

"Listen, darling, today's Tuesday. If you can get yourself to the Four Seasons in Back Bay on Friday, we can meet for lunch and I'll dazzle you with my brilliance while I explain the projects that I need you for. I could use your talents yesterday, but two weeks is tolerable. Don't disappoint me, Sarah. I'm depending on you."

"Don't worry, I'll make it work. Text me the details, okay?"

"Will do, gorgeous. *Ciao!*"

As Sarah had promised Tony on Tuesday, she was now seated on the Friday Red Line train from Braintree to downtown Boston. Leaving her family in New Bedford had been easier than she expected.

She and Ivy had shared a genuinely affectionate good-bye with promises to stay in touch.

She had been mildly surprised that her niece and nephew hadn't complained about her leaving. However, now that they had an ally in their mother, they seemed less dependent on their aunt's understanding of their unique relationship with the Rose Lady.

Sarah had easily convinced her father to drive her back to Braintree so she could finish her book. In fact, he had seemed eager to take a little road trip away from the intensity of life at Brian and Ivy's house .

Father and daughter always enjoyed their time together. This short excursion was an opportunity they both relished.

On the other hand, her mother had made it clear that she would rather her daughter stay in New Bedford. Fortunately, Patrick had persuaded Eileen that Sarah couldn't write with so many people around, and she had a deadline to submit her book to a professional editor. His emphasis on "professional" had won his wife's agreement.

Thank God my father understands my soul-need to write, thought Sarah as the view from the train became increasingly urban. She hadn't told Patrick about her interview with Tony—just as she hadn't shared that information with Kevin.

All anybody knew was that she needed quiet to meet her deadline and that her parents' house was the ideal place to finish her novel.

Kevin was disappointed that she wasn't coming home to New York, but he understood that she couldn't write with him around, either. He was in too much turmoil about his future.

He reluctantly agreed that Sarah was right—he needed his own quiet space to figure out what he should do next.

What *will* Kevin do next? she wondered as she reached the Park Street Station in downtown Boston and transferred to the Orange Line. Perhaps Master Saint Germain or Kevin's druid self, Ah-Lahn, will offer him some guidance.

She hoped so, even as she felt that old twinge of jealousy ripple through her belly. She had to admit that she did envy her husband's abil-ity to contact his former self. She would have to work on that issue, though not at this moment.

Right now, she had their financial future to protect, and that task was sufficient for today.

Seventeen

Kevin was also on the move. The weather on Long Island had cleared, leaving the sky the color of a luminous pearl. Still crisp, yet full of promise. That's how he felt today. Ready to explore Master Saint Germain's prediction of good things to come—that is, if he and Sarah could fulfill their promises to each other and to their masters.

Friday morning was a good time to be out and about, and Kevin was determined to make the most of it. As soon as Sarah had texted him on Thursday morning that her dad was driving her to Braintree, he'd breathed a sigh of relief. That meant she would finish her novel, send it off to her editor, and come home.

Only with both of them in the same location would they try to connect with their masters to discover the meaning of their druidic embodiments, the purpose of the communion with their former selves, and what they were meant to accomplish on behalf of other twin flames.

Full of hope, Kevin had spent the remainder of Thursday installing the biggest doggie door he could find so Hero could access the backyard at will. Once the pup got the hang of pushing his nose against the flap and easing his body through the opening, he'd rushed in and out for hours. Out to gallop around the yard. In to slurp a drink of water. Out to roll in the snow. In to shake off and warm up. Out to do his doggie business. In to flop down for a nap.

Sprite had watched from the safety of the kitchen counter, occasionally reaching down to take a swipe at Hero's tall head as he bounded past her perch. When the pup finally wore himself out, the kitten joined him in the sunbeam that warmed the living room carpet, curling her silky black tail around her little pink nose.

That's where Kevin had left them this morning as he walked the easy mile from his townhouse to Fibonacci's Esoteric Bookstore and adjoining coffee shop. The businesses had opened nearly two years ago in the village center, but he'd never had the time or energy to visit. Now he had both.

There was no missing the bookstore. Fibonacci's was located on a prominent corner—a rounded corner, as it happened—with bright blue trim gracing huge picture window displays of books and art that, to Kevin's well-read eye, reflected the taste of someone dedicated to the depth and breadth of modern and ancient esoteric literature.

He gently pushed open the heavy blue door and stepped into a book lover's wonderland. A delicate sandalwood incense scented the store, creating an atmosphere that Kevin immediately experienced as a heightening of his awareness.

As he strolled along ceiling-high shelves labeled Celtic Spirituality, Jungian Psychology, Classical Philosophy, Poetry, Alchemy, Reincarnation, and Sacred Geometry, he felt his senses tingling in anticipation of an extraordinary event about to take place.

All my favorite subjects! he exclaimed to himself. Why have I never been here before? Of course, he knew the reason, but still. . . . *Everything in its proper time,* he heard his wise inner voice whisper, urging him to explore further.

The store was larger on the interior than it appeared from the street, accommodating large racks of books that Kevin could hardly imagine being gathered in a modern bookstore. The place was a veritable Library of Alexandria.

Past the right-hand window display, a narrow wooden staircase hugged an exposed red brick wall. It led up to an open, second level loft marked "Esoterica & Used Books." In the back right corner was a small alcove for those who wanted to lose themselves in the texture of antique paper and the aroma of real leather bindings.

Kevin felt an enormous impulse to rush up the stairs. Instead, he checked his desire and completed his tour of the first floor.

The loft overhung a lounge area at the back of the store. Here comfortable chairs and sofas were arranged in small groupings around coffee tables where customers could read while enjoying a hot beverage or pastry from the coffee shop that joined the back of the bookstore through an archway made of the same exposed red brick.

Lured by the fragrance of freshly brewed coffee and home-baked pastries, Kevin ventured into another kind of wonderland—Fibonacci's Tea Merchants & Coffee Roasters. This spacious shop was furnished with straight-backed chairs set around authentic, old oak library tables in the center and front of the room with booths upholstered in dark green leather lining the side walls in the back.

The low hum of quiet conversation gave Kevin the feeling that here was an oasis where he could clear his mind and perhaps tap into his own creative intuition.

Exactly what he needed.

And undoubtedly what he would find, he decided, as he gazed at the sage green walls on which were hung what appeared to be a carefully selected gallery of photos, paintings, and drawings depicting geometric designs and examples of spiral shapes in nature and in man-made art and architecture.

Several images, striking in their balance and simplicity, were of the human nude. Additional sculptures and other art pieces were placed around the room on pedestals and shelves.

Just inside the front door, running along nearly the full length of the left wall, a magnificent mahogany bar stood in front of a tall display cabinet made of lighter wood. Here shelves were filled with canisters, tins, and jars of teas and coffees from all over the world. A huge, antique coffee grinder and a modern espresso machine completed the setting.

At the end of the bar nearest the door, a glass-faced display case featured a mouth-watering assortment of baked goods and wraps. Urns of coffee were arranged at the other end of the bar along with the usual condiments and serving utensils. As Kevin would come to learn, these were the only aspects of Fibonacci's that one might call "usual."

He made his way forward to place his order for the coffee and pastry he was now craving, and took a seat on one of the empty leather stools that spoke to the business's former identity as a pub.

He was immediately greeted by a cheerful voice from behind the bar.

"What's your pleasure, sir?" A man of rather indeterminate age and impressive height extended a warm handshake and said in a distinctly Irish brogue, "Welcome to Fibonacci's. I'm Lucky, the owner."

"And lucky to *be* the owner," quipped Kevin with a smile. He returned his host's handshake and introduced himself. "Man, what I would give to run a place like this."

"Who knows? Maybe someday you will," said Lucky, who had already plated a fresh scone with butter and jam and was placing it, along with a cup of hot coffee, in front of a very pleased Kevin. "Here, try this. First order is always on the house."

Lucky's sparkling blue eyes, red hair touched with silver worn in a ponytail that reached down his back, and soft accent made Kevin think of Sarah's description of the *seanchaí*—the storyteller she had met in Ireland. This man was even wearing the sort of khaki shirt and pants that she had described. The only difference was the small amethyst stud in his right earlobe and the diamond pinky ring with stones set in a pentagon shape on his left hand.

Kevin was beginning to think he had stepped into a thin place—a portal out of time where anything might happen.

"Thanks, Lucky. Wow, this coffee is great."

"One of my special blends," said the man with a smile. "My wife, Róisín, calls me the 'Caffeine Alchemist.' She's not here right now, but I know she'll want to meet you."

"You can be sure I'll be back," said Kevin. "The only reason I could tear myself away from the bookstore was because I was hungry. Do you do the buying? I've never seen such a collection of ancient and modern wisdom. I'd like to . . ."

"Oh, sorry, Kevin." His host looked toward the front door and held up a hand. "Excuse me. Don't leave. I won't be long."

Lucky wiped his hands on a towel and quickly moved from behind the bar to the front door. Kevin swiveled on his stool to see what had so abruptly grabbed the proprietor's attention when a young man pushed past other customers who were entering and rushed over to the big Irishman whose large presence halted him mid-step.

"Where is he?" demanded the young man. "Where is Bellamarre?"

Lucky looked him in the eye and said quietly, "Rudy, you know I can't tell you that. There's other folks here, lad. Show some respect."

"I'll show respect when I get some!" Rudy raised his voice. "F. M. dazzles with a few tricks, then won't explain them. I need answers! My life depends on it! I want to see F. M., and you know where he is!"

All heads in the room turned at his outburst. Kevin felt his solar plexus tighten. What was going on here?

At that moment, a tall, stately woman, whom Kevin surmised must be Róisín, came through a curtain at the back of the shop and walked briskly to her husband's side.

"Is there a problem?" she asked in her own soft brogue.

"Oh, I think Rudy here could stand a bite of lunch," said Lucky calmly. "Would you mind the bar, darlin', and I'll see to it."

He moved to Rudy's right side and put his arm around the young man's shoulder. "Come on, lad. Let's talk about this in the back where we have more privacy."

Rudy shook off Lucky's arm. "Don't patronize me, Lucky. I want answers."

Kevin felt the tension in the room bristle. How was the proprietor going to handle this? He was taller than Rudy and more strongly built, but the young man was building up a head of steam that could easily erupt into violence.

Lucky only smiled and angled his body to face him, He lowered his voice even more. "Rudy, we've talked about this. You know if you want contact with F. M. you must learn to control yourself."

To Kevin's amazement, Rudy blew out a deep sigh, gave a weak nod, and calmly allowed Lucky to guide him through the curtain and down a hallway that Kevin now could see led to the kitchen and restrooms. A few customers whispered to each other until it became apparent that no further excitement was forthcoming. Most had already turned back to their own activities.

Several minutes later Lucky emerged alone from the hallway as if nothing had happened. He appeared unperturbed, though Kevin detected an unusual brightness in the man's eyes as he returned to his station behind the bar.

"Sorry about the disturbance," he said. "Rudy gets overly excited sometimes. He usually just needs a sandwich and a bit of reassurance. I gave him both and let him leave by the back door. He's always embarrassed by his outbursts. We don't make a big issue."

Lucky turned to the woman who was standing with him.

"Róisín, this is Kevin MacCauley. Kevin, my wife, Róisín."

"Pleased to meet you, *a chara. Céade míle fáilte,*" said the woman. She extended her hand in a warm handshake that Kevin was glad to accept. Her clear green eyes smiled at him as if she were greeting an old friend. He recognized the hundred thousand welcomes and felt them wash over him like a gentle Irish breeze.

"Thank you," he said and returned her smile.

He suddenly found the unusual open-heartedness of this couple rather overwhelming. They seemed to already know him as he was not so certain he knew himself.

"I'm sure you two will have lots to talk about," said Lucky with a knowing wink at his wife. "However, as I recall, Kevin, you wanted to ask me about the bookstore. And perhaps another, more pressing matter has brought you to us today."

Lucky looked at his guest for several seconds, as if he were seeing more than the physical man sitting on the other side of his bar.

He looked away for a moment, then said, "Róisín, would you fix our friend a cup of the special coffee? Kevin, why don't you take a seat in the far booth. Relax and enjoy the brew. I'll be with you in five minutes. Then we'll have a proper conversation."

Eighteen

Kevin now had even more questions than the ones he'd come in with. They ran through his head as he waited for Lucky to join him.

Who was F. M. Bellamarre? What tricks had he performed that Rudy didn't understand. Why was F. M. not available? Or was he only unavailable to the young man because of his emotional state? What had Lucky really done to calm those emotions? Would he have any insights into Kevin's situation?

And what was in this coffee blend? There was something exotic about the flavor and the sense of well-being that came over Kevin as he drank. If the "Caffeine Alchemist" had served Rudy this beverage, it was no wonder the lad had calmed down.

In exactly five minutes, Lucky set his own cup of coffee on the table and took a seat in the booth across from Kevin.

"You have questions," he said with a friendly smile. "They're scrolling across your forehead like a marquee."

"Sorry to be so obvious." Kevin wrinkled his nose. "Yes, I do. That whole scene with Rudy was odd."

"Not as odd as you might think," said Lucky, "and I will answer those questions soon. But first, tell me what's on your mind that I believe is more urgent than my book inventory."

Kevin laughed. "It's not a short story. Do you have time?"

"I always have time for people and events that interest me. You do. So tell on, and don't spare the details."

"It's been a rather eventful several months," Kevin began. "Events not easy to explain, though I have a feeling you'll know what I'm describing. Judging from the wealth of esoterica next door, would I be correct in assuming that you are more than a little familiar with subjects such as reincarnation, ancient civilizations, mystery schools?"

Kevin could feel the focus of Lucky's attention. The man's expression was inscrutable.

"I am, yes," he answered.

"What about past life reviews, lucid dreaming, ascended masters?"

"Those subjects are known to me and to Róisín—as I'm sure you'd want to know if you are to feel comfortable with us. Don't worry, Kevin, you're in good company here. Tell me about yourself."

"I will appreciate your insight, which I have a feeling is considerable," said Kevin.

His host only smiled and sipped his coffee.

"Okay, here goes," said Kevin. He looked Lucky in the eye and planted both hands on the table as if to steady himself for the confession of his deepest concerns.

"Last summer my wife, Sarah, and I experienced in dreams and visions a series of past life reviews that were centered around our having been druids in first-century Ireland. She was Alana. I was Ah-Lahn. In that life we were married for a short time until Ah-Lahn was killed by an evil druid named Arán Bán."

"You feel these past-life memories are important because . . . ?"

"Because in that embodiment and in others I had mystical powers. Occult knowledge. Insight into other planes of existence and the ability to communicate between this world and the next."

"And you'd like those powers to return?"

"I would. Actually, they are returning—sort of. At least the communication between worlds. I've been having more visions about Ah-Lahn, as if he's trying to tell me something or get me to do something for him. Something that's for me, for Sarah, and probably for other people we know or will meet."

"How do you feel about Ah-Lahn?"

"Impressed. Envious—which is weird if I was him. Curious. Nervous about what I may discover if I let the visions continue. Afraid, I guess, that I might be stepping into a psychic confusion that the masters don't want me to open up."

Lucky leaned forward, his eyes bright.

"Give me the whole story, Kevin. Paint me the picture, especially about the masters you've met. Over the centuries, masters both ascended and unascended have appeared in different forms to those they wish to assist. I'm interested to know who you've seen and in what context."

As easily as if he and Lucky had been friends for centuries, Kevin told his host the full story of how he and Sarah had encountered living memories of their former selves and about his visions of Ah-Lahn.

He talked about Sarah's book and their failed attempt to connect with Saint Germain and Lady Nada, probably because he was on Long Island and his wife was in New Bedford.

As Lucky listened keenly, Kevin felt himself once more caught up in the experience of the events he was describing. He had a feeling that his host was in the scenes with him—not as a participant, but as an unseen observer who understood better than Kevin himself the significance of each event.

"What do you think all this means?" he said at last. He had expected that going into so much detail would have exhausted them both. Instead he was energized and eager to delve into whatever insight Lucky might have to offer.

The big Irishman leaned back in the booth and closed his eyes. He sat silently for a full minute, his hands folded under his chin. His expression told Kevin not to interrupt—only to watch and wait.

When Lucky opened his eyes, they appeared misty, with a faraway look. Another full minute elapsed before he spoke—more to himself than to the man sitting across from him in rapt attention.

"A fascinating journey, to be sure."

He thought for another moment, then turned his attention back to Kevin. "That would be just like F. M. to appear to a former skilled druid as Master Saint Germain."

"F. M. Bellamarre?" asked Kevin. "But I thought from what Rudy said that F. M. was a physical person, not a spirit. Why would he call himself by a different name?"

"Oh, he often uses assumed identities. F. M. Bellamarre is not his real name. Nor is Saint Germain. He enjoys taking on different roles to suit the matter at hand. He's known to have a theatrical playfulness in his dealing with embodied humankind. He says it keeps the dark forces guessing."

"He can do that? Move between spirit and matter and literally move mountains?" Then Kevin remembered his experience outside of the Cave of Symbols and chuckled. "Of course, he can. I've seen him do so."

"He is capable of that and much more," agreed Lucky. "Over the years I've been privileged to join him on some incredible journeys—in my dreams and when fully awake—as it appears you've also done."

Kevin sighed deeply. "You have no idea how relieved I am—and amazed, I must say—to be able to speak freely about this with someone other than my wife. We're still trying to work out what it all means." He finished his coffee. Remarkably, it had not gone cold.

"Honestly, Lucky, in all my reading about ancient history I never imagined such things happening in the twenty-first century—certainly not to me."

"You weren't ready, that's all. It appears now that you are. One does not question the Master about his intentions or his timing. One listens and observes."

"Yes, I can see that," agreed Kevin.

Lucky continued, "Of late, I've witnessed him very purposefully gathering together a diverse group of individuals for reasons he has only briefly divulged. Because I trust him implicitly, over a year ago I volunteered my property as a place for his Friends of Ancient Wisdom to gather for informal discussion and conversation."

"What do you talk about?" Kevin felt a shiver of energy surge up his spine and out the top of his head. In his mind's eye, he could see fireworks.

"The state of the world, the state of our souls, navigating the challenges of living a spiritual life in a grossly materialistic culture. Each member of our community is on a path of soul liberation—some for many years, others only recently awakened.

"We know we have been embodied many times in the past and we are determined to escape this cycle of death and rebirth, or *samsara*, as many Indian religions call it.

"Occasionally, F. M. joins us to conduct a special ritual for world freedom. His services are designed to accelerate our consciousness while our devotion to the cause of freedom he espouses above all other intentions raises the vibration of the community at large. His meetings are extraordinary, I can assure you.

"The Master has made clear that his larger purpose is to help us dispel ignorance wherever it is found—internally and externally. When and how we free our souls is a very individual path for which he seems to have an infinite number of solutions."

Kevin felt his soul leap. His heart beat in almost wild anticipation of attending one of these meetings. He nearly spoke, then checked his enthusiasm. He did not want to appear demanding or disrespectful. The man's response to Rudy was sufficient warning that F. M. was not available for emotional outbursts.

Lucky watched his new, old friend collect himself and smiled.

"Well done, Kevin. You have passed an important test. Self-control is the beginning of wisdom and opens the door to the Master's more material presence. I look forward to the two of you meeting in the physical, as you are already acquainted in the spirit.

"In the meantime, we will watch and wait," said Lucky. "Our next gathering is tomorrow night, Saturday. Please be here at 7:00 p.m. and tell no one where you are going. Our meetings are by invitation only. Yours has been secured and promises more to come."

Early afternoon sun had sent its warming rays into Kevin's living room where he and Sprite and Hero were curled up on the sofa. He hardly remembered walking home, so amazed was he after his conversation with Lucky. Almost like a dream, though he knew he'd been wide awake.

Róisín had sent him home with a cup of another special coffee blend. "This one will ground you," she'd said and chuckled at her own joke. Coffee grounds. Kevin had shared her laugh then and now smiled again to himself. The beverage was working.

At least he was feeling well anchored in his physical body. He would make no attempt to meditate on orbs of light in his fireplace until he received instruction to do so. He was certain more illumination would come tomorrow night and that was plenty soon.

"Isn't it interesting that Sarah is still in Braintree," he mused aloud to his animals. He could almost see the masters directing their paths in a way best suited to them individually.

He and Sarah might be twin flames with a combined mission to complete in this life, but their souls had separate needs. Over the centuries they had made different karma that must be resolved personally. They could love and support each other, but they could not pass one another's tests or fulfill their separate initiations.

Kevin suspected that he and his wife were each doing exactly what was necessary for their individual soul development. He was certain that, when the time was right, Sarah would receive her own invitation to a meeting at Fibonacci's.

Despite his keen desire to tell her about his new friends, he knew without asking that his job was to respect their teachers and honor the individual paths they were being guided to follow—step by amazing step.

He wondered how she was doing, alone at her parents' house. He hoped she was missing him as much as he was missing her.

Nineteen

A raw wind knifed across the Charles River, piercing Sarah's best wool coat as she exited the Prudential subway station and waited for a light-rail tram that would take her to the front entrance of the Four Seasons One Dalton Street hotel in Boston's Back Bay neighborhood.

She would have preferred a taxi, but fares were as prohibitive here as in New York City. Better to economize until she knew she had a job. She pulled her unfashionable, but mercifully warm, knit hat down over her ears and huddled with the others waiting to board the tram.

She had left Braintree in plenty of time to enjoy the train ride into Boston and to explore the stunning, triangle-shaped, curved glass skyscraper where the Four Seasons occupied the first twenty-one floors. She could hardly wait to view the hotel's famous art collection, which had been curated from the finest galleries and institutes in Boston and from around the world.

The tram had been quick, and the hotel was only a few steps away. Sarah still had at least twenty minutes before meeting Tony. Enormous glass doors silently glided open at her approach. She snatched off her knit hat and entered the sleek, marble-tiled lobby. Her breath caught at the scene before her.

An elegantly attired clientele was casually standing or seated in twos and threes. They could have been staged for an advertisement in *Vogue*, so perfectly did the minimalist palette of their chic designer ensembles blend with the lobby decor.

Walls, floors, ceilings, and furnishings ranged in color from dark chocolate brown to gold, grey, silver, and cream, creating an atmosphere of subtle sophistication that spoke of riches, influence, and power.

Thank goodness she'd remembered to pack her Armani suit for the visit with her parents, Sarah congratulated herself. They had planned to dress up for an evening at the symphony, which had never happened. Instead she was walking alone into a world of unsurpassed luxury.

Of course, A. B. would stay in a place like this, she thought as she stowed her ugly hat in her purse and carefully folded her coat over her arm. She could easily visualize her former boss conducting his business over expensive wines and gourmet delicacies featured in the hotel's five-star restaurant.

Tony had invited her to wait in the hotel's lobby rotunda, which served as an introduction to the art collection. An enormous, dome-shaped chandelier fashioned of hundreds of tiny crystals graced a deeply coffered ceiling. Sarah marveled at the play of light that scintillated out from the chandelier. It reminded her of the etheric bridge she had tried to cross to meet Kevin.

That structure was a portal to other worlds. She was certainly in another world, here. For a brief moment, she wondered if she should have accepted Tony's invitation to meet in Boston without telling her family or her husband where she was going.

But then, here was her former colleague, rushing toward her. He was charmingly polished in Prada and full of the effusive enthusiasm she had never been able to resist.

"Sarah, darling, how lovely to see you," he gushed, planting a kiss on both her cheeks. "Looking good, sweetheart. Turn around." He twirled a finger and stepped back to inspect her. Sarah did a slow turn.

"Have I seen that suit before?" Tony peered over his titanium designer glasses. "Of course, I have," he smiled slyly. "I helped you pick it out. You were made for Armani, darling."

"That's right, you did." Sarah had forgotten. "Your fashion advice was always flawless."

"Just part of the service," cooed Tony. "I have to keep my ladies looking their best. And you do, sweetie."

He checked his Rolex watch and placed a manicured hand under Sarah's elbow, smoothly guiding her to a small bank of elevators that offered access to an exclusive corner of the hotel.

"Come along now, darling. You must be famished. Let's enjoy an outrageously expensive lunch and talk shop. I have a surprise for you."

Sarah had expected they would dine in the hotel's world-famous restaurant adjacent to the lobby. Instead, they entered a mirrored elevator that listed a single floor on the control panel. Tony swiped a key card and the car whisked straight up to the twenty-first floor where the door opened directly across from the Presidential Suite.

Tony quickly swiped the card on the suite's door and ushered Sarah into a wide, tiled foyer. He smoothly took her coat and hung it in a closet secreted behind mirrored doors. "Go on in, sweetie, and make yourself comfortable. Lunch should be here soon."

Sarah entered a sitting area furnished in muted tones of beige and navy blue. Her feet sank into thick, cream-colored carpet. This was no ordinary hotel room. To her right was a living room, complete with a gas fireplace where flames danced invitingly.

Dark wood paneling faced floor-to-ceiling curved windows that framed extraordinary views. To her left was a dining room with seating for eight. She noted that the large oval table was currently set for three.

A tall man who had been taking in the expansive cityscape view below, turned to greet her. It was A. B. Ryan.

Sarah gasped at the sight of him. Had she passed him on the street, she would not have recognized him. He must have lost twenty-five pounds. His once salt-and-pepper hair was now completely silver and perfectly styled. His cobalt blue eyes appeared darker than ever, and his expertly tailored grey silk suit fit a body that was toned and tanned.

"Hello, Sarah," A. B. strolled confidently across the room to where she stood transfixed in astonishment and firmly shook her hand. She remembered that the boss valued an assertive handshake and did her best to return his strength with her own.

"Hello, A. B.," she tried not to stammer. "I didn't expect to see you. Tony indicated I would only be helping him."

"When he told me that you'd reached out to him, I decided we all should meet. Your timing was inspired. We need your talents right now. Have a seat by the fire and I'll explain while we wait for lunch."

Tony got Sarah's feet moving by guiding her to a deeply cushioned sofa upholstered in cream-colored velvet and took his place beside her. A. B. pulled up a matching side chair and sat across from them.

"I'm running for office again and Tony is behind on producing the printed materials we need for a big splash. Not his fault. Only a bit of down-sizing in my office." The two men exchanged a knowing glance. "We'll be glad to have someone on board who already knows how I like things done. Right, Tony?"

"Absolutely, A. B. And you wanted to tell Sarah about your other projects." Sarah felt like she was an actor in a scene that everyone but herself had rehearsed.

Exactly on cue, A. B. said his line. "Right. Ursula doesn't think I should let anybody else in on why I'm here in Boston. You remember Ursula?"

"Yes," was all Sarah dared say. She hoped her face didn't betray her recollection of the woman who had run rough-shod over anyone she considered beneath her—which was just about everybody except the boss, who was her lover. Was he now her fiancé? Sarah wondered.

A. B.'s monologue continued. "I may as well tell you because you'll be working on the next projects as soon as we do the big campaign roll-out. That event's easily managed. We've run a dozen times and won a dozen times. We know what we're doing. We just need more people doing it. Aren't you curious about my new adventures?" He licked his lips as if savoring his next triumph.

"Yes, I am," answered Sarah truthfully. She was about to share her surprise that A. B. would allow other interests to pull his focus from politics when lunch arrived.

Tony ushered her to a dining chair that offered an incredible view of the city. He sat on her left with A. B. on her right. She noticed that the boss was positioned where he could watch the foyer. Like a riverboat gambler, she thought. Never sit with your back to the door.

Two liveried waiters silently served an impeccably prepared lunch of shrimp cocktail, roasted beet and pear salad, sole *meunière*, grilled asparagus, and the most delicate white wine Sarah had ever tasted.

For the next forty-five minutes A. B. regaled her with his plans for real estate development. He already had designs on some run-down city blocks he planned to buy up and either convert to condos or raze and build from the ground up.

"Depends on the condition of the structures," he explained while impatiently motioning for the waiter to refill his wine glass for the third time. "Replacing old plumbing and wiring can cost you a bundle. Quaint is highly overrated. I'm in this to make money."

Certainly not to win friends, thought Sarah. She wondered what neighborhoods he was eyeing. She happened to like quaint. A. B.'s enthusiasm for demolition was making her queasy.

He was equally keen, though not as knowledgeable, she noted, about the investments he intended to make in select theatrical productions. His initial deal was with old Boston money—hence the meeting here, rather than New York City.

Sarah was sampling her swirled white chocolate and black cherry dessert parfait when Tony suddenly checked his watch, blanched slightly, and said to his boss, "It's past time I took off. Ursula's expecting me at 2:00 p.m."

"Right," agreed A. B. "Keep her busy for a couple more hours." He turned to Sarah. "I arranged for Ursula to spend some time at the College of Art and Design. Now Tony's taking her shopping."

Tony winked at Sarah and headed to the foyer with a wave over his shoulder. "I'll call you next week, darling. *Ciao*."

Sarah started to get up from her chair. "I should probably be going, too. Thanks for the lunch, A. B."

"No, sit down. You have no reason to leave. Keep me company for a while."

His tone was commanding and suddenly seductive. His hand trapped hers on the table, forcing her back in her chair. His expression went dark and intense. He looked deeply into her eyes and said, "We haven't discussed the terms of your employment—Alana."

Sarah could not move. Her mouth gaped open in astonishment. She was riveted by his gaze and by a heavy energy that blanketed her like a shroud. He'd called her Alana.

A. B. took her immobile hand in both of his. A crooked smile curved his lips.

"Did you think I wouldn't remember you, my girl? I recognized you the day you came to work in my office. When you showed no immediate sign of recalling our long association, I made sure you didn't recognize me and decided to bide my time. I am a patient man. But then you disappeared after your little sojourn in Ireland. Is that where the memories came back to you?"

Sarah was speechless. What did he mean, "I made sure you didn't recognize me?" Her mind was spinning. Her heart flipped wildly in her chest.

"Yes, I can see you remember now." A. B. stroked her hand. "How could you not? You and that husband of yours have been a pain in my ass for a very long time. You're always getting away. I believe we have some unfinished business, you and I—Alana." He practically purred her name.

"Come with me. I'd like to show you the other rooms in the apartment." He pulled her to her feet and firmly wrapped her arm around his where he held it in place. "I find the bedroom especially comfortable."

Oh, yes, Sarah knew him now. There was no mistaking the man's identity or his intentions. Her old nemesis, Arán Bán, was about to have his way with her. Why had she not recognized those dark cobalt eyes or his tone laced with sexual innuendo when she worked for him?

Get out now!!! she heard her inner voice command. She summoned all of her strength and tried to pull her arm free of A. B.'s grasp.

"Let me go!" she demanded. "I need a job, not a lover."

"Call me Arán Bán, Alana. For old times' sake." His tone was silky, his movements sinuous as a serpent.

"No! I'm leaving and I'm not coming back!"

She was surprised that A. B. released her arm and let her hurry to the foyer. He called to her as she grabbed her coat from the closet and yanked open the suite's heavy door.

"Oh, we'll see each other again, and next time I won't take no for an answer. I'll have you yet, Alana. Give my best to Ah-Lahn. I'm sure he'll be delighted to know you came to see me—*alone*."

Sarah could hear him laughing sardonically as she slammed the door and rushed across the hall to the elevator.

"Oh, God, let this work," she whispered, frantically pulsing her finger on the call button. "Please, please, please." At last the door slid open. She rushed in and stabbed the single button she prayed would send the car to the first floor.

Prayer answered, she sprinted across the lobby. Several well-coiffed heads turned and raised their pencil-thin eyebrows in disapproval at the noise her heels made on the marble floor.

She couldn't care less. All she wanted now was to get back to the safety of her parents' home in Braintree.

She nearly collided with the doorman who stood at the hotel's front entrance. "Taxi, miss?" he asked placidly. She nodded like a frantic chicken who had narrowly escaped a hungry fox.

The doorman calmly ushered her outside and waved a white-gloved hand at the next yellow cab in line for a fare. As the car pulled up, Sarah plunged her hand into her purse and dug out a bill—she didn't care if it was a one or a twenty—and stuffed it into the doorman's hand.

He smoothly opened the passenger door and Sarah leapt into the back seat. She was not spending another minute in this city she had always appreciated for the rich charm of its culture.

Stifling a sob, she spoke to the driver, "Park Street 'T' Station."

Would she ever enjoy Boston again? Her delight in its vibrant history abruptly dissipated under the cloud of memories that suddenly flooded her mind—remembering herself as an evil man's prey. She vowed she would not be again.

Twenty

The train from Boston to Braintree had just arrived when Sarah stepped onto the crowded platform. She joined the surge of passengers and pushed her way into the car in front of her before the doors closed. She was surprised to see how few seats remained, then remembered that afternoon rush hour began nearly as soon as morning rush hour concluded.

She moved to the back of the car in hopes of finding a seat where she could regain her composure and consider what in the world she was going to do next. Her heart was still beating wildly, and her body shook, causing her to stumble as the train lurched into motion.

A well-dressed man in his mid-forties reached out a hand encased in soft tan kidskin gloves and guided her to the place beside him. He was impeccably dressed in a cashmere topcoat that matched his gloves and an equally fine scarf wrapped around his neck for warmth.

His light brown hair shone with subtle touches of red and gold. He wore it longish, though perfectly styled. His beard and mustache of the same color were neatly trimmed as if he had recently come from the barber. His manner was gracious, his smile inviting, his deep violet eyes the most intriguingly beautiful Sarah had ever seen on a man.

"Thank you," she said, exhaling wearily as she sat.

"Difficult day?" the man inquired easily—almost as if they were old friends and he'd been waiting for her to join him on the train. He spoke with the resonant musicality of a stage actor. What was such a refined person doing on the Red Line? Sarah wondered.

"Disaster," she answered with emphasis. "And it's completely my fault." She surprised herself by responding so honestly. After her harrowing encounter with a very smooth A. B. Ryan, she should have been wary of opening up to a stranger. Yet there was something about the peaceful countenance of this gentleman, who certainly merited the title, that emitted trustworthiness.

"Would you like to tell me about it?" he asked. "No pressure. Merely an opportunity in case you would appreciate an impartial listening ear. Allow me to introduce myself."

With an imperceptible flick of his wrist—almost like a magician, Sarah thought—he produced a business card and handed it to her. The card was ivory in color and silky smooth to the touch. In the center was a *fleur-de-lys* pattern embossed in deep purple. Under the design she read:

F. M. Bellamarre, A., M.C.

"I don't recognize the letters after your name," said Sarah, turning the card over. Perhaps there was an explanation on the reverse side. "Are you connected with the arts?"

"I am on occasion," said the man. His violet eyes twinkled. "At the moment I am 'Alchemist, Master of Change.' You may call me F. M."

"I'm glad to know that somebody is," Sarah murmured to herself.

"Is what, my dear?"

"A master of change," she replied, shifting in her seat to face him. "I'm overwhelmed with it. My whole life is changing and I've just made it worse." She looked directly into his eyes. "Why did I think I could work for Tony without involving A. B.?"

"A. B. Ryan?"

"You know him?"

"I am acquainted with the man, yes. Is he the cause of your current distress?"

"He is, or rather I am. I should have known better. I should have recognized him. But I never learn. Last summer in Ireland I had an extraordinary peak experience, dreaming of actual past lives that reconciled me with my husband, Kevin. But as soon as we returned home and I started writing—I'm a novelist, or trying to be one—I fell back into old fears and started pushing him away."

She reached out for her seatmate's gloved hand. "What's wrong with me, F.M.? Can you help me? I feel like I'm on the edge of an abyss and I'm frightened."

"I may have a thought or two," he nodded congenially. "Perhaps you should begin at the beginning and we shall see what solutions emerge."

Back in Braintree, evening had fallen imperceptibly while Sarah sat at the kitchen table in the familiar comfort of her parents' home, pondering the day's strange events.

Getting up to switch on a light, she stared at her weary reflection in the darkened window over the sink where she and her mother had washed countless dishes amidst the kind of intimate conversations she had rarely shared with anyone—certainly not with a stranger—until this afternoon when she'd met F. M. Bellamarre.

Had the self-described alchemist suspended time? she wondered. The train ride from Park Street to Braintree normally took little over thirty minutes, and the sun had not been low in the sky when she and F. M. parted company at the station.

The odd thing was that Sarah and her new friend—or was he an old friend?—had been deep in conversation for what must have been two hours. Thinking back now, she remembered how the other passengers had seemed to fade into the background until they reached the end of the line. The train car had grown silent except for the sound of her own voice and F. M.'s occasional question or assurance that he was easily following her story.

She had, indeed, begun at the beginning, as if she were narrating the novel she was finishing about the druids Alana and Ah-Lahn. And, she realized with a clutch in her solar plexus, the novel was also about Arán Bán—the individual now embodied as A. B. Ryan. The man who had tried, lifetime after lifetime, to permanently separate her from her soul's beloved twin.

Nothing she said had seemed to surprise F. M. He had listened with a confessor's patience, yet Sarah suspected he already knew the fullness of her story. There was something so incredibly comforting about unburdening herself to him. As she recounted the details of her life, she had felt herself bathed in an aura of violet light that seemed to erase a great weight from her mind and heart.

Had she also detected a delicate scent of rose, or perhaps violets? She could not know for certain. What she did know was that F. M.'s presence had assured her that he understood not only her past and her present, but most likely her future as well.

Although she felt buoyant of mind and heart, her body told her it was time to retire. She turned off the kitchen light and stood a minute, letting the silence of the empty house settle around her like a soft blanket.

Here was the peace she craved. But would she ever find it in this life? she wondered. She blew out a deep sigh and quietly climbed the familiar stairs to the sanctuary of her childhood bedroom.

She changed into her pajamas and propped herself up in bed. She intended to review the status of her novel, but she could not push her experience with F. M. to the back of her mind.

He reminded her of someone. A person from her past. Perhaps from her lifetime as Alana. Could he have been one of the druids from the doomed community at *Ynys Môn?*

The memories were still vivid of the island that had been Alana's home before she and her mother had fled the invaders who destroyed that glorious seat of druidic learning and massacred their loved ones, including her grandfather, Archdruid Bleddyn.

The most magnificent druid of them all, Bleddyn was incredibly wise, kind, a master of ancient wisdom, one possessed of mystical powers. He was a seer who could look with equal ease into the past and the future—her favorite, most patient teacher.

Sarah's eyes misted as she remembered how he would listen to Alana and converse with her, even when she was only a child. Exactly as F. M. Bellamarre had listened to her today. Could he be . . . ?

He'd said he was an alchemist—a master of change. He certainly had the bearing of a master, an adept. A person who understood the laws of man and nature. Just like her druids.

She dared not imagine F. M. as her beloved grandfather reborn, but she could definitely believe the two men were kindred spirits and teachers of like mind. If F. M. was anything like Alana's grandfather, he would have high expectations of Sarah.

He had made that clear. "Remember," he said, fixing his violet eyes firmly upon her, "you must tell Kevin about your encounter with A. B. Ryan. Much depends upon your courage in this matter."

"I will," Sarah had promised him with a shudder. More fears to overcome. And she *would* overcome them, she vowed to herself and to this remarkable person whom she strongly suspected of being a dear friend of old. She would not disappoint a "wonderman"—for that is what her beloved Bleddyn had been. A magus, a sage, and the most practical, down-to-earth of all the master druids.

Yes, when she returned to New York she would confess to Kevin and pray to *An Síoraí*, the Eternal One, for constancy and a clear mind so she would not waver again.

With this deeper understanding of how her past and her present were indelibly linked, Sarah felt her entire being long to return home to her husband. Starting first thing in the morning she would focus all of her attention on completing her novel quickly so she and Kevin could move on with their lives together—however the future might unfold.

As she snuggled under her flowered comforter, another recollection of F. M. came to her. After they parted company at the Braintree train station, she had been threading her way through the parking lot toward her parents' sedan that she was borrowing when she realized she had never introduced herself, yet F. M. had called her by name.

She'd turned back to ask him how he'd known who she was, but he was gone. Almost like a magician disappearing from sight, she remembered now with a quiet laugh.

He had declined her offer of a ride to his destination, saying that his transportation was already arranged. Just how does a master of change travel? Sarah wondered.

And in exactly what sort of transformation does a modern-day alchemist engage? She would have to ask him next time they met. She hoped that would be very soon.

Twenty-One

On Saturday evening, a cold breeze was blowing off the Long Island Sound, bringing the scent of salt and sea to Kevin's nostrils as he set out from his town house for Fibonacci's.

The stress of anticipation had nearly unnerved him that afternoon. He decided that a brisk walk in the crisp air would center him. Well bundled against the November chill and stretching his long legs, he could cover the mile's distance in fairly short order.

He approached the bookstore entrance and took a deep breath. He pulled himself up to his full six feet in height and pushed open the door. He could almost hear its rows upon rows of books beckoning him with tantalizing keys to his future. Someday he would have time to lose himself here, but not tonight.

Just inside, at the bottom of the stairway to the loft, Róisín met him. A smile graced her lips and crinkled the edges of her deep green eyes.

"Good evening, *a chara*. Come in and welcome. Please go up all the way to the back of the loft, and open the door on the left marked *Private*."

Kevin's heart quickened, as did his pace. He took the stairs two at a time and reached the loft. Here were the volumes of antique esoterica he longed to peruse. The lure of their ancient wisdom pulled mightily on his mind, but, once again, he knew he must proceed where he was invited.

His hand shook slightly as he placed it on the vintage glass knob of the door he was to enter. One more deep breath and he entered another wonderland.

Soft music from a trio of harp, violin, and cello created an ethereal atmosphere, enhanced by a delicate aroma of sandalwood and candle wax that permeated the air. Soft lighting was created by dozens of tapers that had been placed around the enormous space, the size of a ballroom.

In fact, Kevin had entered an authentic, early twentieth-century ballroom, complete with hardwood parquet floors and an immense crystal chandelier sparkling in the center of a painted ceiling that appeared to hold the Milky Way itself in a cobalt vastness.

Kevin stood inside the door, allowing his eyes to adjust to the gentle illumination. He noticed chairs for about twenty-five people at the front of the room, though few of the other guests were seated. Most were gathered in small groups, engaged in conversation that hummed with congeniality—another kind of warmth.

As he looked around for Lucky, he felt tears prickle behind his eyes and a shiver run up his spine. To his surprise and delight, as he observed more closely, he could see that the ballroom was filled with familiar male and female faces who now turned in his direction and nodded as if his presence here tonight were expected and welcomed.

Kevin stood stock still in utter amazement. As he returned the respectful nods, he realized he could call many of the guests by the names they had worn over nineteen centuries ago. Others he recognized from more recent times.

Had he entered a portal to other dimensions of reality? Yesterday he had suspected Fibonacci's of being a thin place. Now he was certain of it. Why else would he suddenly be able to identify friends from former lives—compatriots with whom he had shared many, many experiences?

He felt his heart leap, his soul quicken. These were kindred souls gathered from ages past into an unlikely place. Or was Fibonacci's the perfect location where no one would suspect an assembly of mystics to come together on a Saturday night? In a way, he felt as if they had been meeting this way for centuries, if not millennia.

As he continued to gaze about the room, he also found himself missing the faces of a few he would have expected to be included in this gathering. Sadly, he did not see Ah-Lahn's best friend and fellow druid, Riordan. In recalling episodes for Sarah's book, he had wondered why their paths had not crossed in this life. Perhaps they would yet.

The answers to such questions were the grail he hoped to find among these friends of old.

Yesterday Lucky had called them a diverse group. An apt description, Kevin concluded, observing their wide variety of attire and grooming preferences, some casual, others more formal. Many of the guests were around his age—in their mid-thirties and or early forties. A few were significantly older and a handful were much younger.

A sense of wistfulness clutched briefly in his chest. Here were the sort of companions Ah-Lahn had wished for his estranged son, Tadhgan. Kevin shook off the weight of that reflection and greeted Lucky.

"Welcome, my friend," said the big Irishman. "It's grand to see you here." He vigorously shook Kevin's hand and pulled him into the room to be welcomed by those who obviously recognized him and now nearly overwhelmed him with enthusiastic handshakes and embraces as if they had all recently returned from a long voyage.

"Ah, here's Craig, just moved to New York from Ireland. He especially wanted to see you," said Lucky. He excused his friend from some other guests and motioned to a strongly built man who strode over and looked at Kevin intently.

The fellow was dressed in an Irish fisherman's knit sweater over faded jeans. His hair was long, the color of burnished copper, pulled back in a ponytail similar to Lucky's. He was probably in his late thirties, but his full beard and bushy eyebrows made him look like a timeless warrior Celt. He wore no rings on large, workman-like hands.

Apparently satisfied with his observations, Craig grabbed Kevin's right hand and arm in the double handshake of friendship and laughed heartily at his quizzical expression.

"Ah-Lahn, my friend. Do you not remember your old *taoiseach*?"

Kevin looked more closely and a light dawned.

"Cróga!" He practically shouted the name of the tribal leader whom Ah-Lahn had served as *ceann-druí*, or chief druid, until the time of his death.

"That would be me." They embraced, slapping each other on the back, then stepping back a pace, each one taking in the sight of the man before him. "Grand to see you . . . Kevin, is it? Well, a rose by any other name . . . right, Lucky?"

"Right you are, Craig," answered their host with a hearty laugh.

"I'll have to tell my brother I met you," beamed Craig. "Maybe your presence at Fibonacci's will entice him to the States for a visit. If I can get him over here, I'm hoping this group will pull him out of his monk's habit and into the twenty-first century."

"Your brother is a monk?"

"He is, yes. Rory, my younger brother—Riordan, your old druid partner."

Kevin's mouth fell open. Questions tumbled out. "Riordan is your brother? How did that happen?" He winced. "Obviously, I know how babies are made. I'm just surprised that you would be brothers in this life. Where is he a monk?"

Craig looked off into the distance past Kevin and began to speak of their former lives as if they were yesterday's memories.

"After your—that is, Ah-Lahn's—untimely departure from this world at the hand of Arán Bán, Riordan became *ceann-druí* and my right hand in the *túath*. We had a rough go of it at first. I thought him too reserved and he thought me too determined to expand my territory. We eventually worked out an understanding that served us well enough, though we both missed you for as long as we lived.

"Master Saint Germain told me we had karma from previous lifetimes. He said we'd done well to resolve it in the millennium's first century rather than carrying it into the twenty-first. I'm glad we did. We still fought as brothers will when we were lads in this life, but we always knew that love and respect lay at the base.

"He's a good man, is Rory. I just wish I could get him away from those old Irish monks. He's holed up in an abbey near Limerick—like he's hiding from something, though I can't for the life of me figure out what. And he won't say."

"You've met Master Saint Germain?" Kevin felt his heart thumping.

"I have, yes—as have many who are here tonight. Others know him only as F. M. Nobody has quite figured out why he appears one way or the other. Lucky is mum on the subject. If you ask F.M., you can sometimes catch a bit of a twinkle about his eyes. I've personally only heard him say, 'As each one requires.' "

Craig continued, "Exactly as each of us requires. That's what we're all about learning. It's the main reason we're here—to find out what our souls need to learn and become in order to finally take our leave of this bright blue sphere called Earth.

"Grand to see you, Kevin," repeated Craig, pumping his arm again. "Looks like Lucky is ready to start the program."

Indeed, the other guests had taken their seats and Lucky was standing in front of a long table set at the far end of the ballroom. The table, Kevin now observed, was decorated like an altar and covered with a white linen cloth woven with threads of gold in spirals and other Celtic symbols.

On the altar were placed a large crystal chalice in the center, twin amethyst crystal geodes on either side, and several statues he recognized as angels, saints, and divine beings from a variety of spiritual traditions.

On the wall behind the altar was hung an enormous metal disc the color of brushed gold. In fact, it was gold. Kevin was sure of it. The vibration was too pure, too powerful to be other than the substance he knew the alchemists of old believed to be precipitated sunlight.

At the center of the disc was a faintly etched figure out of whose upraised hands streamed luminous beams that scintillated in the flickering light of double spiral candelabra that stood as tall as a man on either side of the altar.

As Kevin observed the disc more closely, he felt the figure gazing out at him with an expression that emanated the Divine Love he had experienced in the presence of Master Saint Germain. Surely, this is the face of *An Síoraí*, the Eternal One, he thought, as he took the empty, front row seat that Lucky motioned for him to claim.

Fascinated, he watched and listened as Lucky turned to face the altar and delivered an invocation that made the hairs on Kevin's neck stand on end. Shivers ran up and down his spine as if he were hearing an echo from antiquity.

He remembered that invocation—could have spoken it himself. Uncle Óengus, Ah-Lahn's druid mentor, had opened a ritual with the same words on the day that Ah-Lahn had been murdered by Arán Bán. Kevin's soul quivered at the call.

O Spirits of East and West, South and North, give ear, we pray, to our supplications. Angels of our world and the next, bless this assembly with your protection and inspiration.

Beloved An Síoraí, may the words of our mouths and the deeds of our hands bring health and abundance to all our people and safety to our homes, our leaders, and those we love both near and far, here with us and in gracious Tír na n'Óg, Land of the Ever-Living.

Having thus spoken, Lucky turned around and began to address the congregation. The silver highlights in his hair shone like a halo in the light of the great sun disc behind him.

"Dear Friends of Ancient Wisdom, we come together as lovers of the great Light of Freedom, the true nature of our souls. Together let us give the OM. As we blend our voices, may we also harmonize our minds and hearts.

"Please place your attention on the divine spark that illumines your individual being. See that flame expanding until it fills your aura, this room, this city—all the way out to the entire planet and beyond."

Closing his eyes and inhaling deeply, Lucky's clear tenor voice sounded the ancient syllable that was the essence of all creation.

O-M-M-M-M.

A vibrant chorus joined in, ranging from deep bass to high soprano. The participants took turns breathing so the OM continued in a perpetual, harmonic intoning as if a giant organ were playing a chord in every possible register.

Kevin joined the chorus and placed his attention on the center of his chest, which grew warm as his heart chakra began to spin. Soon, his whole body was vibrating. The OM was both in him and around him. He was instrument and receiver; singing and being sung.

As the OM continued, the atmosphere in the room pulsated with waves of vibrant energy that bathed the group.

Kevin relaxed into the exquisite sensation and noticed in the center of his chest the same tripartite, flame-like plumes of rose, sapphire, and sun-lit gold that he had observed in Master Saint Germain—though not nearly so large. Nevertheless, the flames were spinning and expanding, filling his being with their radiance.

He found he could not move his body. In fact, he was not certain he had a body. The plumes spun faster and faster, growing wider and taller. Then suddenly they shot down to the base of his spine, then up and out through the top of his head, exploding like fireworks in a shower of light rays in every color of the rainbow.

Kevin's gaze was drawn up to the center of the gold disc that was shimmering before him. Clearly smiling at him with a sublimely benevolent expression was the face of *An Síoraí,* the Eternal One.

Bathed in unspeakable love, he felt the figure wordlessly convey:

You are recognized and you are loved. Go forth in that knowledge, my son. I AM with you always. I AM your Highest Self.

Kevin had no idea how long the meditation lasted. It could have been ten minutes or ten hours. All he knew was that eventually the ethereal vision faded, and the perpetual OM diminished to a whisper.

No one moved from their seats for many minutes. Lucky remained standing before the people, his face shining with a glow that surpassed any description of bliss Kevin had ever imagined.

After another space of indeterminate time, Lucky faced the altar once more and said a prayer for the protection of the spiritual light they had invoked. He carefully extinguished the candles, then turned, bowed his head, and pressed his hands to his heart in the gesture of *Namaste, the light in me honors the light in you.*

Lifting his gaze, he looked out serenely at the congregation. "Thank you, Friends, for your participation in our service this night. May the blessing of our Master be with you as you return to your homes in silence and in peace."

Without another word, he walked down the center aisle and stood by the ballroom entrance while the Friends of Ancient Wisdom filed out, descending the bookstore staircase and passing silently out into the crisp night air.

As Kevin made his way past Lucky, the man slipped him a business card that was printed on expensive ivory stock with a glossy purple *fleur-de-lys* embossed on the front.

Enjoying the possibility that yet another mystery might be revealed to him tonight, he pocketed the card until he could reach the peaceful warmth of his own home. Once he had shed his heavy coat and turned on the fireplace in the living room, he sat in his favorite chair. Only then did he turn the card over to see that an invitation had been written on the back in a fine hand:

F. M. Bellamarre requests the pleasure
of your company at Fibonacci's Coffee Shop
tomorrow, Sunday, at 1:00 p.m.
Bring your questions.

Twenty-Two

Kevin felt a bit foolish driving the few blocks from his town house to Fibonacci's for his meeting with F. M. Bellamarre. However, the weather had changed again on Sunday morning, now promising snow and ice.

He preferred not to arrive looking like a polar expedition survivor. Instead, he wore his best charcoal dress slacks, hunter green cashmere sweater, and tweed sports jacket.

He was nervous about meeting F. M. Another foolish notion, but he couldn't help it. Imagine being able to converse with the Master here in the physical. The implications were staggering.

His visionary encounter with Saint Germain had been miraculous and heartening. Still, the thought of seeing the Master in a flesh-and-blood presence sent shivers of excitement up and down Kevin's spine. He shook his head at his childishness. He was acting like a little boy about to meet Santa Claus. Another ridiculous thought.

He was quite certain the Master did not hand out trinkets for good behavior. Although he had been the very soul of kindness and grace as Saint Germain, Kevin knew that the path of soul liberation he espoused was rigorous, demanding individual discipline, focus, and a strong commitment to the purposes of the Masters of Light who were known as the Great White Brotherhood because of the white light in their auras.

Remember who you are, Kevin's wise inner voice admonished him. Or at least who I used to be, he thought. Casting his mind back in time, he recalled the gatherings of druids he had attended as Ah-Lahn. In fact, he had conducted many meetings of the Druid Council when he held the office of *ceann-druí* in his *túath* of *Tearmann*.

He parked his car a few doors down from the coffee shop and sat in silence, resting his hands on the steering wheel, while he considered what he wanted to ask F. M. Bellamarre. Last night he had composed a list of questions and this morning had discarded most of them as trivial or impertinent.

There were a couple of matters he wanted to discuss with Róisín. Otherwise, he had a single question for the Master. He got out of his car and made his way to the encounter he hoped would be the watershed moment he was praying for.

Lucky had sent him a message this morning suggesting that he might want to arrive early. "I won't be at the shop until nearly 1:00 p.m.," he had texted, "but Róisín will be there. She'll appreciate the company. Come have coffee and a chat until F. M. arrives."

So, Kevin found himself sitting at the bar, engaged in deep conversation with Lucky's wife. They had barely spoken on Saturday, but today their discussion flowed naturally into the questions he hoped she would answer.

"Can you tell me what it's like to be a modern-day alchemist?" he began while she brewed a fresh urn of coffee.

Róisín's face lit up at the question. Her expression was always cheerful, though never so enthusiastic as when she was asked to share some of her knowledge, which Kevin discovered was topically broad and philosophically deep.

Despite the mass of silver curls that shimmered on her head like a crown, her alabaster skin and glowing cheeks gave her a youthful appearance. Her dark green eyes seemed to observe everything, regardless of how mundane it might appear.

"Each part of the material cosmos is important to the whole," she remarked in answer to Kevin's unspoken observation. Apparently, mind reading was also one of her skills. "The world's stability depends upon the integrity of its minutest particles. *An Síoraí*, the Eternal One, loves each atom unconditionally. Such is the foundation of alchemy.

"We do not change lead into gold out of antipathy for lead. Rather, we love its elements so completely that we offer it the opportunity to come up higher into a more refined molecular structure."

Róisín let that thought sit for a moment while she plated a blueberry muffin and made an Americano for one of the Friends of Ancient Wisdom who was having a late breakfast at the end of the bar.

She returned to where Kevin was considering her last statement and continued. "The same alchemical principle is true for mankind. You'll see how people change for the better in the Master's presence. The fire of his love simply burns out aspects of personality, behavior, or consciousness that keep the soul earth-bound."

"Yes, I've felt that myself," said Kevin, remembering how peace and a lightness in his being had come over him when he first met Saint Germain.

Róisín topped off his coffee without looking at his cup. Instead her gaze seemed to reach into his heart. "The alchemy of change is a matter of love and of loving so deeply that naught but love remains—whether animal, vegetable, mineral, or human."

"I can see that," said Kevin. He sipped his coffee and pondered the idea that gold could be created by love. He was again reminded that the alchemists believed the radiant mineral to be precipitated sunshine.

That concept might be a stretch in the physical realm—although last night's golden disc emanated that quality. But it was certainly a plausibility in the spiritual. The sun's energy is light. *An Síoraí*, the Eternal One's love is light. Things equal to the same things are equal to each other. Infuse the lead of human consciousness with enough love and you can transform it into the gold of Divine Wisdom.

Kevin brought his attention back to Róisín. He suspected that she'd been watching the thread of his thoughts as they spun out in his mind.

"I have read about the Wonderman of Europe who appeared in many European courts before and after the French Revolution. Shocking as it is to my outer consciousness, it appears that I am soon to meet this person, in the flesh."

"And you'd like to know how to address him," suggested Róisín.

"I would," said Kevin. "Depending on circumstances, the Wonderman used different names, including Comte Bellamarre. However, he has been most frequently recorded in history as the Comte de Saint Germain. I'm curious as to why he doesn't use that name here."

His hostess warmed to the subject.

"Of course, we know that Saint Germain or 'Holy Brother' is more a title than his real name. That bit of information remains shrouded in mystery. So we address him as he appears to us individually or if we're gathered in a group.

"He prefers a less occult moniker when dealing with the Friends of Ancient Wisdom. Over the years, we have learned that novice members may not have purged their minds of the world's prejudices against him."

"Such as?" Kevin knitted his eyebrows.

Róisín gestured for the teen-aged barista who was helping her to assist the "To-Go" customers at the end of the bar. Then she lowered her voice so that only Kevin heard her.

"Sadly, the name of Saint Germain has accumulated a heavy weight in the form of gossip, misunderstanding, and outright falsehoods about the Master's true character.

"Throughout the centuries he has been accused of the filthiest dark arts, his name carelessly bandied about in historical works as well as in popular fiction. Though some writers have understood the sanctity of his being, how tirelessly he works on behalf of mankind's freedom, and the purity of his intentions, many more have slandered him.

"He finds it easier to work in the modern world as F. M. Bellamarre so that newer students are less likely to make a sudden leap in judgment, either for or against him, depending on what stories they have heard and believed."

"I had no idea," said Kevin.

"Our Master is all too aware of how easily humans can make karma with him by entertaining any number of critical thoughts that plague the mass consciousness. He does not wish to be the source of additional burden to an otherwise striving soul.

"We of the Friends work very hard at rooting out those shards of negativity so that, when we are privileged to be in the Master's presence, the experience is pleasant for him as well as for us."

Kevin swallowed hard. For many years he had tried to maintain a harmonious inner and outer world. He hoped those efforts would prove successful. In his appearance as Saint Germain, the Master had not chastised him for his thoughts. However, the physical plane was more conducive to error than the etheric where they had met.

"I can understand F. M.'s reasoning," said Kevin thoughtfully. "One more question: Can you tell me what F. M. stands for?"

A playful smile teased Róisín's lips. "A joke among the Friends is that it means 'frequency modular.' And here he is!"

Róisín looked up and beamed at the elegant gentleman who approached the bar. Kevin had not heard him come in.

He immediately recognized the grace of posture and grooming, the sparkling violet eyes, the welcoming demeanor. F. M. looked exactly like a less luminous Saint Germain—the main difference being his attire. Instead of a pure white robe, he wore a light tan cashmere top coat and soft kid gloves which he removed with a nod to Róisín.

"Good afternoon, F. M." she said, as Kevin stood to greet the Master. "May I present Kevin MacCauley, though I believe you already know each other."

"Indeed, we are acquainted, are we not, Kevin?" said F. M., extending his hand in a warm handshake. A shiver of vibrant energy rippled up Kevin's arm into the center of his chest where it sparkled out to his entire body as if his blood were suddenly made of champagne. He felt instantly enlivened and surprisingly at ease.

"Yes, we are, Sir. Thank you for inviting me today."

"Thank you for accepting. Not everyone does, you know."

"Really? That surprises me." Kevin furrowed his brow.

The Master's expression became thoughtful. "The opportunity to choose one's next step comes to each soul as their destiny requires. Some are more courageous than others."

He returned his gaze to Kevin.

"Now, with regards to our conversation, I had hoped to be present at last night's gathering of the Friends of Ancient Wisdom. However, events in the Capitol demanded my attention. In any event, I find that discoursing in the physical can lend a more practical air to the discussion. I believe you have questions, which I will be pleased to answer. Let us take a seat in the back booth where we will not be disturbed."

Kevin wondered how they could possibly have a private conversation when other members of the Friends were likely to stop by for one of Róisín's delicious pastries and the special coffee she brewed only on Sundays. He hadn't seen Rudy at last night's gathering and was concerned that the agitated young man might suddenly disturb their discussion.

However, as soon as he and F. M. were seated with hot beverages graciously served by Róisín, the sounds of customers coming and going seemed to fade into the background, almost as if the Master had drawn around their communion a curtain which no untoward human thought or feeling could penetrate.

Twenty-Three

The secluded booth where the Master and his guest sat across from each other was upholstered in dark green leather, reminding Kevin of the deeply sheltered oak groves where Ah-Lahn and Alana had slipped between the veils of time in their reviews of past lives.

For a while, the two men remained in silence, peace descending around them like the quiet of a forest blanketed in new-fallen snow. Such was the still, contained atmosphere F. M.'s presence created. Exactly as Kevin had experienced in his ethereal encounter with Saint Germain.

He felt free in his soul, comfortable in the Master's presence without fear or artifice or affect. Surrounded in F. M.'s aura, he was fully himself—Kevin and Ah-Lahn fused into a total being—as if he had become his True Self.

Exactly how long the sensation of wholeness lasted, he could not say. Time out of time was most definitely a quality of communion with the Master, even in his flesh-and-blood form.

Gradually the experience faded. Kevin blinked open his eyes and looked around. He and F. M. were seated as they had been. The Master was calmly drinking his tea, observing his guest with an expression of compassionate understanding.

"Is this what you wish to achieve, my son?"

"It is." Kevin answered slowly, his gaze going within as he explained. "I remember who, or rather how, I used to be as Ah-Lahn. And though I have thought the return of his powers was what I was seeking, I now see that is no longer my sole desire.

"Being aware of what I was, I feel myself half a man. Mediocre. Separate from my true identity. Disappointed and afraid that I'm not fulfilling my destiny as an individual or in my marriage.

"I wonder if Sarah doesn't feel the same. We've shared our recent dreams and visions, but we don't seem able to hold onto the magic we found in Ireland. Time after time, the essence of our oneness comes tantalizingly close, but then it slips away—like a ship that never reaches safe harbor.

"Now my intuition warns me that Sarah may be in danger. Unfortunately, I can't identify the problem and I can't reach her while she's finishing her book."

Kevin paused, his eyes momentarily half-closed in contemplation. His heart abruptly ached with a desire he could hardly bear. His voice caught in his throat as months of uncertainty threatened to overwhelm him. Desperation made him unashamed to reveal his deepest emotion to the Master. Were F. M.'s eyes also glistening?

"I miss my wife. My Sarah. My other half. She is the breath of my soul, the person who kindles my love as no one else. How in this world or out of it do we stay together? We've lost each other so many times—I cannot bear it again."

Kevin took a deep breath, doing his best to calm his emotions.

"I'm sorry to be so overwrought, Sir. But do you know what it's like to love someone more than life itself and still not be able to complete the union? One of us is always at a distance. Even now, Sarah is in Massachusetts, apparently reluctant to come home. I cannot go after her again. I thought we were fine last summer when we came home from Ireland. But we're not okay now, and I don't know what to do."

As Kevin poured out his heart to the Master, he became aware of F. M. returning the flow in an earnest exchange—a soul kinship that gave him the courage to continue.

"I keep thinking that if I could consciously integrate my present self with my druidic self—which seems to have split off from me—I would know what to do and how to be in this life. And how to achieve true oneness with Sarah. Does that make sense?"

"Perfect sense, my son," replied F. M. "I understand your plight. I myself spent hundreds of years without the solace of my beloved at my side as I strove to free my soul from the rounds of rebirth. Someday I may tell you the story. For now, please accept that I know the pain of separation from one's twin flame. Until the hour of spiritual reunion, love's victory is not complete and the ache is real."

F. M. may be a wonderman, thought Kevin, but he has a tender heart. He could see from the seriousness in the Master's eyes that here was an immensely powerful being who had not forgotten what it was like to be human, and who extended his love in ways that his students could scarcely fathom.

"This is the path each of us must walk," explained F. M. "We have lived in golden ages. We have been priests and priestesses of old. On many occasions we have possessed profound knowledge and healing powers. We have also fallen short of the mark in other embodiments.

"We now live in an age in which we must retrieve those fragments of soul that have—as you correctly perceive—split off. Our shared destiny as Friends of Ancient Wisdom proclaims the integration of all our past and present selves."

"Is there a way to this integration?" asked Kevin. The longing for union with the totality of his being swelled in his chest as a pressure that made his breath hitch. His soul reached out for the Master's guidance— for the fullness of his unconditional love.

F. M. contemplated the genuine desire of the man before him and spoke plainly. "There is a way forward, if you will take it."

Kevin inhaled deeply. "I will."

"Very well, then. Here is my suggestion."

Although the figure of F. M. Bellamarre remained visibly with him in the booth, Kevin had no doubt that the ascended-master presence of Saint Germain was delivering to him the opportunity of a lifetime.

A fortnight remains until Sarah returns from Braintree. When she comes home, she may be troubled, not quite herself. She will have certain things to discuss with you—as you have your own matters of concern.

In these conversations you must maintain absolute equanimity so you may assist Sarah in doing the same. The future of your service as members of our Brotherhood depends upon that harmony.

These issues are critical to your individual souls and to your work as twin flames, both in the physical and in the etheric journeys that each of you has experienced—and which we desire to see you enhance.

Kevin did not hesitate. "We will do our best. Both of us. I know Sarah's true heart."

F. M. nodded in approval and continued. As he laid out his instructions, Kevin could see in his mind's eye everything unfolding exactly as the Master described:

Follow these guidelines and I prophesy that all will be well between you. Even so, your actions will determine the circumstances under which we may meet again.

In your meditations during the next fourteen days, visualize your entire being surrounded by violet light consuming all burdens, anxieties, doubts, and fears about what the future may hold for you and your beloved.

Sound the *OM* as you visualize and repeat the affirmation *I AM Light!* until you feel that pure energy moving in, around, and through your entire being.

See yourself opening your heart to Sarah and keeping it open when she returns home, no matter what may threaten to transpire between you that is not harmonious.

Your repeated practice of this visualization will create a pattern of consciousness that you will more easily retain when you and your wife meet again.

Remember what Róisín told you about the fire of love that melts the lead of human consciousness. Be like the sun and shine without ceasing, inviting all that is not of the Light to be transmuted into the gold of your Higher Self—the presence of *An Síoraí*, the Eternal One, the great I AM within you.

Both men were silent for several minutes, the radiance of the Master Alchemist's words shimmering between them. At last they rose together and F. M. prepared to take his leave.

"Please contact Lucky when you and Sarah have overcome any resistance to fully opening your hearts to one another in harmony. Although the stakes are high, I have faith in you and your beloved. I will hold the vision of your success."

He grasped his guest's hand and arm in the druid's double handshake of friendship as if they had been parting this way for centuries. Again, a ripple of vibrant energy ran up Kevin's arm and anchored in his heart.

The Master bowed slightly and slipped through the curtain that led to the coffee shop's back door without the notice of any of the patrons in what was now a very busy and noisy Sunday afternoon at Fibonacci's, where Lucky and Róisín were both working the bar.

Kevin returned to his seat in the booth and leaned back, gazing at the photos and paintings of natural and man-made spirals that covered every available bit of wall space.

His attention was drawn to a very old photo of the spiral staircase that had been miraculously constructed in 1878 at the Loretto Chapel in Santa Fe, New Mexico. Built by a mysterious carpenter in answer to the nuns' prayers to St. Joseph, the staircase contains two 360 degree turns and rises twenty-two feet from the chapel floor to the choir loft above without visible means of support.

My life keeps turning like that giant spiral, thought Kevin to himself. I pray I'm moving up the staircase, not down.

Twenty-Four

Sarah had told Kevin not to expect to hear from her while she prepared her book manuscript for the editor Gillian had found.

There were still some loose ends to resolve—the biggest problem being her uncertainty about the final chapter. However, she assured herself, if the editor was as skilled as Gillian promised, they surely would figure out the book's ending together. No point in forcing a conclusion that was inconsistent with how circumstances would have evolved for the story's main characters.

Nevertheless, Sarah spent an entire morning spell-checking, reimagining a few paragraphs, adding and subtracting modifiers, toying with the idea of chucking the entire project in the trash, then pulling back from the brink before doing anything so foolish.

Finally, she agreed with herself—there was no one else around to object—that she had fiddled long enough. She printed off the final section, slipped the pages into a FedEx box, and addressed it to Gillian's office in New York.

New York. How odd to think of returning there. In her mind, home was a million miles away. She was still enfolded in the delicious, timeless, spaceless atmosphere of imagination that being a novelist evoked in her.

But then, the manuscript was packed. She was no longer writing. And all the anxiety that process had held at bay came rushing in.

She missed Kevin, but also dreaded seeing him again. She had to face her fear of telling him about her appalling encounter with A. B. Ryan. And worse, they now needed a plan for supporting themselves financially because her scheme to earn a paycheck had been a disaster.

"God, I feel so stupid," she said aloud to the empty house. Then jumped like a shot had been fired when the doorbell rang.

Lest she change her mind at the last minute, she had decided to schedule a FedEx pick-up instead of dropping off the package herself. Now that the driver was waiting at the door, she had to will herself to hand him the package—reluctantly releasing it from her fingers as if he were taking her first-born child off to a foreign country.

An apt metaphor, she thought. The novel was her first-born, and even now she couldn't quite bring her creation to term.

But the book wasn't still-born, she assured herself. This baby only needed a midwife—Gillian's famous editor. All she needed to do at present was pray the woman wouldn't laugh at the pieces of her soul that lay naked on every page.

To make sure there was no turning back from the book's destiny or her own, Sarah ran outside in her stocking feet to watch the FedEx truck disappear around a corner six blocks away. Then she walked slowly back into the house and closed the door on this chapter of her life.

Now that she'd shipped her book to Gillian, Sarah found herself wandering around the house, all too aware of being alone and feeling empty, spent, directionless. And wondering if she'd made the right decision to stay in Braintree to help her parents with the twins.

As expected, Eileen and Patrick were bringing Kerry and Kaitlyn to stay with them while Ivy and Brian recuperated without the unrelenting needs of two bouncy four-year-olds.

Lacking inspiration or energy for any other activity, Sarah made a cup of tea and went to her room. Sitting on her bed with the stuffed panther, Ba, at her side, she tucked her feet under the floral comforter that encouraged sunny thoughts and took up her journal.

Words came slowly at first. Yet as she relaxed and let random thoughts flow, a communion with her muse took shape.

Despite writing an entire novel about Alana and Ah-Lahn, I seem to know more about the druid than the druidess.

Are we always so blind to who we are? We never see ourselves as others see us. Looking in a mirror, our image is reversed. A photo may capture a moment in time. Video is better. But somehow, we remain two-dimensional. Avatars in a computer game, manufactured replicas of some element of real or imagined self of our own design.

The mesmerism is so complete, we do not realize we've been programmed, boxed, marketed, and sold as a false self-image we have accepted without question. We live in a prison of our own creation. Others may see the bars that keep us bound, though we do not.

How to break free? Alana never did—even with her knowledge of the unseen, her attunement with Nature's seasonal cycles, her ability to shift shapes and commune with elemental life. With all those powers, she did not truly know herself. And that ignorance left her incapable of truly loving Ah-Lahn with the full depth of her being—simply because she never plumbed that depth. Not all the way.

She had tried. Oh, how she tried to go deep into their love. There were moments—even days and weeks—when the power of his love for her had broken through the barriers she denied.

In those hours, her love for him flooded out in torrents and frightened her. How could she adore him so completely and still be herself? Would the fire of his being so burn that she would be completely consumed?

"And am I talking about Alana or Sarah?" she said aloud to her wise inner voice. The pen felt like a flame in her hand as she wrote:

You speak of both Alana and Sarah. You are in the same quandary as your former self and will remain so until you embrace the enormity of your capacity to love with the fullness of the Divine within you. Release Alana's fear and Sarah's. Only then will you see your True Self reflected in the eyes of your twin flame.

The pressure building in Sarah's chest took her breath away. She clutched her left hand to her breast and covered her mouth with her right as if she dared not utter the truth she had written.

Her heart ached with yearning. She was homesick for her husband, for the affectionate understanding that sparked to life between them when they were in tune with one another's souls.

Not surprisingly, she also longed for Ireland. The thin places of Éire were calling her with mysteries yet to be unfolded. Would she and Kevin ever return to the site of their recent reunion?

The people, the music, the language, the land, the sea, the sky—each element in its way spoke of her soul's true nature. There was a way to her inner truth. She knew it. Through the yearning that poured out from the depths of her being, she believed Kevin would agree.

Suddenly exhausted, Sarah gathered Ba in her arms and curled up in the comforter's garden softness. Her auburn tresses spread out like copper fire on her pillow as she dozed.

She dreamed of Ireland, of oak groves, of the sounds of Uilleann pipes playing in the distance, of the peaceful breathing of her beloved. She ached to feel his body next to hers. Her twin, her Ah-Lahn.

Coming half awake, she sat up abruptly and proclaimed out loud, "No! I long for my *Kevin!* And I'm going home as soon as possible!"

With a fiery determination kindling in her soul, she snuggled back under the covers. And as her body sank into a deep sleep, she vowed to take the train home to New York, to whatever awaited her there.

Twenty-Five

Sarah had gone to bed early—more like falling into oblivion and sleeping like the dead, she observed the next morning as she inspected her rumpled appearance in her bedroom's full-length mirror.

Thankful to be well-rested, she'd been up long before the sun, surveying the house, taking inventory of the wreckage from her two-week campaign to finish the novel.

Upstairs, only her own bedroom and bathroom showed signs of habitation. Unfortunately, the entire downstairs—kitchen, dining room, living room and den—looked as if the invisible battalion her mother often cooked for had materialized and bivouacked, occupying every nook and cranny of the Callahan's spacious home.

Unread newspapers, stacks of unopened mail were piled in the hallway. The garbage can was filled to overflowing with empty pizza boxes and Chinese take-out containers. An assortment of beverage cans were scattered in what could only be called wild abandon. Left alone to write, Sarah did not cook, but she ate—constantly, from the looks of things. And she did not bother to clean up any more than was necessary.

Sensing her mother's potential horror at returning to find that her pristine home had been invaded by starving gypsies, Sarah had dusted, mopped, vacuumed, and polished like a dervish. The dishwasher was full and humming, the first floor restored to pre-invasion order.

Only she and her bedroom showed the effects of the battles she had waged with inertia, fear, and the final stages of a writer's frantic attempts at completion. The bedroom could wait behind a closed door. Her own appearance could not.

A panicked glance at her watch launched her into the shower and clean—well, mostly clean—clothes that had not been slept in. She had just managed to pull her damp hair into a clip when she heard the front door open and her father's shout, "Sarah! We're home!"

She hurried downstairs to find the twins wriggling out of their coats and their grandmother's grasp. Kerry and Kaitlyn rushed to her, nearly knocking her back onto the stairs. Four amazingly strong little arms grasped her around the knees, hugging her wildly—exclamations pouring out on top of each other as usual.

"Aunt Sewah! We're here for two whole weeks!"

"We get to bake turkey cookies."

"And help with Thanksgiving dinner."

"Grampa's going to play games with us and build a Lego castle and, and, and . . ."

Sarah looked up from the twins' excited chatter and into the faces of her parents. Eileen was beaming with at least as much enthusiasm as the little redheads who were jabbering away while clutching their aunt.

Patrick raised his eyebrows with a weak smile and offered a bewildered shrug. Sarah thought he looked like a man contemplating escape to a remote and peaceful desert island.

Extricating herself from the twins' embrace and regaining the full use of her legs, she kissed her mother on the cheek. "Hi, Ma. I'm glad to see you."

"You, too, my girl," Eileen said, her cheeks flushed from the cold air. "Kerry and Kaitlyn, come with me to the kitchen. We'll make hot cocoa while Grampa and Aunt Sarah unload the car."

"Yay!" The twins didn't have to be asked twice.

"Come on, Dad, we have our orders," said Sarah with a grin as she grabbed her hat and coat from the hall tree and opened the front door. "I'll help you bring in the . . . good heavens! Did you leave anything at Brian's house?" The back of the SUV was crammed with suitcases and every imaginable item of children's entertainment paraphernalia.

Patrick gave a weary smile. "Your mother wanted to be sure we brought everything the kiddos might need."

"I think you succeeded," Sarah laughed as she grabbed a large tote bag in each hand. She admired how precisely the SUV had been packed. No wasted space and no extra space either.

"Did you finish your book?" her father asked as they carried the final load of bags and suitcases upstairs.

"As well as I could," Sarah replied. "I'm hoping for editorial miracles on the way to print. Pulling together the final chapters was a struggle."

She set down her burden in the children's room and turned to her father, drawing comfort from his calm presence as she had done since her earliest memories of this parent she adored.

"Dad, I know I said I'd stay a couple of days to help you and Ma with the twins, but I really need to go home."

Patrick studied his daughter's face with interest. Something in her eyes had changed. A certain look of resistance was gone. So was the undertone of grief. The expression that gazed back at him was softer, more balanced than he had observed in many months.

"I'm glad to hear it," he said at length. "You miss him, don't you?"

"More than I ever have. He's lost his job, you know? Or maybe I didn't tell you. He was laid off in an office coup. I need to be with him."

"Is he looking for another job?"

"I'm not sure. We haven't seriously discussed what he's going to do. There really hasn't been time with the car accident and my finishing the book. He's getting a good severance and benefits for a while, so he doesn't have to rush. I just want him to find work that makes him happy."

"Let me know if you need any help," said Patrick, giving her shoulders a firm squeeze.

"Thanks, Dad. All I need right now is a ride to the station tomorrow in time for the morning train to New York. I'd like to be home in the afternoon. And, Dad? Don't worry. We'll be fine."

"My Fairy Queen," he said. Two sets of hazel eyes misted as father and daughter hugged each other.

"Grampa! Aunt Sewah! Where are you! We finished our cocoa and we're ready to play!" Insistent little voices shouted from downstairs, piercing the moment's reverie.

"Maybe you could set up an obstacle course in the backyard. That would tire them out," suggested Sarah with a laugh.

"No?" she answered her father's grimace. "How about I take the first shift here? It won't take me long to pack, so you can get settled—or as settled as this crew will let you."

She headed downstairs, calling to her niece and nephew. "Okay, you two. Aunt Sarah's here. Let's go to the den. I want to hear the latest about the Rose Lady."

As a matter of fact, Sarah had not been able to get the full story about the twins' initial interactions with Lady Nada before she left New Bedford. They had shared the story of their mother seeing the Rose Lady in her temple. However, Sarah wanted to know how the twins' relationship with the lady master had begun.

She suspected there were other details Kerry and Kaitlyn hadn't told anyone. She intended to find out as much as she could from them before she returned to New York.

How did Lady Nada interact with four-year-olds when they were alone? Was there a connection between her recent visions and Kevin's and the adventures the twins went on—apparently quite regularly?

She was as excited to learn whatever the children were willing to tell her as they were to do the telling.

Twenty-Six

Sarah could have chosen to fly from Boston to New York. Travel time would have been much shorter than the nearly seven hours she would be riding trains from Braintree to the Long Island station where Kevin would pick her up for a twenty-minute drive home.

However, she liked going by rail—especially these days. The trains had been modernized to accommodate electronic devices. The windows were larger for viewing the countryside, although the scenes on this route were mostly grey and urban. And the seats were larger. This made a difference. Sarah needed time and space for her mind to expand, to process the many events that had taken place since she'd left home nearly a month earlier.

The train car she'd chosen was relatively empty with a comfortable seat in the middle of the coach where she wouldn't be bothered by cold drafts from other passengers opening and closing connecting doors on either end.

There was something soothing about the slight swaying of the train and the subtle metal-on-metal sound of wheels moving steadily along tracks that had been laid many years before. For Sarah, the railroad felt historical, an important link to the nation's past.

She was heading into a future that must embrace the ancient history that she and Kevin had lived together. Despite their conversations about what he had learned from Saint Germain, she was unsure as to how that process would unfold. Only that it must.

At the moment, her focus was on making sense of the story Kerry and Kaitlyn had told her about Lady Master Nada, the Rose Lady.

Sarah smiled as she remembered how eagerly the twins had scrambled up on the sofa in their grandparents' den. She had barely seated herself in a chair across from them before their recollections came spilling out. They seemed intent on making sure she knew every detail of their adventures with their special friend.

"The Rose Lady wears a long pink dress and a gold crown and sandals," reported Kaitlyn who knew the importance of facts. Mommy and Daddy had taught her that.

"She doesn't have wings," added Kerry, a note of disappointment in his voice. "Fairies are supposed to have wings."

"She's not a fairy," corrected his sister. "She's a goddess, isn't she Aunt Sewah?"

"Yes, that is true," agreed Sarah. Explaining to them that Nada was also a lady master would wait for another time. "When did you first meet her?" This is what she really wanted to know.

"After Kerry stopped wetting the bed at night," said Kaitlyn with a sideways glance at her brother who squirmed slightly in his seat.

"That must be a long time ago," said Sarah, looking at her nephew. She knew the twins had both been potty trained for nearly two years.

"A *very* long time," said Kerry with emphasis.

"I'm sure it was," said Sarah, changing the subject. "Kerry, can you tell me where you saw the Rose Lady?"

Kerry took a deep breath and spoke, his clear child's voice picking up speed as he explained: "In our room at home. We weren't sleepy and then there was a big ball of pink light and the Rose Lady was in it. She walked over to our beds and she said hello and she knew our names. And she said she was going to show us pretty places and not to be scared. Katy was, but I wasn't. I was very brave."

He puffed out his chest and folded his chubby little arms over his chest, nodding to himself in satisfaction.

"I was only afraid 'cause she was in our room," said Kaitlyn, raising her chin and sticking out her lower lip. "Mommy and Daddy say not to speak to strangers."

"But we already knew the Rose Lady," Kerry disagreed. "When you see somebody in your dreams, they're not a stranger when you see them in your room."

"You've seen her in your dreams?" asked Sarah. "When was that?"

"Since we were two," said Kaitlyn, doing her best to get in a word.

Kerry still had more to say. "She takes us to her home in the sky and it's really big and white and it sparkles and there are flowers and it smells pretty and we get to play in the fountain and. . ."

"We've met your babies, Aunt Sewah," interrupted Kaitlyn as soon as her brother took a breath.

Sarah's own breath caught in her throat. "My babies?" How did they know about the babies she had miscarried?

"Uh-huh, last summer," said Kaitlyn, nodding her head. "A little boy and a little girl. They told us they're your babies. They couldn't stay with you before 'cause you have to do something for the Rose Lady's friend."

Sarah clutched her heart. Tears brimmed in her eyes.

"Don't cry, Aunt Sewah," said Kerry, reaching out his little hand to pat her knee. "Your babies are happy in heaven. They got to practice being in your tummy and they promise not to go away next time."

"The Rose Lady is helping them decide who gets to grow in your tummy first," said Kaitlyn. "They love you and Unkka Kebbin and they watch you all the time."

"How do they do that?" asked Sarah, wiping her eyes with the heel of her hand.

"On a movie screen in a pretty room with soft chairs," said Kaitlyn. "We get to go there sometimes. We watch you too. Sometimes you wear funny clothes. The Rose Lady says it's 'cause you do things for her and her friends. She told us we can help them, too, when we grow up. She says you'll show us how 'cause we're like you and Unkka Kebbin."

"Mommy and Daddy aren't twins, so they don't understand us yet like you do," said Kerry matter-of-factly—and then added in a distracted tone, "Did you know your babies like to play games?" His attention was being drawn to the kitchen where sounds of Eileen making lunch were getting louder.

"How can they do that if they're babies?" asked Sarah.

"Sometimes they look older," explained Kerry, who for a minute appeared to his aunt as the fine young man he would become.

Sarah leaned back in her seat on the train and chuckled to herself. There was definitely magic afoot when the twins were involved. And more details to ponder.

She pulled out her journal and made a few quick notes so she could discuss this amazing report with Kevin, especially the idea of her getting pregnant again. The twins seemed to say that would happen. Could she go through the anxiety of a third complicated pregnancy?

A hundred questions raced through Sarah's mind. Taking a deep breath, she wrote down the most important ones:

If Kaitlyn and Kerry are twin flames, how are we going to help them—or any other twin flames, for that matter?

What is their dharma—their mission?

Do they have anything to do with our trying to merge with our former selves?

Did we know these souls when we were druids or earlier?

How do they relate to our babies—who promise not to leave the next time they are conceived?

Sarah had changed trains at Penn Station and was now seated in a comfortable car on the Long Island Railroad for the last leg of her trip.

She would be glad to be home. Her heart fluttered eagerly in anticipation of telling Kevin everything she had learned from the twins, and her stomach lurched when she thought of the difficult conversation they must have as soon as possible.

She willed herself to remember the hope and confidence she had felt in the presence of the man she sensed was a teacher of the caliber of Alana's grandfather Bleddyn. F. M. Bellamarre had made it clear that she must confess her encounter with A. B. Ryan, and she had promised him she would. She would not let fear stop her from doing what was right.

Kevin was waiting on the platform when Sarah's train arrived. He had always enjoyed the anticipation of meeting friends or family at the station. Greeting his wife was the best.

She was back-lit by the setting sun when he saw her. Her hair was down, glowing like an auburn halo in the golden rays of winter's late afternoon. He hurried over to help with her bags, which she set down as soon as she saw him.

His hair had grown, and she could tell he had shaved and trimmed his mustache. A nice touch. His blue-green eyes were fixed on her face, serene and calm like deep pools. He had never appeared so Celtic.

They stood looking at each other for a moment.

"My love," he said with his whole heart, and they were in each other's arms. She sank into his embrace. He held her as if he would never let her go, then leaned down and kissed her deeply.

"Are you ready to go home?" he said at last.

"More than you can imagine." She picked up her carry-on and smiled at the sensation of gratitude for Kevin's affectionate support that swept through her whole being.

Grasping the handle of her large roller bag in one hand, he put his other arm around her as she rested her head on his shoulder. At last, she was home, fitting herself into the curve of his body that always felt empty unless she was nestling there.

Sarah was determined not to let her trepidation about confessing the A. B. Ryan episode spoil the ride home. She decided to tell Kevin about her conversation with Brian's children before launching into troubled waters.

He laughed at her description of the twins' relationship with each other and the adults—Kaitlyn putting on her best grown-up demeanor and Kerry's unabashed enthusiasm for adventure and snacks.

When Sarah mentioned them seeing the babies she had lost, he gripped the steering wheel more tightly. She thought some of the color drained from his naturally ruddy complexion.

"They really said the babies promised not to leave next time?"

"Uh-huh."

"Can you handle a next time?"

"I'm not sure. That was the last thing I expected them to come up with. I have to think about it. *We* have to think about it."

"You know I won't pressure you, Hon."

"I know and I'm grateful. We'll decide together, okay?"

"Okay." Kevin's hands relaxed. He and Sarah took a deep breath at the same time and laughed.

She knew they would need a lot more of that synchronicity when they got home.

Twenty-Seven

Sarah's homecoming was punctuated by shrill barks and a loud thud as she heard Hero's huge paws hit the front door.

"You'd better stand behind me," said Kevin with a laugh. He quickly opened the door and stepped in front of her so seventy pounds of eager, adolescent canine didn't knock her to the ground.

"Down, boy! No jumping! Sit!"

Hero slammed his bottom on the front step, whined, and wagged his tailed furiously as Sarah scratched his head. She dared not bend over to pet him. He was much bigger than she remembered and, she thought, probably stronger than she was.

"Better let him run off his excitement," said Kevin knowingly. "Hero! Backyard!" At that command, a flash of hair and paws galloped into the house, skidded through the kitchen, and launched his body through the doggie door.

"You've got to see this." Kevin set Sarah's bags inside and closed the front door. He beckoned her to the kitchen window where she could watch the pup's antics. Hero was racing around in circles, stopping every few seconds to roll around in the snow. Then he would leap up into the air and run around some more.

"I'll call him back inside in a couple of minutes. Meanwhile, I think somebody else wants to say 'Welcome home.'"

"Meow!" said Sprite loudly as she curved around her mistress's legs and then jumped straight off the floor into her arms.

"Hello, my sweet kitty. You've grown too," said Sarah, cuddling the purring feline. "Are they eating us out of house and home yet?"

"Not quite. We can afford to feed ourselves for another couple of months. By then, one of us is probably going to have to go to work."

"Uh, that's something I need to talk to you about, Kevin."

"What, working? No worries yet." He opened the back door and called to Hero. "Come here, Buddy. Shake off on the porch. Good dog. Inside. Lie down while I dry you off." Kevin grabbed an old bath sheet and began toweling off the dog. Both of them were grinning.

"His training is really coming along," said Sarah, stalling for time.

"We've been working on obedience. He's too big to spoil."

"Are you taking him to puppy school?"

"No. He's so much bigger than the other puppies, the instructor took one look at him and suggested we do private training. That's too expensive, so I bought a video and we're making progress. Aren't we, Buddy?"

The dog thumped his tail on the floor and looked adoringly into the man's eyes. When Kevin declared, "Dinner!" Hero jumped up, his big body all a-quiver

"I'm starved," said Kevin, opening the oven door to check the food he was cooking. "I'll bet you are, too. I know the fur kids are. It's that time of day. Oh, you wanted to talk about working. Can that wait? The lasagna is just about ready."

"You made lasagna?"

"I bought frozen lasagna and put it in the oven. Does that count?"

"It certainly does," said Sarah, kissing him on the check. "And, yes, the work discussion can wait."

"Good. Go freshen up. I also bought a bag of salad and cheesecake for dessert. I'll feed the kids now and you in ten minutes."

"Thanks, I am hungry," Sarah admitted with a sigh. She was in no hurry to ruin their evening.

"Nice meal, Kevin. You're welcome to do the cooking from now on." Sarah peeked over her coffee cup and snickered at his wrinkled brow.

"Sorry, Hon. I can't afford to spoil you either. At least not after tonight. Bring your coffee and come with me. I think it's time we had a snuggle now that you're home. I've missed you, Sarah."

He pulled out her chair and led her to the living room sofa. He switched on the gas fireplace and sat beside her. He put his arm around her and was surprised when he felt her body stiffen.

"Kevin, would you mind sitting over there while we talk?" She indicated the easy chair adjacent to the sofa.

"Why? Did I do something wrong? I thought you liked dinner." He frowned at her change in tone. Why did she look afraid and ashamed?

"I *loved* the dinner. And you didn't do anything wrong. I did. That's what I have to talk to you about."

"Okay, give me a second here." Kevin took a deep breath and imagined them both enveloped in violet light as F. M. had instructed. He let his awareness drop into his heart. A door opened and he silently invited Sarah to walk in.

"What is it, Hon? Don't be afraid. I am here."

"And I," she surprised herself by saying. This was the way they had greeted each other on Atlantis, and as Alana and Ah-Lahn. She clasped her hands in her lap and began.

"I've been really stupid and I'm so sorry." She held up her hand as he began to object. "No, Hon, let me get this out while I can. I should have known better but I thought I could manage."

"Manage what?"

"Not what—who."

"Who, then?"

"A. B. Ryan."

"Him? How? Why? I thought you'd never have to see him again."

"So did I, but that's not how circumstances unfolded. I wanted to help you, Kevin, so you didn't have to take a job that made you unhappy. I called Tony—you remember—one of the senior writers I used to talk about?"

"Sort of. What does he have to do with anything?"

"Well, I called him to ask about doing some freelance writing for him, though not for A. B. Tony thought that was a great idea. It just so happened that he was going to be in Boston at a conference of some kind, so I took the train from Braintree and met him at the Four Seasons Hotel in Back Bay."

"That sounds okay," said Kevin. "We definitely could use the money. As long as you didn't have to interact with A. B."

"That's what I thought. But then when I got there, Tony whisked me up to the Presidential Suite." Kevin lifted his eyebrows.

Sarah gulped, her courage nearly fleeing the scene. "Yes, I know, very fancy. You should have seen the art collection in the hotel lobby."

Kevin pressed her to continue. "So Tony whisks you to the Presidential Suite, and . . . ?"

"So Tony ushers me into this gorgeous apartment and there, standing by these huge windows looking out at the city, was A. B. Ryan. I couldn't believe it. He looked so different from how I remembered him. That should've been a clue that they'd tricked me."

"Did you leave as soon as you saw him?"

"No, I didn't. And that's why I feel so stupid. Why did I stay?"

"Why did you?" asked Kevin, his voice cooling.

"I shouldn't have, but it was almost like he was weaving a spell—he and Tony together."

In Sarah's mind she was suddenly back in the hotel with her adversaries. Nerves got the better of her, and she began talking fast like her little nephew, Kerry, when he was excited.

"A. B. started bragging about how he was running for office again and going into real estate development and theatrical investments and how he needed me on the job because I already knew how he liked things. And lunch was fabulous, and I got caught up in the prospect of working on high-powered projects again. That's how he hooked me."

Sarah gasped for a breath and came back to herself. Kevin was staring at her, his expression consciously neutral.

"I thought you were over being impressed with that sort of thing."

"So did I. And I did sort of come to my senses when Tony got up to leave. I tried to go, too, but then A. B. . . . then he . . ."

"He what?" Kevin clenched and unclenched his fists, doing his best to calm his breath. "Sarah, what happened? Did he hurt you?" He dared not give voice to what he feared might have taken place.

"No, I got away before he could do . . . anything, though he clearly wanted to. He was gripping my arm and steering me toward the bedroom when I shook him off. Actually, he let me go. But he called me Alana."

"He what?" Kevin's eyes went dark with alarm. He looked at his wife in disbelief. "Are you sure he didn't hurt you?"

"No, but he was frightening. He smirked at me when he called me Alana and said he'd have me yet. He was so cold and threatening. And he called you Ah-Lahn. He said we were a pain in his ass and had been for centuries. I don't know what he can do to us, but I was so scared.

"Kevin, A. B. Ryan is *Arán Bán*. He was absolutely gloating when he revealed his true identity. I don't know why I never recognized him when I worked for him, except that he didn't look like this before. In Boston he was definitely Arán Bán—all slick and serpentine. And those dark, dark eyes—gazing at me like he was trying to hypnotize me."

Kevin was on his feet again, pacing, ready to defend his wife. Then he caught himself. Remembering the Master's instructions, he took a deep breath and visualized the room bathed in violet light.

Sarah sat frozen. What would she do if Kevin couldn't forgive her? At last, he spoke. His tone was serious, but there was kindness in his eyes.

"Did Arán Bán make any other threats against you or me? If he didn't, I'm not sure what action we can take." Except talk to F. M. Bellamarre, he thought to himself.

"No. Once he let go of my arm, I got out of there as fast as I could. But I felt absolutely filthy and like such an idiot."

She shuddered violently. Kevin moved to her side on the sofa.

"Come here," he said, opening his arms to her. She moved to him and leaned her head on his chest. He felt her tears on his shirt and drew her closer, allowing her apology to flow.

"I'm so sorry, Hon. I'll never do anything like that again. I should have told you what I was doing, but I wanted to surprise you. I wanted to be a hero. Like that silly dog," she laughed through a sniffle.

"Sarah, look at me." Kevin held her away from him and focused his eyes on hers. "I don't blame you. I know you wanted to help me, and I thank you for that. But we need to work out our future together, okay?"

"Okay. I'm not going anywhere. I love you, Kevin. Soul to soul."

"Never to be separated again," he agreed. "I love you, too, Hon. Now, can we go to bed? I'm tired and your eyes are drooping. Besides, I need to hold you for a long time."

"And I need to be held."

You wouldn't think that two people who've been through what we have would be shy with each other, thought Kevin as he got ready for bed, but here we are.

He had turned discreetly toward the wall to don the pajamas he hadn't bothered to wear while Sarah was with her family, while she had gone into the bathroom to change into her nightgown.

Now they were standing on opposite sides of their queen-sized bed, looking as awkward as newlyweds. A new phase of life was beginning and they both knew it.

Sarah had meant to describe her meeting on the train from Boston with the distinguished man whom she was certain was an old druid. But after confessing the terrible encounter with Arán Bán, she simply didn't have the energy. Instead, she smiled sleepily at Kevin and climbed into bed. "I'm ready for my snuggle if you are."

"Ready," he said and joined her.

He had intended to tell her about his experiences at Fibonacci's. But as soon as he was finally holding her as he had longed to do for weeks, he decided that conversation could wait.

Besides, he didn't have the authority to invite his wife to join the Friends of Ancient Wisdom. That prerogative lay with the Master. When the time was right, Sarah would receive her own invitation into the mysteries that he, himself, was only beginning to understand.

Sarah nestled into the curve of Kevin's arm and drifted off to sleep— her head resting on his chest, the soft beat of his heart soothing her into the comforting peace of being exactly where she belonged.

He breathed a deep sigh, pulled up the covers, and joined his soul's twin in slumber.

Twenty-Eight

Snuffle, snuffle, snort. Snuffle, snuffle, snort. Snuffle, snuffle, snort. Snuffle, snuffle, snort.

The sound of soft snores in her ear and the feeling of warm breath on her neck woke Sarah from a lovely dream that evaporated as soon as she squinted open her eyes. The bedroom she was once again sharing with Kevin was still dark, except for the ambient glow of a streetlamp outside their window.

She didn't remember her husband being a snorer. Or a bed hog. Why was she clinging to barely six inches of mattress and why was Kevin's arm resting so heavily on her head? She put a hand up to move that arm and made contact with a small furry body that began to purr at her touch.

She switched on the bedside lamp and rolled over to admonish Kevin for letting the cat sleep on her pillow—right into the warm, wet nose of Hero, who woke up as she turned and gave her mouth a big, good-morning slurp.

"Ew! Kevin!" Sarah groaned and wiped her mouth, trying to shield her face with her hands. "What are these animals doing in our bed?"

He opened one eye and mumbled groggily. "What? Too early. Go back to sleep. Why is the light on?"

"Wake up!" Sarah raised her voice. She tried to reach over and shake him, but seventy pounds of dog was still intent on giving her wet kisses. The cat was perched on her pillow, hissing at the commotion.

"Kevin! Get your dog off of me!" She pushed Hero just hard enough that he rolled over on his back and then all the way over onto Kevin, sending the man sliding to the floor. The dog leapt off the bed and, deciding this was the best morning game he'd ever played, started joyfully licking his owner's face.

"Argh! Hero! Stop! Sit! Down! Backyard!" groaned Kevin. With the last command he managed to extricate himself from the exuberant canine who rushed downstairs and out his doggie door.

From a crumpled heap of blankets on the floor, Kevin looked up into the face of his wife. Sarah was leaning over the edge of the bed and laughing so hard her whole body was shaking.

"Good morning," she said in a sing-song voice. "Is this how you've been starting your day since I've been gone?"

"No, it isn't," said Kevin. He scrambled up on the bed and fixed her with a sly grin. "Neither is this, but I'd like to make it a habit—starting right now."

He reached over and pulled her to him. Cradling her in his strong arms, he kissed her tenderly. When she did not pull away, he deepened the kiss and felt her body welcome his—heart to heart, soul to soul.

He would have urged her further, had Hero not come bounding back into the room from his outside doggie duty. He plopped both huge paws on the bed and began whining with an expectant look in his big brown eyes.

"Sorry, Hon," said a clearly disappointed Kevin. He shook his head as Sarah eased out of his arms. "It's breakfast time for the fur kids and they don't take no for an answer."

"I can see that," she said with laughter sparkling in her hazel eyes. Not to be left out, Sprite started rubbing against her arm and purring eagerly. "And since you made me dinner last night, I'll cook you breakfast this morning. Then we can discuss future sleeping arrangements—or possibly the purchase of a larger bed."

Husband and wife were lingering over their second cup of coffee after the hearty breakfast Sarah had fixed. A surprisingly sunny November day had dawned, and they hadn't quite decided how to spend it.

"That was so much better than cold cereal," said Kevin with a blissful sigh. He folded his hands on the table and closed his eyes, savoring the feeling of a warm, full tummy.

"Don't get up, Hon, I'll take of these," said Sarah, teasing the very contented man who showed no signs of clearing their plates. She loaded the dishwasher, then came back to the table.

"I have something else to tell you about what happened while I was gone, on the train to Braintree after the disastrous Arán Bán encounter."

Kevin's eyes flew open. His face blanched.

"No, nothing else horrible, Hon, I promise," said Sarah. She reached across the table and put her hands on his. "This is really quite remarkable, especially since I've been living in the mystical world of druids for so many months. I think I met one on the train from Boston."

"Tell me," was all Kevin could say. He watched his wife's expression for signs of danger. Seeing none, he allowed himself to relax and listen to the story she eagerly began to unfold.

"You remember Alana's grandfather, Archdruid Bleddyn?"

"The one who was killed in the destruction of *Ynys Môn* along with her father, Carwyn?"

"Uh-huh." Sarah closed her eyes and tented her fingers at her lips. She was remembering how much Alana loved the man who had been her most beloved mentor, before she met Ah-Lahn.

Kevin waited silently until she brought her attention back to him. He well knew the powerful emotions these recollections could evoke.

"What about Bleddyn, Hon?"

"I think I met him on the train. Or someone who reminded me of him as he might be in today's world. There was something about his presence, his kindness. The way he listened. The wisdom I felt him impart to me without saying word.

"I told him all about Alana and Ah-Lahn and about A. B. Ryan being Arán Bán—the whole story. Somehow explaining myself to this man, who watched me with his extraordinary violet eyes, was like going to confession. I felt absolved of my sins when we got off the train. Can you imagine?"

"I can," said Kevin simply. There was only one person he could think of who fit this description. A wave of gratitude swept through him, heart and soul. Sarah had been protected after all. He should not have been surprised. F. M. Bellamarre definitely got around.

He wondered—Had his own faithful meditations on the violet light made a difference in the Master's ability to look out for his beloved? Somehow, he believed they had.

"Anyway," Sarah continued, "this amazing person named F. M. Bellamarre gave me the confidence to tell you about my stupid mistake. In fact, he more or less demanded that I tell you. Not in an onerous kind of way—but in a manner of such quiet authority, such dignity and honor, that I couldn't imagine doing other than what he said I must. Does that make sense?"

"Perfect sense. Did he say anything else?" Kevin could hardly contain the excitement bubbling up in his breast. Was now the time he could tell Sarah all about Fibonacci's? *Not yet,* he felt the voice of inner wisdom speak into his heart. *Let her disclose the Master's words.*

"He only said that much depended on my courage in this matter. And then he disappeared—just like the master druids would cloak themselves in the *féath fíadha* mist. I didn't detect any vapors around him, but he vanished as if there had been."

"Have you seen him or anybody like him since then?" asked Kevin carefully.

"No, I was too busy finishing my book. But you know, now that you ask, there were a couple of times as I was trying to figure out a particular scene that I could almost see him in my mind's eye or hear him inspiring me with what I should write and how I should write it. I believe that's the main reason I was able to finish in two weeks. Extraordinary, don't you think?"

"Absolutely," said Kevin. He got up from the table and put his coffee cup in the dishwasher. "Come on, Hon. Let's bundle up and take Hero for a run on the beach. It's a great day to be outside."

Twenty-Nine

The next week was a busy one. Sarah was frequently on the phone with her new editor, Samantha, getting acquainted, asking and answering some basic questions about how they would proceed together to finish the novel.

She was comforted that Sam, as the editor liked to be called, wasn't concerned about the story's ending. "We'll know what to do when we get there. These stories have a way of revealing their conclusions when good, clean editing paves the way," she commented cheerfully.

Kevin was spending a fair amount of his time working on Hero's training to ensure the safety of their furniture and any potential future visitors.

"I think this dog grows overnight. I swear he's bigger this morning," he commented with a rueful smile. Hero came dancing in from the backyard, slurped a big gulp of water from his bowl, drooled half of it across the floor, and flopped down under the kitchen table where Sarah was sitting.

She scratched the dog's big head and laughed up at Kevin who stood by the kitchen counter, pouring himself a cup of coffee. Then she grew serious. "Now that we're home together, do you think we should try stepping into a light orb to contact Master Saint Germain or Lady Nada?"

"No, let's get through Thanksgiving and then see what happens. Do you mind if we don't do the big family dinner thing this year? You've just been with your folks, and I'd like to beg off driving to my parents' house."

Sarah agreed. She was happy to let her Massachusetts kin take care of each other. Eileen had already phoned to say that Millie and Jack were driving Brian and Ivy up to Braintree for feasting and football. That would be plenty of company for the Callahan household.

"We could take the train from Grand Central," she offered.

"Really? You just spent a whole day getting home on the train."

"I know, but Poughkeepsie is only two hours away, not seven. It's something else, isn't it? Your father?"

"Yeah," Kevin sighed and drew out the word. "I haven't told my folks about losing my job, and I really can't face my dad's disappointment or his sermons about being responsible and practical."

Sarah understood her husband's reluctance. His father, George MacCauley, had recently retired as vice president of the local bank in Kevin's hometown of Poughkeepsie, New York.

His sister, Margaret, had married a banker like their father. The son-in-law, Terrance, had come from money and knew how to make more—a talent George admired and wished that his own son possessed.

Kevin's mother, Miriam, had also retired that year from teaching middle school English. Despite George's opinion that a man should pursue a practical career, she had instilled in her son a love of the written and spoken word and an appreciation for the music and culture of his Irish ancestry—especially its poetry.

Her son also loved the quaintness of Poughkeepsie's historic areas. Only ninety miles from New York City, it was a world apart. Even as a child, Kevin had been fascinated by its history. He could feel the past on every street. There was a continuity of life here with people who had forged their lives in a new nation nearly three hundred years earlier. They had created community out of wilderness by ingenuity, inspiration, and faith in their connection with Providence.

Kevin had acquiesced to his father's wishes and taken a major in business and finance. He'd also written some poetry, read about Irish history, and discovered a passion for classical and esoteric philosophy.

After college, he had gone to New York in hopes of using his business skills in support of the arts. However, his first job had been with Karl and Greta Nordemann, who were growing their financial services business. He had stayed with them for nearly ten years until lately— which is why he didn't want to see his father.

"I'll call my mom. I can blame our absence on my temperamental novelist-wife," Kevin said with a wink. Sarah made a face at him that made him laugh.

"Seriously, I'll explain that we need some time together after all the drama with your brother's car accident. I'll probably tell her about losing my job. She'll understand. I may even let her break the news to Dad—as long as she promises to stop him from calling me until I've got something new lined up."

Sarah stood and put her arm around Kevin's waist than patted him on the chest. "Good plan. Now, Mr. Finance, how about helping me figure out how we can afford to feed ourselves, my kitty, and your monster dog."

For the next hour Kevin and Sarah put their heads together on ways to economize. When their brains got tired of stretching pennies, they took a break and brainstormed possible careers for him to pursue so she could continue writing.

Sarah made a pot of tea and found some cookies in the pantry. Returning to sit adjacent to her husband at the table, she folded her hands under her chin and assumed a pensive expression.

After wrapping her brain around money matters—not her strong suit—she was more than a little punchy. Her opening ideas were not particularly helpful.

"Let's imagine what you could do besides crunching numbers. How about . . . lumberjack?" Kevin wrinkled his nose.

"Ferryboat captain? Lifeguard?"

"It's winter."

"I was thinking of the indoor pool at the gym. If you didn't want to get wet, you could be a fitness trainer."

"Yes . . . I could do that . . . for a while anyway." Kevin shrugged.

"You could, but you shouldn't," said Sarah, turning serious. "I want you to be happy in your work." She laid her hand on his shoulder. "What would you *like* to do? Forget about money. What would feed your soul?"

Kevin leaned back in his chair and looked into a long-held dream. "I've always wanted to teach. Or own a bookstore. Maybe both."

"Really? What would you teach? Can you teach in a bookstore?"

"That's something I wanted to talk to you about. I was waiting for the right time. Guess this is it."

Kevin had been unsure of Sarah's response to the offer he'd received from Lucky last week. The fact that she wanted him to be happy in his work opened the way.

"You remember Fibonacci's?"

"The coffee shop and bookstore you've wanted to visit?"

"Right. I've been spending quite a bit of time there while you were working on your book. I've been learning a lot from Lucky and his wife, Róisín, the couple who own both businesses. I'll tell you more about them later. The great thing is that Lucky offered me a part-time job that could eventually lead to my taking over the businesses when he retires, which might be in the next year or so."

"Honey, that's fabulous! How did it happen?"

"I'll tell you. It was almost as if somebody had scripted the event," Kevin began with a smile. Sarah refreshed her cup of tea and settled in for a story. This promised to be a good one.

Lucky is the kind of person you immediately feel comfortable telling about your life. The first day I met him and Róisín, I mentioned that I'd lost my job with Nordemann Financial. He asked what sort of work I did there and fairly quickly asked if I'd look over his investments and charitable giving strategy.

Of course, I jumped at the chance. So last week we spent a morning reviewing his portfolio. We both had questions and I offered to do an in-depth review if he didn't mind my going over his books. That's a lot for somebody to trust you with when they hardly know you, but he did.

That was Monday morning. After lunch—Róisín makes a great sandwich, by the way—I was sitting at a table in the coffee shop with Lucky's laptop when a young man, a college student, sat down.

Everybody shares tables at Fibonacci's, so that wasn't unusual. What caught my attention was the fellow's obvious frustration over whatever he was studying on his tablet.

I couldn't help inquiring. 'Tough subject?'

'Not tough, pointless,' he grumbled. 'I'm a philosophy major. The Greeks. Classics. So why do I have to take a geometry course? I'm studying their words and ideas, not shapes or spacial relationships.'

'Maybe I can help.' I offered my hand. 'I'm Kevin.'

'Noah.' He returned the handshake with a wary nod.

'Take a look around on the walls,' I suggested. 'What do you see?'

'Spirals. Lots of spirals. Pyramids, crystals. Five-petaled flowers, fruits, and starfish. What does that have to do with philosophy? Looks like geometry to me.'

'It is geometry, and many of these shapes were identified by Plato as being the foundational components of the universe—fire, air, water, and earth. These essences were the basis for his theory of forms or ideals.'

'Okay, but why all the spirals?' asked Noah.

'Lucky, the owner here, could tell you more, but he's busy right now.' I could see he was alone at the bar, making lattes and serving pastries for a flock of students who had come in all at once.

'Here's what I've learned from him,' I said to Noah and told him what I knew about the origins of Fibonacci's.

'Several years ago, when Lucky first came to America from Ireland, he studied with an old alchemist named Joshua. In addition to conducting the ancient experiments for turning physical lead into physical gold, Joshua was also seeking a correlation between Plato's Ideal Forms, the Golden Ratio, the Pythagorean Theorem, and the Fibonacci number sequence.

'He wanted to know how those concepts might correlate with the transformation of the lead of human consciousness into the gold of Spirit.

'He owned an extensive library of occult works and vintage esoterica which Lucky inherited when Joshua died suddenly two years ago. Many of those volumes are now in the loft next door. The old alchemist also collected much of the art you see on the walls here as examples of what he believed to be the synthesis of all of the ancients' theories.

'Lucky explained to me that there are minute but significant differences between the various spirals. That being said, however, there is an underlying synchrony that he and I find fascinating—that is the importance of the number five in each of these perspectives.

'Pythagoras adopted the five-pointed star as the symbol for his esoteric school at Crotona, Italy. The fifth of Plato's solids is based on pentagons. Three plus two is the fifth combination in the Fibonacci sequence.

'Da Vinci created a detailed study of the five-petaled violet flower. The Golden Ratio can be calculated using the square root of the number five as one of the variables.

'I've, personally, seen a photo of a gold crystal that appeared to be made of five-sided shapes, though they weren't perfect pentagons. When you get a chance, take a look at the pinky ring Lucky wears—it's a pentagon.'

'Wow, Kevin, you know a lot,' said Noah after I finished Lucky's story.

'Not as much as I'd like,' I assured him. 'I'm still learning, and I hope never to stop. I'm fascinated by the confluence of different branches of knowledge and experience. And I like sharing what I know with others who aren't satisfied with living in ignorance of the ancient and often mysterious origins of our society.'

'This may sound weird,' ventured Noah, 'but would you be willing to talk to some of my classmates? A bunch of us are struggling and I think you could help us. I don't know why our professors aren't making these connections.'

'I think you have to be a bit of a mystic to want to see the connections. Modern thought tends to be reductionist—flat. The juice is in the complexity.'

I felt like Noah and I had made a good connection, so I

agreed, 'Sure, I'll be happy to meet with you and your friends. Here's my cell number. Text me with some options and we'll find a time to get together.'

"That's how it happened," said Kevin, beaming at Sarah. "We're having our first meeting on Friday after Thanksgiving. Lucky thinks it's a great idea. He's already creating a special shelf in the bookstore with titles my students may find interesting and that we can explore as a group."

Sarah's heart rejoiced as she listened to the excitement in Kevin's voice. His face was aglow with an enthusiasm that had been missing for a very long time. When he said "my students" she felt illumination dawn for both of them.

"Honey, this is great! I'm so happy for you. I can't wait to meet Lucky and Róisín myself. When can we stop by Fibonacci's?"

"How does Thanksgiving sound?"

"Really?"

"Yes. I've been hoping for an invitation that would include you, and it came in this morning's mail." He took both her hands in his.

"Hon, there is so much more to tell you about what's going on at Fibonacci's and what I've been experiencing there with the Friends of Ancient Wisdom. But the full story isn't mine to tell. We'll go to Lucky's pot luck dinner on Thursday and let the mystery unfold from there."

Sarah wrinkled her brow and stuck out her lower lip in mock disappointment. Kevin laughed and handed her the invitation.

"Trust me, the revelation will be worth the wait."

Kevin & Sarah MacCauley are invited to celebrate Thanksgiving with the Friends of Ancient Wisdom on Thursday, 1:00 p.m. Lucky and Róisín will provide turkey, fixings, and beverages. Please bring an entree, side dish, or dessert to share.

Thirty

K evin, you have *got* to tell me more about the Friends of Ancient Wisdom. We'll be there in no time, and I need to know what I'm walking into."

Sarah cradled a sweet potato casserole on her lap and looked insistently at her husband as he drove them to Thanksgiving dinner. He'd been mum about details since receiving their shared invitation, saying only that he couldn't predict her experience.

"Okay," he acquiesced. "Since we're nearly there, I can tell you that I have met many friends—people I knew as Ah-Lahn and a few others from more recent embodiments."

"Really? That's incredible. You mean like from our life reviews? How is that possible? Did you just walk in and, *Poof!*, you're back in time?"

"Almost. There is something about entering Fibonacci's—at least when you're invited to a particular event—that opens your third eye. Sometimes a little, other times a lot, depending on your soul's need at that moment. I'm as eager as you to find out who you'll recognize.

"When I showed up for my first meeting of the Friends of Ancient Wisdom, I definitely felt like I was stepping into a life review—or onto the set for a movie about your book. Except the individuals I met weren't characters on a screen. They're real people who have awakened to some of their past lives—and who just happen to be friends we've known for centuries."

"Like who? Who did you meet?" Sarah's heart was racing now. Had Kevin seen Archdruid Bleddyn? If he had, why didn't he say so when she told him about meeting F. M. Bellamarre? She was becoming annoyed at being kept in the dark.

"That first Saturday I recognized Cróga, the tribal chieftain that

Ah-Lahn served as chief druid. There were men and women from the Druid Council and fellow monks from the awful days of Clonmacnoise monastery. Even a couple of old Vikings who seemed relatively benign this time around."

"I can't believe you didn't tell me." Sarah looked out the car window at Fibonacci's store front as Kevin pulled up to the curb.

"Hon, I wasn't *allowed* to," he tried to explain. He shut off the engine and put his hand on her shoulder. She turned to him, a wounded expression on her face.

"Believe me, *not* telling you has been a real test. I'm sorry if that hurt you. All I can say is that Lucky was emphatic that each person's introduction to the Friends is unique and must not be preempted, even by their indulgent spouse." He stroked her cheek. His expression begged her to understand.

"Honey, you haven't been indulgent in any of the lifetimes I've known you." Sarah chuckled and blew out a sigh. "I get the point. Let the mysteries begin."

Kevin opened the coffee shop's heavy wooden door, and Sarah entered another world.

Fibonacci's was decorated with twinkle lights festooned around every window. The archway leading to the adjoining bookstore was outlined in tiny bulbs, inviting entrance into what appeared to Sarah as a magical land she suspected of being peopled by elves and fairies and fantastical beings who shimmered in the white lights that sparkled from every corner.

Intoxicating aromas filled the air with spices savory and sweet. Long tables were piled high with an enormous roast turkey, a prime rib, casseroles, vegetables and salads of every variety, and a separate table loaded with desserts.

Kevin had expected Sarah to be enchanted by her initial experience at this unusual place of business that was truly a portal to other planes of consciousness. However, he did not anticipate being overwhelmed by the next person he would recognize from his embodiment as the druid Ah-Lahn.

He heard Craig call his name and, momentarily forgetting Sarah, allowed himself to be introduced to a couple of former Celtic warriors. He didn't recognize them, but found them to be very congenial fellows.

Likewise forgetting Kevin and not realizing that he had left her side, Sarah was gazing at the general splendor of the decorations when a friendly young woman with long blonde hair and sparkling green eyes approached her.

"Here, I'll take your casserole and . . . Sarah!'

"Debbie?! What are you doing here?"

"I might ask you the same, except I heard from Róisín that you'd received your invitation. Welcome to the Friends of Ancient Wisdom."

"Thank you. Are you a member of this group? How long have you been coming here? Did you know about Fibonacci's when we worked together? Sorry, I have so many questions."

"I don't mind," said Debbie, her green eyes beaming warmth and recognition. "Yes, I am a member. I've been coming here for about a year and a half. And, yes, I did know about Fibonacci's when we worked together, but inviting you was not my prerogative. Now that I see you've been invited on your own merit, I'm very happy to share what I know."

She smiled broadly and extended her hand to Kevin, who was hurrying over to rejoin his wife.

"Ah, this must be the husband I've never met, I . . ." Debbie's eyes went wide. Her voice caught in her throat. "Ah-Lahn?!"

She and Kevin stood staring at each other, their mouths gaping. Tears suddenly sprang into their eyes as each beheld a soul mate from long ago. Despite Sarah and Debbie having been co-workers, her friend and her husband had never met in this life.

"Dearbhla, my dear friend. I can't believe it's you," exclaimed Kevin. They embraced like the long-lost friends they were and then put their arms around Sarah, gathering her into the family they had been.

"Hon, this your co-worker? When you were writing about Alana's aunt, did you not figure out that Debbie was the seer and Ah-Lahn's great friend?"

"Not a clue," she said shaking her head. "Debbie, did you know?"

"I had an inkling. When you first asked me about your panther spirit guide, I wondered. I've known for a while that I was a seer with the ancient Irish druids, but the details have only recently filled in since I've been coming to Fibonacci's.

"When you never came back to work after being in Ireland, I let the subject drop. We didn't really stay in touch, so I had no idea what you were writing. What *have* you been writing, Sarah?"

"Our story—all of us. You, me, Kevin, others from when we were druids. Oh, my God, my head is spinning. Debbie, why didn't I recognize you? Kevin, this is so fantastic."

"This is the magic I was studiously *not* telling you about," he explained. His blue-green eyes were wide and sparking. "But, Debbie, if you've been a member of the Friends, why haven't our paths crossed?"

" 'Everything in its time,' as F. M. says. I've been moving and helping my sister set up her health food store. I haven't been here . . ."

"F. M.? F. M. Bellamarre?" interrupted Sarah. "You know him? Is he here?" She whipped around to Kevin. "You've met him, haven't you? And you didn't say anything when I told you about my conversation with him on the train."

"Yes, I have met him," he admitted. "And before you get mad at me, remember, I was sworn to secrecy."

"You've already been introduced to F. M.?" Debbie wanted to know. "Where? How?"

"On the train from Boston to Braintree. Oh, my God, Debbie. I know I keep saying that, but oh, my God! You won't believe what happened with Tony. I'll have to tell you later. It's too long a story." Sarah held her hand to her heart. "So, you both know F. M. Bellamarre. Is he one of the Friends?"

"He's our spiritual leader, the one who brought us all together," said Debbie with a tender warmth in her voice. "He is responsible for your invitation—a credit to your own state of consciousness. We earn our proximity to the Master, as I see you have done."

Debbie nodded to the end of the room where several people were gathered in conversation. As if he heard his friend's comment, F. M. turned and looked directly at Sarah. Excusing himself from the others, he made his way through the crowd that parted before him as naturally as if he were directing their movement.

"Greetings, my dear. We meet again," he said with a slight bow, his voice as melodious and reassuring as Sarah remembered. The Master took her hand and nodded to Kevin, who relinquished her arm which he had been holding to steady her—and himself.

"I had the pleasure of sharing a short train ride with Sarah when she was leaving Boston a few weeks back. You were in somewhat of a flurry, as I recall. I trust events in your life are more settled now. Did you finish your book?"

Sarah managed to find her voice. "Yes, I did. At least enough to send the manuscript to my editor." She stammered and wondered if she should curtsy to this elegant man whom Debbie called her Master.

"F. M. . . . Sir . . . I . . ."

"You have questions," he interjected with violet eyes twinkling. "All will be answered in time. Now, please enjoy your meal and our fellowship of old friends. There are many here who are eager to greet you. At this moment I am called elsewhere, but I will return this evening and we will speak at length. There are particular matters we must discuss pertaining to our conversation on the train."

Sarah's head continued to spin, and she had to work to keep her mouth from gaping as she was greeted by many friends of old.

More than once, her eyes filled with tears in recognition of individuals who had been dear to her in the times of happiness and sorrow that make up a life lived to the full. For such had been Alana's experience in her short time with Ah-Lahn and throughout her subsequent career as a masterful druidess.

Debbie and Craig—whom she also recognized as Cróga—joined her and Kevin at a booth in the back of the room. Throughout their meal their conversation bubbled in enthusiastic recollection of several shared lifetimes—for they had been together in more than their druidic embodiments.

They were finishing their desserts when F. M. reappeared.

Sarah observed that he could move in and out of various groups without being noticed except by those with whom he wished to speak.

Otherwise, he seemed to be invisible to the other guests.

Debbie and Craig excused themselves so the Master could sit across from Sarah and Kevin. Without further introduction, he began to unfold the instructions that would change their lives forever.

His tone was conversational, though the subject was deadly serious.

Thirty-One

I often think the brothers of shadow are more self-aware than the children of light," F. M. began. "Even mature sons and daughters of *An Síoraí* fail to understand the depth of hatred the dark ones hold and constantly perpetrate against the Divine Light that lives in our hearts.

"With regards to Arán Bán, his hatred is personal. By now, you must have realized that he will do everything in his power to separate the two of you—to destroy you, either singly or together."

"He's certainly made that clear in the past," said Kevin. He shuddered as images of Ah-Lahn's murder flashed before his inner sight. "But somehow I never thought to be concerned for our safety in the twenty-first century."

"Let me explain," said F. M. "What we are dealing with here is an individual who, like Lucifer himself, at one time had great light. That attainment afforded him a more than ordinary opportunity to forsake his evil ways and once more embrace the Divine.

"However, the age has turned. Those like him, who have consistently chosen the left-handed path and tempted the children of *An Síoraí*, the Eternal One, to forsake their spiritual inheritance, have reached the end of opportunity to wield their negative power."

"But A. B. seemed to be brimming with power when I encountered him in Boston," said Sarah. "Especially when he revealed himself to me as Arán Bán."

"And his shocking you was one of the many ways these individuals steal the very life essence from those they would control. They siphon off energy from good people, like you, who unwittingly support their nefarious deeds."

"Then how do we combat them?" asked Kevin.

As he and Sarah looked on, F. M.'s aura became visible to them. A violet glow emanated from him. His voice grew deeper, more resonant, and he spoke with the unmistakable authority Sarah had witnessed in her first conversation with this remarkable being. She and her husband were spellbound as the Master continued a discourse of great import.

Now, in this new age, we must enlist sons and daughters who, for eons, have been enmeshed with these fallen ones. You and others must separate out and embody your own True Self. Until then, you are in the line of fire, so to speak, and the ripcord of karma cannot be pulled by the Great White Brotherhood.

The union of twin flames is one of our most powerful tools for liberating those who are caught in veils of illusion—not realizing they have been duped by forces of self-centeredness and greed to relinquish their innate soul freedoms.

Dear ones, you must understand that the death of the soul is the aim of these dark ones. They are sly in their subtle misinterpretation of compassion. They are immensely skilled at confusing well-meaning people into sympathy for the devil himself—convincing them to accept mediocrity and ignorance while allowing themselves to be perpetually distracted by the world's entertainments.

Kevin and Sarah looked at each other in dismay. How often had sympathetic ties—even with friends or family—convinced them to take positions or engage in activities that they later discovered were not in alignment with their highest principles.

The Master read their thoughts and smiled. Yes, he said to himself, these two will do well in the commission for which they have long been preparing.

F. M.'s countenance brightened. His violet eyes seemed to throw out sparks of love and encouragement. Now, as he spoke, his words created images in his listeners' minds to help them understand what lay before them.

A thrill rippled through Kevin's body. He could feel himself and

Sarah being lifted into a state of consciousness not unlike a life review. The Master painted the picture:

> If souls only knew the glories, peace, happiness, and love that are the treasures of union with *An Síoraí*, the Eternal One, they would turn from the impostor of freedom and run to the arms of their own Divine Presence. The great I AM is the true source and goal of all of life. This is the message we are pledged to convey.
>
> A terrible rending took place with Ah-Lahn's murder. That event was never meant to be. It caused a set-back to your souls and to the Brotherhood's plans. The shock of Arán Bán's preempting of these plans opened the door to darkness that came upon the druidic communities and the entire Celtic culture.
>
> Alana and Ah-Lahn were destined to be a bulwark of illumination for other pairs of twin flames who depended on their support in those days—and who await you now, though they know it not. They will need your strength to find their own. To fight their own battles and to win Love's victory.

"Who are these people?" asked Sarah when the Master paused. She could feel her heart chakra spinning in anticipation—though of what, she was not certain. "How will we know whom we are to help?"

F. M. smiled reassuringly and engaged them in conversation before continuing with his instructions.

"You will know them when your paths cross. Some you know already as dear friends of old. However, before you can be of extraordinary assistance to others, you two must be united in the mastery of your own wholeness. In order to safely combat the intentions of Arán Bán and those like him, you must be whole as individuals and as a couple."

"How do we do that, Sir?" asked Kevin. Here was the crux of the Master's discourse. He could feel it in his soul, and he knew that Sarah was linked with him in that insight. They had never been so united.

"Yes, my dears, you understand perfectly." F. M. inhaled deeply and amplified the images he had put before them. His violet eyes were clear and kind as he unfolded the details of the extraordinary commission he would be asking them to accept.

Some rents in the fabric of soul and mind can only be mended where they occurred—where the akashic records yet remain. The Brotherhood has determined that you will most likely achieve that reunion in Ireland at the time of the winter solstice.

You will be returning to the site of your previous mastery and of your tragic demise. The records must be cleared and the divine plan restored to your twin flames.

We are not activating old patterns of consciousness. Your souls have matured since the first century. Yet there is significant life force trapped as soul fragments in the records of that embodiment that need to be revealed, retrieved, and transmuted to enable your work and service in this life.

F. M. observed his listeners carefully. Good, they are still following, he said to himself. Their attention bodes well for what is to come.

What you have remembered so far—and have done well to recall and record—is only a fraction of the adeptship you each achieved. Master druids like Ah-Lahn knew how to create the *féath fíadha* mists and other marvels of spiritual alchemy.

This wisdom is locked on the etheric plane in an aspect of being some call the soul's treasures in heaven. The term we use is causal body. We would have you gain access to that knowledge for the rituals you must perform and partake of while in Ireland.

Until you leave for the land of Éire, we ask that you fast and pray and be open to what *An Síoraí*, the Eternal One, will inspire upon you through your True Self, which is the seat of your intuition.

Sarah and Kevin had not expected to return to Ireland so soon. Although F. M. was presenting them with a challenging mission, the opportunity to visit the land that was home to their souls thrilled them beyond words. They hung on his every word.

Listen carefully, for here are your instructions: Under the Brotherhood's direction, you will find the grove used by Master Druid Óengus where Alana's life reviews took place. There you will perform a certain ritual that only a very few druids knew.

If all goes well, you will merge your present consciousness with your past attainment as Ah-Lahn and Alana. You were well on your way to achieving the balance of masculine and feminine in your beings. Your task now is to complete what you began.

Sarah turned to Kevin, her eyes wide. He met her gaze and blew out a deep breath. Still, in the Master's aura, fear did not disturb them.

His instruction to them complete for now, he dissolved the images he had shown them and resumed a more conversational tone.

"You are not alone, my dears. As you make your preparations, we will keep a watchful eye on Arán Bán. He is not the source of the darkness that opposes you, but over the centuries he has proved himself a willing tool of that force.

"We do not expect him to attack you—at least not yet. However, he is a master of cloaking his intentions, which is why you, Sarah, did not recognize him until he threw off his disguise in Boston."

She knitted her brow. "I wondered why he appeared so different. Until he turned and spoke, I would not have recognized him."

F. M. continued. "The bombastic politician you previously worked for in New York was an illusion which he has used quite successfully for many years. He must be feeling very confident to now reveal his actual appearance.

"That is good news for the Brotherhood. When the dark ones overplay their hand, the victory of the Divine Light is nigh. Sooner or later, Arán Bán will meet the fullness of his karma, as must each soul in the course of events both human and divine.

"We intend to be ready for that eventuality and so will you. There are no guarantees, and this process does place you in considerable danger. However, be assured that we of the Great White Brotherhood will do our utmost to protect you."

Three very intent souls took each other's measure and were grateful for the commitment they felt on the return current of their attention.

"Now, my dears, I will leave you to your thoughts," said F. M. "Fear not. You would not be presented with this assignment if you were not able for it."

He stood to depart. The couple found their legs and managed to stand with him. Sarah had a sudden inspiration.

"Sir, before you go, may I ask you one more question?"

"Of course. I will answer if I am able."

"I hope you don't think me impertinent, but I must ask. Are you Saint Germain?"

"What does your heart tell you, Sarah?"

"Though I had thought you might be the reembodiment of Alana's grandfather, Archdruid Bleddyn, my heart, my soul, my intuition all say you are the great alchemist, Ascended Master Saint Germain—friend and colleague of our Lady Master Nada."

F. M. beamed at Sarah and Kevin. "From this day forward, whenever possible, I shall meet you in that form, beginning tomorrow evening." He laid a hand on each one's shoulder and looked at them as a father beholding his precious children.

"Trust your attunement, my daughter and my son, and you will pass every test with flying colors. Until we meet on the other side of a crystal bridge, I wish you Godspeed."

Ever gracious, as F. M. departed, he paused to say good night to Lucky and Róisín, who were sipping tea by themselves at the bar. Sarah tried to watch the Master leave, but when she looked away for a moment, he was no longer there.

Thirty-Two

Fibonacci's coffee shop was as peaceful as a chapel after mass. All of the food had been put away. Tables and chairs were set up for Friday morning's early customers.

Kevin and Sarah quietly gathered their belongings and looked around—their hearts full of wonder. The twinkle lights cast a magical glow around the empty room. Still, no one would guess the fullness of the transformation that had taken place here this evening.

Of course, Lucky and Róisín had some idea—at least that F. M. Bellamarre had presented their friends with an opportunity that would change their lives—that had already changed them, judging from the look of otherworldliness each one wore like an inner smile. They hugged Sarah and Kevin and walked them to the front door.

The MacCauleys drove the few blocks to their home without speaking and entered this place of sanctuary with a quiet dignity that even their animals seemed to understand. Neither Hero nor Sprite rushed to greet them, as was their normal behavior.

Instead, they lifted their heads from where they were sleeping in the living room. With a signal from Kevin, they quietly followed their humans outside to the backyard where they all stood in the cold night air, looking up at the sky.

Kevin put his arm around Sarah's shoulder. She had her arm about his waist. The night was partly cloudy with only a few stars visible. Urban light pollution hid most of them from view, but husband and wife could see the vast array of the Milky Way in their mind's eye.

"Do you remember how Alana and Ah-Lahn used to meditate on that great river of light?" said Kevin.

"Billions and billions of stars. A crystalline bridge right there in the heavens, just waiting to carry us all the way to *Tír na n'Óg*, Land of the Ever-Living," mused Sarah.

"Are you worried?" asked Kevin.

"Concerned, yes. Aware that we may be in danger. I trust Saint Germain, and yet I am beginning to understand that there is only so much he can do in certain situations," answered Sarah. "Until tonight I really had no idea. I guess I'd always thought of ascended masters as omniscient and all-powerful. They are more limited by what we humans do than I would have thought."

"I know," said Kevin, looking at the few stars that winked between clouds. "Despite his ability to walk among us as F. M. Bellamarre, we are the ones responsible for our own karma and for fulfilling our reason for being."

"Look, Hon, a falling star." Sarah traced a blaze of light that suddenly shot across the horizon. "I wonder what that sign portends and for whom? I know the Masters will do everything in their power for us, but soul liberation is still a do-it-yourself project, isn't it?"

"It is," agreed Kevin, "but not completely solo. We have each other. I've got you, Sarah." He pulled her closer.

"And I've got you, Kevin. Come what may."

"Come what may, beloved of my heart."

Before Kevin and Sarah could follow F. M.'s instructions for crossing the crystal bridge where he would join them in his ascended presence as Master Saint Germain, Kevin was committed to meet with the philosophy student Noah and any of his friends who wished to discuss the connection between the geometry class they found superfluous to the classics they preferred.

After Thursday's big Thanksgiving dinner, business at Fibonacci's coffee shop was slow on Friday morning. All the tables were back in place and only a hint of yesterday's sumptuous aromas remained. Lucky looked up from behind the mahogany coffee bar. He smiled and handed

Kevin a freshly brewed Americano.

"Here, try this new blend. One of the Friends brought me some beans from Costa Rica. It's a variety I've not tasted."

"Mmmm, it's good," said Kevin sipping slowly. "Nice body. Strong, but no bite."

"Speaking of bite, are you ready for your guests?" Lucky nodded to the front door that now opened to admit five college students, one of whom was Rudy. "Did you know Rudy was one of them?"

"No, is that a problem?"

"Not unless he makes it one, which I don't think he will. He's been in a good space recently. By the way, he doesn't know you were here the day of his outburst about F. M."

Kevin nodded and walked over to greet the young people he hoped would make up his first study group.

"Welcome to Fibonacci's, gentlemen and ladies," he said, extending a warm handshake to three young men and two young women who looked around curiously.

"Noah, good to see you."

"Thanks, Kevin. I brought Jenny with me. She's in our philosophy class. You made a big point of the number five, so we included the ladies. Hope that's okay."

"Absolutely," agreed Kevin. "Glad to have you join us, Jenny."

"Glad to be here," she responded easily.

"I'm Finn and this is Valerie." All six-feet-two inches of healthy Viking genes returned Kevin's firm handshake. He pulled off a well-worn stocking cap to reveal a full head of wild red hair and smiled broadly. "Thanks for meeting with us. Noah says you know a lot."

"We'll find out, won't we?" said Kevin, turning to the blue-eyed strawberry blonde beside him. "Valerie, do you have a special interest?"

"She's all numbers, numbers, numbers," offered Jenny. "And Finn, of course." She wrinkled her nose at Valerie, who responded in kind.

Kevin laughed. He liked these people already. Taking a cue from Lucky, he turned to Rudy as if they hadn't met. "And you are?"

"Rudy. Have I seen you here before? How come Lucky's letting you teach?" He shouted across the room, "Hey, Lucky, I thought teachers had to be one of the Friends. What gives?"

"Kevin's okay, Rudy," called Lucky from behind the bar. "He's been around a long time, just like you and me."

"If you say so," said Rudy with a shrug. "So, Kevin, what are you going to teach us? If F. M. won't see me, I guess you'll have to do."

"Hey, man, let up, okay?" Jenny gave Rudy a sisterly punch in the shoulder. "Sorry, Kevin. This guy can't help acting like his name—Roood-eee."

"No worries," said Kevin, casually waving away any concern. "I expect we'll all learn from each other. I'd like to hear about your courses and then share some of my own interests. Lucky just made a pot of coffee. Why don't you grab a cup, and we'll convene at the back table. Then, we'll see where this goes."

Kevin poured himself a fresh cup of Lucky's brew and made his way to the table. There was something so familiar about Rudy, but nothing he could identify. The third-eye awakening he had occasionally experienced at Fibonacci's was not active at the moment.

After a quick survey of which courses the five students were taking, Kevin decided to lead with the image his intuition had suggested this morning when he woke up. He pulled out a drawing and set it before the group.

"Since Noah's first question to me was, 'What does geometry have to do with philosophy?' I thought we'd start here. Anybody know what this is?"

"Da Vinci's illustrations of Plato's Solids that he drew for Pacioli's *De Divina Proportione*, published 1509," said Valerie without hesitation.

"That's right, Valerie," said Kevin, as surprised as the others.

"Show-off," said Jenny with a good-natured smirk.

"I could have told you, if you'd asked," retorted her friend. "I'm also into shapes, not just numbers."

"So's Finn," laughed Jenny, taunting her fellow student who blushed as red as his hair. She'd caught him admiring a shapely brunette across the room.

Kevin let chuckles ripple through the group, then brought them back to the discussion.

"What else can you tell us about the Solids, Valerie?"

"Without getting into the math. . ."

"*Thank* you!" sighed Noah with emphasis.

"Without getting into the math," Valerie repeated, "these five shapes form the basis of Plato's Theory of Everything. It's in the *Timaeus* dialogue."

"Professor Gilderstein says not to start with *Timaeus*," Finn objected. "We're doing the *Republic* instead."

"Then why do we have to take geometry?" Frustration was getting the better of Noah.

"Maybe Gilderstein doesn't like math either and hopes somebody else will teach it," said Jenny, rolling her eyes.

"You're all missing the point," said Rudy, pulling at his sandy colored hair and standing up abruptly, nearly knocking over his chair.

"Which is?" asked the other four students in unison.

"The point is that Plato and Pythagoras were looking far beyond physical shapes or mathematics. Their philosophy was more than cosmology or a description of the universe, which is what Plato called the dodecahedron—the fifth shape based on pentagons," he explained. The others looked at him blankly.

"Number five. Don't you get it?" Rudy declared. His voice grew more insistent as he paced back and forth in front of the table where his friends sat frozen in amazement at his passion.

"Pythagoras posited a Harmony of the Spheres, but he wasn't just pointing out music or planets. He was talking about the fifth dimension of consciousness. Mind. Spirit. Soul.

"You guys! That's what we're here for! To follow the great thinkers, the masters, the druids, the alchemists! They all understood! Why can't you?!"

His eyes wide, he looked pleadingly at Kevin who nodded slowly. Now he knew where he'd seen this excitable young man before. That encounter was from a much earlier period in history than the outburst he had witnessed two weeks ago in this coffee shop.

"Wow, Rudy," said Jenny at last, breaking the silence.

"I think we understand more than you realize," said Valerie. She reached out for her friend's hand, then looked across the table. "Well, maybe not Noah."

Everybody laughed. The tension in the room released, and Rudy sat back down.

"Man, I had no idea you were so deep," said Noah.

"Me, either," agreed Finn.

"So, Kevin, where do we go from here?" asked Jenny. "Now that Rudy has blown open the discussion, what do you recommend?"

Stall for time, thought Kevin to himself.

Instead, he answered her challenge, "We'll take a quick break. Rudy has definitely pointed us to some fascinating topics, which, conveniently enough, are contained in many of the volumes in Fibonacci's Esoteric Bookstore.

"Let's meet back here in five minutes. Then I suggest an exploratory expedition next door. I suspect the topics of our future discussions may leap right off the shelves at us."

Four students headed for the coffee urns. Rudy hung back.

"I know you, too, Ah-Lahn," he said, his brown eyes dark and direct with the meaning that Kevin caught immediately.

"Yes, Tadhgan, my son. I believe we have a few things to work out between us, do we not?"

"We do—*Dad*," said Rudy with a smirk. He turned on his heel and joined his friends at the coffee bar where Róisín had just appeared with a plate of freshly baked scones, butter, and strawberry jam which the students and Kevin quickly devoured.

Thirty-Three

Later that night Kevin sat with Sarah in their living room, warmed by the fire burning brightly in their fireplace. He was staring intently into the flames.

"You're not about to step across the crystal bridge to meet Saint Germain without me, are you?" asked Sarah.

"What?" Kevin blinked and turned to her.

"You've been focusing on the fire without saying a word. I'm just making sure you're not leaving your body before we complete the ritual we're supposed to do tonight."

"Oh, no, nothing like that," said Kevin, rubbing his eyes.

"Something's captured your imagination."

"It has. A situation to keep in your prayers."

"About our assignment from Saint Germain?"

"Not directly."

"Are you going to make me guess?"

"No, sorry." Kevin blew out a breath and rolled his shoulders. "Do you remember Ah-Lahn's son, Tadhgan?"

"How could I forget? What a heartbreak that was—for Arán Bán to use him so cruelly as a way to punish Ah-Lahn. What about him?"

"He's one of my students—Rudy. He's a bright lad, as Lucky would say. Occasionally defiant. Cynical, but curious. He's one of the Friends of Ancient Wisdom, but F. M. seems to keep him at arm's length, which annoys the lad."

"If that's true, why do you think he's part of your class?"

"Opportunity to balance karma, is my first thought. And something much deeper. He recognized me as Ah-Lahn. Even called me 'Dad' with a heavy dose of sarcasm. I have no idea what to do about him except be real. He's got radar for anything phony. And he's well read. Today he challenged the others to consider some profound subjects. I'm going to let things play out and see what happens."

"Is there anything I can do—other than pray?" Sarah was remembering Alana's difficult past with Ah-Lahn's son.

"Send him love. I'm sure you'll have occasion to meet him."

"I wonder how he'll respond to me. Tadhgan harbored intense resentment toward Alana. Of course, we know our connections date back to Atlantis and probably further than that. Have you crossed paths with him since druid times?"

"No. It's almost as if the Masters have kept us apart until now.

"Then we'll hope for a final resolution," said Sarah. "Thanks for telling me, Hon. I could see the concern on your face. If you carry a burden, so do I. Remember that."

"I will," said Kevin with a knowing wink. "Especially since that's been my message to you for quite a while now."

Sarah wrinkled her nose and gave him a quick hug. "No more secrets," she agreed. "We're indelibly linked. No doubt about that."

"Are you ready to meet Saint Germain?" asked Kevin.

"I am."

As a precaution against psychic intrusion into their plans, F. M. had indicated that the Brotherhood wanted them to commune with him in his ascended presence as Saint Germain in the refined atmosphere of the etheric. Before calling them across the crystal bridge where they would meet, he would lead them in a powerful meditation.

"You will not see me," he had said. "Instead, you will hear me as the voice of your own inner wisdom."

So it was as they sat in silent contemplation, following the Master's instruction as if he were with them in their home:

Close your eyes and see yourself as a pure white candle with a
wick composed of golden filigree rising from your crown chakra

at the top of your head and extending up to *An Síoraí*, the Eternal One—the Presence of your Highest Self who is sending forth rays of Divine Love to bless your meditation.

Together, focus intently and repeat with great devotion the fiat *LIGHT! LIGHT! LIGHT!*

As your intonation accelerates and intensifies, experience a tripartite flame igniting in your heart chakra as plume-like flames of pink and blue with a gold flame between them.

See these plumes joyfully spiraling around each other as they illumine the essence of your True Self.

Now, join hands and turn your attention to the radiant orbs of light in your fireplace dancing like enlivened Christmas balls.

Notice how the pink and blue orbs which you have witnessed previously are merging to create a larger, single sphere that scintillates with shades of violet, purple, and ruby.

As the sphere expands to encompass your combined consciousness, allow the sensation to intensify and draw you to the orb's center.

As Kevin and Sarah completed the ritual, they were transported out of their physical bodies by the Master's powerful words reverberating in the depths of their beings. They now stood side by side in their light bodies, bathed in an impenetrable aura of ineffable radiance and joy.

A crystal bridge shimmered into form, and they heard the invitation they had longed to receive:

> *Cross over in answer to my call, beloveds, as I, Saint Germain,*
> *embrace you in the fullness of my ascended being.*

With the speed of Mercury, they hurried over the span that lifted them ever higher into the consciousness of their Divine Master. As they penetrated the veil between this world and the next, their forms were subsumed in sensations of unconditional acceptance, total forgiveness, and eternal hope for the ultimate victory of their mission that scintillated from the aura of Saint Germain.

As if in answer to the questions which had dissolved from their minds upon hearing his melodious voice, the Master began his instruction, offering their souls unsurpassed insight into the necessity of and potential for the work to which he was commissioning them:

When individual souls embody or when we ascended masters materialize a visible form, we leave a goodly portion of our spirit essence in the etheric—to hold the balance for our earthly endeavors and as a magnet to draw us back to our Source.

In this life, you each brought to earth much of the spiritual attainment you have garnered over many lifetimes in your druidic embodiments and in some others, though not as much as we had hoped.

Unfortunately, the attack on the druids in Ireland wore down your souls, even as the continual flood of black magic and witchcraft has worn down the very soul of Éire herself.

Kevin took Sarah's hand and held it tightly. The murderous intent of the brothers of shadow directed against them and those they loved had, indeed, left a mark, which they were still working to dissolve.

The Master observed their reaction and sought to console them.

Fear not, beloved ones. The spiritual essence remains—in you and in the land; in etheric octaves and in the memories that have been revealed to you in order that you may reclaim the wholeness of your Reality. This is the quality of soul you see reflected in the characters of Alana and Ah-Lahn.

In many ways they are archetypes for your True Self. However, as individuals, they were not able to fulfill their dharma, balance their karma, or achieve the higher degree of personal mastery that was their destiny and that remains yours to complete.

Due to several circumstances, they did not fully overcome certain momentums that have repeatedly separated them—as you two have experienced in this life.

You are aware of being embodied on Atlantis where you both possessed considerable mastery in your roles as priest and priestess in the Temple of the One Light. Your souls also suffered fragmentation then. However, we must work with more recent events before we can deal effectively with those records.

The couple brightened somewhat. The Master was not leaving them comfortless. Still, his countenance was serious as he explained what would take place in Ireland.

This is a delicate operation—to bring the attainment of Alana and Ah-Lahn forward without Sarah and Kevin becoming mired in the past.

As a result of events in that lifetime, a portion of your druid selves remain in the grove of Master Druid Óengus. You must retrieve those portions and integrate them into your present consciousness.

Once you achieve reunion with a greater percentage of your spiritual reality, you will be able to inspire and instruct other sets of twin flames who long to find their way home to the Divine Presence you know as *An Síoraí*, the Eternal One.

Kevin felt his heart leap at the Master's words. Here was the opportunity he had prayed for—to reclaim spiritual powers that had been lost through time, and to use those powers in service to life. Sarah squeezed his hand as her heart answered his.

Here was hope they had not experienced for centuries. But what exactly did this hope mean for the present and the future?

Saint Germain answered their unspoken question.

The Brotherhood desires you to walk the earth as modern-day mystics—as were alchemists and druids of old—to fulfill your dharma and help other pairs of twin flames do the same.

Please understand that the power of twin flames united is double or triple what either soul could accomplish alone, even in a community such as we have gathered at Fibonacci's.

We intend for you to become all that *An Síoraí* would have you be and for you to take your place on the ladder of adeptship with other members of our Brotherhood. We would see you unfettered, dear ones. May you heed the call of your Divine Source, for that is your soul's surety in these perilous times.

Consult your True Self for the way ahead. Attend the still small voice of inner wisdom—as you have both accomplished to greater or lesser degree in each of your lives.

Implement its guidance and observe how the frequency and volume of that voice intensifies until you find yourselves in ongoing conversation with the best of you, rather than being distracted by the idle chatter of mass consciousness that will do its worst to derail you.

Kevin and Sarah now understood why the Brotherhood wanted Saint Germain to give them this instruction in an etheric atmosphere. So often had they each felt the noise of human nonsense attempting to impinge upon their meditations, even during the rituals of prayer and meditation they practiced daily.

Two hearts swelled in gratitude for this opportunity to receive teaching directly from the Master—who immediately expanded his aura, infusing the couple with a portion of his own essence. He knew they would need every assistance he could possibly give them.

Be humble in the presence of ancient wisdom, for we have at our fingertips the origin of the Grail mysteries. May you be as Parsifal—pure, though not fools. We would have you take illumined action that sees through the tricks of the arch-deceiver and his minions.

Love each other as I love you, and you will overcome the wicked one who is possessed of dark intentions. He harbors ill will against you and yours, as well as against those you are destined to assist on the pilgrimage to eternity.

"Could Arán Bán ever change?" Kevin asked when the Master paused. "I remember Ah-Lahn feeling compassion for the man's soul because he had made such terrible choices lifetime after lifetime."

"There is always hope," answered Saint Germain thoughtfully. As he continued his discourse, his aura grew more vibrant, filling the couple with his radiance that shimmered with incredible spiritual power.

The Creator never stops loving his creation. But at some point, that pure love becomes a judgment, a cease-fire action that disarms the individual.

One more opportunity is given for that rebellious soul to come into alignment with the Divine Self of its origin. If that does not happen, a trial is held. From throughout cosmos, masters ascended and unascended are called to give testimony regarding the individual's actions throughout the ages.

If that one is found guilty, members of the Great White Brotherhood are summoned to witness the action known as the Second Death. A flame descends from the Godhead from whence have come all souls. The personal identity is dissolved, and its energy is returned to that Absolute Source.

Sarah and Kevin gasped in realization that a soul could be lost as a result of persistent, malicious choices.

The Master continued the instruction they must have for the protection of their souls and the fulfillment of their mission as twin flames. These advanced teachings had rarely been given outside of ancient mystery schools or druid groves.

Your shock is understandable, dear ones. Dissolution of a soul is used only as a last resort and is never the desire of the Brotherhood. I can assure you that attendance in the chamber where the judgment is delivered is a sobering experience.

Sadly, it is possible for a soul to fail. When that occurs, we do not rejoice, though other devoted individuals will have been saved by the interruption of malevolent forces.

When an identity has chosen eternal destruction—for that snuffing out is ultimately a personal choice—we become even more committed to the liberation of every other soul who has been caught up in the lies and illusions of the fallen ones.

Saint Germain paused and focused his brilliant violet eyes on this man and this woman who had been his friends for many thousands of years. Though the couple remembered not even a fraction of the adventures they had shared, in this age of rapid change the three of them needed each other as never before.

Kevin and Sarah, your part in this drama is dangerous. We do not require it of you. Although, should you accept, our gratitude will be great. However, you must know that, having come this far, you have been targeted by the brothers of shadow. To do nothing may put you in greater peril than moving forward.

We of the Great White Brotherhood have anticipated this point-counterpoint, for the battle has always been thus. Please know that in any situation you may call forth a mighty manifestation of light energy, especially of the violet flame. When you do, use my name: Saint Germain. When you call, I will answer.

So now, beloveds, what is your decision?

Kevin and Sarah looked deeply into each other's eyes. A spark passed between them. "We accept the assignment," they said in unison.

"Then kneel, my son and daughter, and receive this sealing of your minds and hearts for the fulfillment of your commission," said Saint Germain solemnly.

He took from his hand the amethyst ring set with diamonds and rubies and placed it first on their crown chakras and then on their hearts while intoning words in an ancient tongue that filled their beings with light and caused the very ethers to vibrate.

For several minutes, the Master stood before the twin flames in whom he was investing unprecedented energy and trust. Once more he expanded his aura, surrounding them in a radiant sphere of blue, white, gold and violet light—a guardian action that would remain with them for as long as they maintained their harmony and communion with his heart. It was all he could do for now.

As Sarah and Kevin felt themselves being gently returned to their physical bodies, which had been resting peacefully in their living room, they heard the Master intoning the words of *An Síorai*, the Eternal One:

Time is short.
The ship has sailed.
The captain gazes across the open sea
as dawn breaks o'er the horizon.
Once more the ancient call resounds.
May true hearts answer as in the past
for the sake of future-present.

Thirty-Four

Pebbles on a long stretch of rocky shore crunched under Sarah's boots as she walked slowly down her favorite beach, skirting the lacy foam that tipped the waves at low tide. She was bundled against November's cloudy chill, yet she relished the whip of wind against her cheeks.

If she closed her eyes, she could imagine herself on the other side of the Atlantic. In Ireland. Listening to enormous waves crashing against steep cliffs in the primordial antiphon that relentlessly sculpted Éire's shoreline into the tapestry of textures that never failed to pull on her heart.

She would be there soon. With Kevin. Her strong, handsome Celtic husband who was currently hurling a soggy tennis ball for his big dog, who was growing up to look just like a wolfhound. She had warned him not to let Hero get wet in the cold. However, from the looks of them both, their car was going to smell like damp canine for a long time.

The man and his dog, she laughed to herself. They need each other. "Just like I need you, sweet kitty," she said aloud.

"Meow," answered Sprite from her cozy nest. She was tucked inside Sarah's jacket with only her silky head peering out.

When Kevin had suggested a romp on the beach for Hero, Sprite had made it clear that she did not want to be left out of the family outing. So Sarah had created a sling from an old pashmina and then buttoned her jacket around the kitty's body so she'd stay put.

Both females looked up in time to see man and dog come galloping toward them with Hero well in the lead.

"We're cold and hungry," Kevin laughed breathlessly as he caught up and playfully brushed his mustache over Sarah's pink cheeks.

"It's a good thing you're training him," she said while trying to hold off Hero's exuberant greeting. "With those long legs, you'd never catch him if he decided to run off."

"I know. But you're a good boy, aren't you, Buddy?" Hero answered with a happy "Woof!" and danced alongside his humans as they walked back to their car.

"Have you thought any more about our attending the meeting at Fibonacci's tonight?" asked Kevin. "Lucky's text said there was no ritual planned, only community and conversation."

"I don't see any reason why we shouldn't," answered Sarah. She looked off into the distance, listening. "I haven't picked up any negative energy. After our experience with Saint Germain yesterday, I wasn't sure we should go out. But I think we'll be fine. My still small voice is silent on the matter."

"Mine, too," said Kevin. "I'd like to talk to Lucky and Róisín about our assignment from Saint Germain—unless there are too many people around."

"While we're there, I want to ask Debbie about some essential oils for the fur kids," said Sarah. "And for something to combat *Eau-de-Wet-Doggie,*" she said holding her nose.

"Sorry," said Kevin. "I'll give him a b-a-t-h when we get home." Hero woofed happily from behind the back seat of their SUV. So far, he hadn't learned to spell.

Later that day, Kevin and Sarah were sipping hot cocoa while a clean, dry, and less odoriferous Hero snoozed under the kitchen table. Sprite was purring contentedly on her mistress's lap.

"I think I've figured out something about Rudy," said Kevin thoughtfully. "While Hero and I were romping on the beach, it came to me why Ah-Lahn's son, Tadhgan, and I haven't crossed paths since the first century in Ireland."

"Really? I've wondered about that," said Sarah.

"What came to me about that incarnation is that Tadhgan's trying to perform like a master druid without the training or attainment probably severely damaged his chakras.

"His death was so traumatizing to his soul that he's been asleep for all these centuries—almost like doctors will put critically injured patients into an induced coma for a while so they can heal. I think that's what the Masters may have done for the lad."

"That means Rudy is picking up where he left off as Ah-Lahn's son," suggested Sarah. "I can see how that would be the case. That could explain why he would have the emotional challenges you've described, and why he would recognize you."

"Exactly," agreed Kevin. "And I'm thinking about the subjects he insisted the philosophy students take up. We know he was a priest on Atlantis. He also would have absorbed occult teachings in Egypt, probably in Greece, and definitely in Ireland. So he's brought an affinity for those cultures into this embodiment."

"Fascinating," said Sarah. "I look forward to meeting him."

Kevin raised his eyebrows. "Be careful what you wish for."

Only a few members of the Friends of Ancient Wisdom trickled into Fibonacci's coffee shop Saturday evening, which was fine with Kevin and Sarah. They were still plumbing the depths of what Saint Germain had told them, and they had some questions for Lucky and Róisín.

In daily life, the pair kept a low profile and simply presented themselves as proprietors of a successful coffee shop and esoteric bookstore. However, Kevin was quite certain they were people of considerable spiritual attainment—most likely adepts in their own right.

As the two couples, joined by Debbie, sat together at a table in the center of the room, Sarah took note of a unique behavior within this community of old souls. The Friends of Ancient Wisdom exhibited a profound respect for one another's private conversations—almost as if each small group drew a cloak of silence around themselves so they could speak candidly without others overhearing.

As she looked around the room, an insight came to her that the practice was not for keeping secrets. Rather, it was for ensuring openness between individuals who might have personal karma to resolve with one another, as well as for those who might have a particular service to perform for the Great White Brotherhood that involved only one or two other people.

Lucky's voice brought her back to their conversation. "You two wear the Master's blessing like a mantle."

" 'Tis true," agreed Róisín. "Your chakras are glowing. Do you see how they're sparkling, Debbie?"

"I do. You look like violet light bulbs."

"I sense your questions," said Lucky, "and must tell you that most of them are not mine to answer. However, there are a few things I can tell you by way of warning."

Although Sarah and Kevin were determined not to let the vibrant energy in their hearts sink, a ripple of concern briefly clouded their auras.

"Never fear," said Lucky. "The Master would never have entrusted you with such a mighty assignment if you weren't able for it in attainment and attunement."

"That's a relief," said Kevin.

Sarah nodded. "I felt Saint Germain's confidence in us when we met him across the crystal bridge. Still, on this side, human doubts try to creep in."

"Keeping those doubts at bay will be one of your greatest tests," said Róisín. "I can tell you for certain that life will never be the same. People will likely love you or despise you—and most won't know why."

"It's the light and the Master's presence with you," explained Lucky. He reached over and took his wife's hand. "Hold tight to your harmony, my friends, because things will start happening around you, through no fault of your own."

He brought Róisín's hand to his lips and kissed it. They looked deeply into each other's eyes and smiled knowingly.

Oh, yes, thought Sarah as she watched them. They have shared many challenges in this life and countless others. Probably more than we can even imagine.

Lucky released his wife's hand and continued speaking.

"Until you've completed this commission, I'm thinking you should limit your interaction with other people. I was going to suggest that I take over for Kevin with the philosophy students, but that could raise questions we're not inclined to answer right now."

"Thanks, Lucky," said Kevin. "I agree. And I also feel that my working with the students as much as possible is integral to future aspects of our commission."

"Just be careful," said Lucky. "You two must learn to tuck in your auras and keep a lower profile in daily life."

"You do that, don't you?" said Sarah. "I'm amazed at how normal you appear—for adepts," she added.

The couple tipped their heads in acknowledgment and smiled. "Ah, yes," said Róisín, "but then we haven't had an evil druid trying to eliminate us, as you apparently do. We've only recently become a threat to the brothers of shadow because the Great White Brotherhood is anchoring more light at Fibonacci's, and more people are joining the Friends of Ancient Wisdom."

"Saint Germain is definitely gathering his network," added Debbie. "We all feel it. What will happen as a result is anyone's guess. I don't think even the Master knows for sure."

"The free will of humans is always the X factor," agreed Lucky. "And here comes one now. Let's greet our brother and welcome him to our table. The lad needs all the love we can give him."

They all turned to see Rudy coming in the front door. He stood for a moment, scanning the coffee shop. When his eyes landed on Kevin, he gave a crooked grin and walked over to their table.

Lucky and Kevin immediately rose and extended warm handshakes to the young man.

"Hey, Teach," Rudy said to Kevin and nodded to the women.

"Good to see you, Rudy," said Lucky. "Take a seat between Kevin and me." He poured the lad a cup of coffee from the carafe Róisín had brought to the table.

"Rudy, I'd like you to meet my wife, Sarah," said Kevin as casually as he could manage.

"Hello, Rudy," said Sarah. She reached in front of her husband, extending a handshake. When Rudy reciprocated, she took his hand in both of hers and looked him in the eye. "I'm glad to see you. Shall I say, 'Again'?"

"Why not, Alana," replied Rudy. "We do know each other."

"Yes, we do," agreed Sarah. "And I hope this time around we can be friends." Despite Lucky's warning about keeping a low profile, Sarah unconsciously opened her heart to this young man who had hated her in the past. All she could feel for him was a profound, motherly love that simply flooded out to him.

Rudy pulled his hand away from her grasp and abruptly pushed his chair back from the table. He stood staring at Sarah and her husband. Everyone held their breath, wondering if the lad would lose his temper. Instead, he spoke, but with hurt in his eyes and a quaver in his voice.

"You've been hanging with F. M., haven't you?"

Neither Kevin nor Sarah dared answer.

"You don't have to say anything. I can tell. People get all sparkly-eyed when they've been with him. Did he show you his cloud trick? You know—where he concentrates and pretty soon visible points of light start gathering around each other until the atmosphere goes misty, and then he disappears?"

Kevin started to speak but checked himself at the strong *No!* he heard from his voice of inner wisdom.

The pain in Rudy's voice increased as he rehearsed the complaint Kevin had heard from him during his first visit to Fibonacci's. What can I do to help the lad get past this stumbling block? he wondered.

Rudy's voice great louder. "I've asked F. M. how he creates the mist, but he won't tell me. You know what he said? 'When you can create a calm forcefield, you will be able to learn.' "

"That's true for all of us," said Kevin, taking a risk. "I don't know about you, but if my mind is agitated, I'm dumb as a rock." The others at the table rewarded his attempt at humor with a polite laugh.

"You really set yourself up there, Teach," said Rudy with a sly grin.

"And you get points for restraint," said Kevin, matching his tone. He gestured for Rudy to resume his seat. To everyone's surprise, he did.

Kevin decided to keep the lad talking. "What else did F. M. tell you, Rudy?"

"No games?"

"No games. I'd like to know."

"Whatever." Rudy shrugged, but went on. "He told me I already know how to create a cloud—like the *féath fíadha* mists the druids used to precipitate. All I have to do is remember. But how am I supposed to remember if he won't help me?"

"I've had a similar experience," said Kevin. There was genuine sincerity in his voice.

"You're kidding." Rudy had his eyes fixed on the man who had been both friend and father to him in the past.

"No, I'm not." Without thinking, Kevin placed a hand on Rudy's shoulder. "I can't tell you how many times in the last few weeks I've sensed the absence of a power or a skill or a certain 'knowing' that I can almost touch—but not quite.

"When I've been with F. M.—and, yes, I've had that privilege—I could feel that he knew exactly what I was missing, but he wasn't going to give me the answer.

"I got the impression that if he simply revealed what I wanted to know, I wouldn't accrue the good karma of self-discovery, and he might accrue negative karma for short-circuiting the requirements of my personal path."

"Huh," Rudy grunted. "I never thought of that."

"That's why we're a community," offered Lucky. "So we can share insights that others might never discover on their own. Masters like F. M. Bellamarre aren't allowed to smooth out every boulder in our path. Their job is to teach and bring us together for mutual understanding."

"That's why we're all here," added Debbie, more to herself than to anyone at the table.

"Huh," said Rudy again. He rubbed the back of his neck, thinking. Could he trust what these people were saying? We'll see, he decided.

He pushed his chair away from the table—more gently this time—and addressed Kevin. "I gotta go. See you next Friday, Teach?"

"I'll be there. I'm wondering if you'd bring a list of books you think the philosophy gang should start on. You had some good ideas."

"Yeah, okay." Rudy took a large swallow of coffee and left quickly. Several at the table noticed a slight spring in his step.

"Well done," said Sarah quietly when Rudy had gone. She leaned over and kissed her husband's cheek. She was sparkly-eyed, just as the lad had observed.

"No celebrations yet." Kevin shook his head. "I'm afraid that Rudy and I—and you—have some serious hills to climb before we come to the resolution our souls have needed for over twelve thousand years."

Thirty-Five

The outside temperature was frigid, the skies were grey, and the wind was raw on the Monday after Thanksgiving. Inside Fibonacci's Esoteric Bookstore, the atmosphere was warm and cozy.

Business had been slow all day, so Sarah had volunteered to mind the store while Lucky took Kevin to a sporting goods shop that he guaranteed sold the perfect day packs for the MacCauleys' upcoming trip to Ireland.

This afternoon Hero was snoozing behind the counter while Sarah finished some paperwork before she headed home for the evening. The doggie didn't like being left alone at the MacCauleys' house, so, as part of his socialization training, Kevin had been bringing him to work.

Hero wasn't allowed in the coffee shop where food was served, but he was becoming a popular fixture in the bookstore. The regular clientele were very fond of him, and new customers were quickly assured that his size only meant there was more of him to love.

He was always ready for a belly rub or a scratch behind the ears, and he gave out plenty of kisses, especially to children whose heads were at the same height as his.

He and the youngsters got along famously. In fact, he had recently completed a couple of successful "Paws to Read" sessions with some neighborhood children who read to him while he listened intently, never judging if they stumbled on a word. He was especially keen when they showed him their picture books or brought him treats.

Near to closing time, the bell on the front door jingled and Rudy walked in. Hero immediately got to his feet and put his paws on the counter to see who of his buddies might have come to visit him.

"Jeez, that's a big dog," said Rudy, his brown eyes wide as moons.

"That he is," answered Sarah with a smile, "and he's still growing. We're thinking we may have to get him a social security number so he can continue working in the store."

"Does he bite?"

"Not unless you do," she laughed. "I'm getting ready to close up. Were you looking for a particular book?"

"I'm looking for Ah-Lahn."

Normally Sarah would have told Hero to take his paws off the counter, but something in Rudy's tone told her to let him stay where he was. She noticed the hairs on the back of the dog's neck were standing on end—a reaction that almost never happened.

"Kevin isn't here right now," said Sarah. "He and Lucky are out, but they should be back fairly soon. Can I help you with anything?"

"Naw, this is between Ah-Lahn and me."

Odd that he's using Kevin's druid name, thought Sarah. She felt her own hackles rising. "Okay, you're welcome to wait. You might want to check out the books that Lucky has added to your study group's shelf."

"Stop trying to be helpful, Alana," snapped Rudy. "I haven't decided if I want to talk to you or not."

Sarah's own eyes went wide as she felt herself pushed back by the intensity of his reply. She automatically raised her hands and did her best to strike a conciliatory tone.

"Fair enough. But you know, Rudy, we're not really Ah-Lahn and Alana. Kevin and Sarah are different people, living in the twenty-first century."

"Yeah, well I know the druids and that's what I want to talk to my father about."

"I understand," said Sarah—though she really didn't. She was becoming concerned, but she wasn't going to force a conversation. Instead, she began shutting down the cash register and computer in preparation for closing the store.

"No, I don't think you do understand," said Rudy. Frustration was edging into his voice.

"Well, at this moment I do happen to be available, if you'd like to explain to me what I'm missing," said Sarah firmly. She was not going to be bullied. "I'm locking up now. You're welcome to leave. Or if you want to talk, we can sit in the lounge until Kevin and Lucky return."

"Okay." Rudy grumbled, but he didn't offer to leave.

"Will you close the blinds for me?" asked Sarah, trying a different tactic. When the lad surprised her by complying, she locked the front door, flipped over the OPEN sign to CLOSED, and turned on the night-time lights.

"Hero, come," she said to her canine companion and walked to the back of the store. Before she closed the door connecting to Fibonacci's, she'd half expected Rudy to go into the coffee shop. Instead, he followed her to the bookstore lounge. They each sat in a wing-backed chair and were silent for several minutes.

Hero planted himself at the side of his mistress and rested his head on the chair's arm where he could watch the scene unfolding before him. Sarah scratched her dog behind his ears and waited.

Rudy had turned his body away from her and was staring into the bookstore with an intense look in his eyes. His brow was furrowed, he was clenching and unclenching his hands. He appeared to be thinking very hard about something.

Sarah had hoped he would start talking. Instead, he abruptly stood up and whipped around.

"This is stupid. I have nothing to say to you."

Sarah let out a deep breath. "Okay, I get that. But can you tell me why you have nothing to say to me?"

She was doing her best to remain calm so as not to further upset this volatile young man. At the same time, she could feel her inner wisdom guiding her to keep him talking.

"Because I hate you," said Rudy, raising his voice unsteadily. He started to tremble, and his face was flushed.

Hero stood up and growled. Sarah held his collar. "Sit, Hero. Rudy's not going to hurt anybody." She hoped that was true.

"I don't hate you," she said with as much kindness as she could muster.

"No, but you never loved me, Alana."

Sarah now realized that she was not addressing Rudy in the present and probably hadn't been since he entered the store. He had flipped into his former self—Tadhgan, Ah-Lahn's son. Judging from the half-crazed look in his eyes, she figured she had better go along with his fantasy.

"Tadhgan, I would have loved you, if you had let me."

"Not the way I wanted. I would have married you."

"You know that wasn't possible. Your father and I are twin flames— two halves of the same whole, as we have been since the beginning of time. Will you sit, Tadhgan, and tell me what you remember?"

"You mean besides now, in Ireland?"

"Yes. Do you remember other embodiments when you and your father and I have been together?"

"No. I can feel things from the past, but when I try to remember, all I see is mist. My mind is all foggy." He almost whined the words.

"Then I can't reveal any details to you that are not mine to reveal. All I can say is that things that we both misunderstood happened a very long time ago. You thought we betrayed you. We didn't, but I never realized how much you loved me. I couldn't have changed my feelings for my twin flame, but I could have been kinder to you."

Rudy was looking at her, but Sarah could tell that he wasn't really seeing her. She went on and prayed that Kevin would return soon.

"Tadhgan, your misunderstanding was not my fault. We've never abandoned you. Twelve thousand years is a long time to carry that resentment. It only hurts you and makes you vulnerable to difficult situations."

"Like what?" the young man demanded and stood up again.

Thank God, he said something, thought Sarah, but she didn't like what she was seeing. He was sweating. His breathing was shallow. His face was growing redder.

She also stood, still holding Hero's collar, sensing the tension in his body. Despite her trying to maintain a conciliatory tone, the dog was muttering a low growl.

Sarah could feel her voice starting to shake, but she continued to keep her heart open to Rudy as best she could.

"Like growing up without a mother. I know that was tough on you, Tadhgan. But Ah-Lahn and I are here for you. I'd like to be your friend, if you'll let me."

"I don't believe you!" he cried. "You're lying, like you always do! I hate you! I hate you! I hate you!"

Sarah screamed and ducked as he raised his hand to strike her.

Hero gave one enormous bark and lunged forward. In an instant he had pinned Rudy to the floor and fastened his teeth around the young man's arm as he tried to protect himself from the fury of the beast whose wolfhound genes had kicked into action.

"Hero! Stop! Heel!" Sarah cried, to no avail. She was no match for a seventy-pound dog and was sure he would have killed her would-be assailant had Kevin and Lucky not come barreling into the lounge.

It took both of them to dislodge the dog's teeth from Rudy's arm and pull him off of the young man's body. Lucky was able to drag Hero a few feet away and instantly calmed him with some Gaelic words that left the hound panting and licking the big Irishman's hands.

Kevin had eased Rudy into one of the wing-backed chairs where the lad sat dazed and staring. The man looked up from where he was kneeling and demanded, "Sarah, are you alright?" She was shaking, but nodded in the affirmative.

"Good. Can you make it to the coffee shop? Ask Róisín for some water and say that we need something stronger to bring Rudy back to himself. You can tell me what happened later."

Unable to speak, Sarah hurried into the coffee shop and ran right into Lucky's wife, who had been prompted to go over to the bookstore.

"*A chara*, you're pale as a ghost." She put her arm around Sarah's shoulders and guided her to a bar stool. "What's happened to you?"

Sarah was gasping for breath and could hardly speak. "Rudy. He turned into Tadhgan. He tried to hit me. Hero pinned him. Kevin said, 'Get water and something stronger.' "

Róisín nodded and shook her head. "I was afraid something like this might happen after the way he acted on Saturday." She reached under the bar and pulled out a small vial containing an amber-colored liquid. She put two drops into a glass of water and handed it to Sarah.

"Drink this while I mix what Kevin needs."

In less than a minute she held a to-go cup containing one of her special teas in her left hand. With her right hand she gently nudged Sarah off her bar stool and quickly led her into the lounge.

"Róisín! Thank God!" Kevin leapt to his feet and wrapped his arms around his wife. "I was afraid Sarah might have collapsed."

"She's a bit wobbly, but she'll be fine," said Róisín. "I've given her something to calm her. You take her and your brave dog home. Lucky and I will see to Rudy. We'll set him to rights and feed him a meal, and then we'll drive him back to his mother's house. We know where he lives, but he wouldn't want you to see the place."

"Here's your mighty warrior," said Lucky as he handed Kevin the dog's leash. "He'll want his dinner and a lot of affection tonight—as I expect you and Sarah will. Hero's not sure what happened. I don't think he's fully experienced himself as a wolfhound before. I told him he did a fine job of living up to his name."

"Yes, you did, you big sweetheart," said Sarah. She bent down to kiss the dog's nose, but missed as she swayed into Lucky, who caught her and decided he'd better help her stay vertical.

"Here, *a chara*. Let's get you to your car. Your man will take you and the great beast home. Kevin, call me in the morning and we'll figure out what to do between now and when you leave for Ireland."

The next morning, Lucky and Kevin decided that the Irishman would handle the philosophy students' study group on Friday, after all. With Sarah and Kevin leaving for Ireland in less than ten days, the couple needed all of that time to pull themselves back together.

The friends also agreed that Rudy should be encouraged to continue participating in the study group.

Lucky explained. "When Róisín and I were driving the lad home last night, I told him that I expected him to show up for the discussion on Friday. He grimaced at first, but then he promised he would be there because you wanted him to bring a list of books to share with the other students.

"Honestly, I don't think he remembers very much of what happened yesterday. That's why I didn't say anything about there being no hard feelings between you and him and Sarah.

"I've seen such things before when a soul has been damaged by traumatic events. I don't think you'd call what happened to Rudy a psychotic break, but it was close. It's a good thing your big dog tackled him. That snapped him back into the present."

"No kidding," said Kevin. "Did Rudy say anything about his actions or ask any questions?"

"He wanted to know why he was at the bookstore. I told him he'd come in to see you and then, while he and Sarah were talking, he'd fainted because he hadn't eaten.

"In truth, I think lack of food may have triggered this episode. I can't tell you about his home life, as that story isn't mine to tell. But I can say that his mother is also a damaged soul, and she doesn't take care of Rudy."

Kevin raised his eyebrows.

"I realize he's not a child," explained Lucky. "They live together as sort of mutual caregivers—which is more like the blind leading the blind. Many days, neither one of them remembers to eat."

"That's a shame," said Kevin. "What can we do to help him? I'm certain that we've come together at Fibonacci's to resolve the karma between us. I can still feel the weight on Ah-Lahn's heart over his son's tragic death. I hope the two of us—and Sarah—can find the forgiveness our souls want and need."

Lucky felt his friend's sincerity. "Róisín and I will do everything in our power to help you. We had already taken Rudy under our wing before you joined the Friends. We'll keep a close eye on him. And you know we're very good at that," Lucky added with a chuckle. "Rudy needs Fibonacci's, and your philosophy students need him."

"I agree," said Kevin.

"Don't worry," said Lucky. "F. M. has taken a particular interest in this soul. He hasn't told me why, except to say that there is a karma that must play out here. He's also watching very carefully."

"Thanks, Lucky."

"You're welcome, Kevin. Now, go rest up for your trip."

Thirty-Six

After the dramatic events at the bookstore, Saint Germain had not made contact with Kevin or Sarah, but they were certain the Master was well aware of what had transpired.

"I can feel his presence around me," said Sarah on the afternoon following her ordeal with Rudy. She was sitting on the sofa in their living room, drinking the cup of tea Kevin had brought her. Sprite was nestled next to her and Hero was snoozing at her feet.

"Róisín's healing potions are definitely bringing me back to myself."

"Thank God," was all Kevin could say.

"The whole thing was so unreal," said Sarah. She patted the sofa for him to come sit next to her.

"Are you sure you want to talk about it?" he asked. "You're still pale. I don't want you upsetting yourself."

"No, I'm fine now. I couldn't talk about it before, but you need to know what happened."

"Okay, but stop if telling me is too much."

"I will. So, Rudy came in looking for Ah-Lahn, which I thought was strange since we had all been together the day before in the coffee shop. I could have asked him to come back another time because I was closing up, but the prompting of my inner guide told me to keep talking."

Kevin shook his head. "I'm not sure that prompting was very wise this time."

"I know," agreed Sarah. "Yet I can't help feeling that Rudy's state of mind was something that needed to be revealed."

"That could be," said Kevin thoughtfully.

"Anyway, he started getting really agitated. Then all of a sudden, he became totally unreachable. As I think about it now, the energy was exactly the same as when Tadhgan was trying to reproduce a druidic feat and got overtaken by that terrible force that killed him. If Hero hadn't jumped him, I'm afraid something similar might have happened. It was terrifying."

"And the energy affected you, too," said Kevin. He shook his head and smiled at her. "My Sarah. I dare not let you out of my sight."

"I think that's a good idea," she agreed as he folded her into his arms and kissed her tenderly. Hero nuzzled his way into the embrace, and Sprite moved onto Sarah's lap where the kitty began to purr loudly.

We have time to prepare for Ireland, Kevin thought to himself as he held his family to his heart—but just barely.

A few days later, thanks to their friends, both seen and unseen, everything was in order for Sarah and Kevin's departure for Ireland.

Róisín had arranged their itinerary, including flights, hotels, and rental car. In their absence, Lucky would continue to facilitate discussions with the "Pythagoreans," as the philosophy students had dubbed themselves at their last meeting. Debbie would be house-sitting and keeping Hero and Sprite company.

Today, as Sarah and Kevin finished packing, Debbie was sitting cross-legged on a comfy, overstuffed chair in their bedroom. In a few minutes she would drive them to JFK for their red-eye flight across the Atlantic.

"Miraculous!" she exclaimed when Kevin showed her the envelope he'd received by courier that morning. F. M. had provided a special gift.

"This is a miracle!" Debbie repeated. "Nobody gets a last-minute pass for winter solstice at Newgrange. The lottery is drawn in September and this year they had over thirty thousand applications. Talk about an alchemy! F. M. must have pulled a rabbit from his wizard's hat. Your ticket is for solstice morning. I suppose our Master has also guaranteed perfect weather."

"I'm sure of it," chuckled Sarah, zipping her suitcase closed. "The structure is certainly magical. My short visit there last summer was amazing. I could sense that the people who built Newgrange over five thousand years ago must have had more profound purposes in mind than its being a passage tomb. That's what they call it, you know.

"I don't think tour guides like telling non-pagans that the sun's journey down the passageway to illumine the central altar was likely a fertility ritual to ensure abundant harvests for the next year."

Sarah cast her mind back to her experience of only a few months earlier when she had stood with other visitors in complete darkness inside the Neolithic structure. The immensity of silence had quickened a felt sense of ancient presences.

She had been in such a place before. She'd felt it last summer, even before discovering her druidic past. Knowing what she knew now gave her shivers. What was waiting for her and Kevin at the season's turning?

Her friend's voice called her back to the present.

"I can't wait to hear all about it when you return," enthused Debbie. She shifted her gaze to Kevin, who was shaking his head at his dog and Sarah's cat. Hero was sitting on the floor next to their friend with his head in her lap while Sprite had managed to drape herself about her neck and shoulders.

Debbie answered his quizzical expression. "Don't worry, Kevin, I won't totally spoil them. I know Hero needs his discipline. We're just getting acquainted, aren't we kids?" she smiled, stroking them both affectionately.

"You certainly have a way with animals—visible and otherwise," laughed Sarah with a wink at her seer-friend.

"Have you seen your panther recently?" asked Debbie as she stroked Sprite's head. "Not this little one. The magnificent, full-sized one."

"No," said Sarah. "Except for a dream I had about Alana's overcoming her fears, Sprid hasn't made an appearance since we adopted Sprite. You don't suppose the panther is jealous, do you?"

"I've never felt that about her," said Debbie. "I think she's practical. If you need her, she'll show up. I'm certain of that."

Another shiver ran up Sarah's spine. What were they getting themselves into? From the Master's description, there was plenty to fear from dark forces that opposed a reunion with their druid selves.

However, they had accepted the challenge, and Saint Germain had produced a minor miracle to ensure they got to Newgrange on time to complete the commission he had assigned them.

"Speaking of the unseen, Sarah, I almost forgot to give you this." Debbie held out a small zippered pouch with an envelope attached. "It's from Róisín. You haven't been coming in to Fibonacci's, so she asked me to bring it to you. She said not to break the seal on the pouch unless you need to, but go ahead and read the card."

Sarah opened the envelope and pulled out a single note card. She could hear Róisín's voice. The extraordinary woman wrote exactly as she spoke.

Sarah, *a chara*, keep this kit with you at all times while you're in Ireland. 'Tis for a single emergency, so don't open it till then. Have no fear, you'll be sure of the right time. Perhaps you won't need it. If you do, there's a tincture to be taken immediately and a bit of an old hazel wand to bind on a wound in case of injury.

Be wise, *a chara*, and you and your man will be safe.

Slán abhaile. May you come safely home, *Róisín*

Debbie stood, gently extricating herself from the fur kids' affections. "Be careful, you two, and come back to us safely," she said. "I know Saint Germain will do his best to protect you. However, we also know that old serpent, Arán Bán, might show up at any time. I couldn't bear to lose either of you again."

The three of them embraced, each trying not to imagine that this might be last time they would see each other.

As if on cue, Hero jumped up and put his paws on Kevin's shoulders. Sprite wound around their legs, purring loudly.

The three humans laughed through misty eyes and nodded. Yes, by Saint Germain's grace, they would make it through this test.

"Don't worry, Debbie, we'll be back." Kevin put a reassuring hand on their dear friend's shoulder.

"I guess we'd better go now," said Sarah. She turned to her husband and their eyes met. Resolve sparked between them and he hugged her to him.

"*A ghrá,*" he whispered, kissing the top of her head.

Only Debbie noticed that Kevin said "My love" in Gaelic—something he did not normally do.

Thirty-Seven

The overnight flight to Dublin was surprisingly restful, their arrival uneventful. Kevin had scoped out a restaurant in the airport and was eager to get there. "Just feed me a full Irish breakfast and I'll be ready to drive," he assured Sarah as he led the way through the crowds of passengers from all over the world.

"I'm glad you don't mind driving on the left," she said as they sat down in a corner booth. "I know they say, 'driver in the middle,' but if I had to drive, I'm afraid it would be 'driver in the muddle.' When we got back from Ireland last summer, I could hardly cross the street, let alone remember to keep the car on the right side of the road."

"No problem, I'll get us there, especially with a navigator," said Kevin, perusing the menu a fresh-faced waiter handed him. "Don't forget, I had to find your cottage on my own in the dark last summer. Arriving at Uncle Óengus's grove should be a snap."

Sarah knew he was making light of the challenges that no doubt awaited them, but she appreciated his confidence—even if he didn't totally believe his own words.

Over breakfast they discussed Sarah's desire to detour through the Wicklow Mountains to explore Glendalough, the serene medieval monastery she had visited last summer. However, when they briefly meditated on the notion, their intuition said it was too dangerous. Besides, they would need all the time allotted to complete their commission and return home safely before Christmas.

Kevin would be driving them along the coastal motorways to Wexford, where they would spend one night before heading north up the River Barrow to where they hoped to find the ancient druid's grove. They must be rested for the initiations that awaited them.

As they pulled into their hotel overlooking Wexford harbor, they could feel the pull of ancient memories calling them. Somewhere near this bustling urban center, Alana and Ah-Lahn had lived in the first-century settlement called *Tearmann*. For a while it had reflected its name, "sanctuary"—that is, until Ah-Lahn met his untimely death.

Again, the voice of inner wisdom warned them not to stray into unpopulated areas. They were free to explore some of the sights in the historic Viking town, but they should avoid old castles. They must not allow themselves to be affected by the heavy akashic records in such places.

Their one indulgence was a visit to the Irish National Heritage Park—which felt as if they were stepping into *Tearmann* after all, so familiar were the thatched dwellings and the layout of the park.

They were tempted to stay overnight in the ring fort but decided they might inadvertently slip between the veils of time and miss their opportunity to merge with their druid selves.

Instead, they opted for an archery lesson and an educational experience with the birds of prey, who reminded Sarah of her dream encounter with a wise snowy owl.

More jet-lagged than they expected, they slept late the next morning. After Kevin's insistence on taking time for another full Irish breakfast, they quickly made their way along the expressway to Minaun at the confluence of the rivers Barrow and Suir.

Although they both remembered Uncle Óengus looking to his right to gaze upriver, Kevin wanted to see if by looking across the Barrow from the River Suir side, they might recognize a familiar setting. It was also possible that their recollections were mistaken about which bank of the river the master druid's *túath* of *Cois Abhainn* had occupied.

After several hours of hiking around various points on Strand Road, Sarah shook her head. "There's nothing here. We didn't expect there would be, but I'm glad we checked."

"Me, too," agreed Kevin, putting his arm around her shoulder. "We're just getting started. It's only an hour back to Campile. Let's ask around there. We may find something at Dunbrody Abbey or closer to where the rivers meet close to a big power station."

Although well aware of their rigorous timelines, they turned south at New Ross onto a rural, two-lane road and adopted a more leisurely pace. The call of the Irish countryside had them pulling over every few miles to peer through breaks in the thick, native foliage at grassy fields where herds of cows or sheep grazed peacefully on the other side of homely fences nearly overgrown with gorse and fuchsia hedges, now brown in December's chill.

After a brief rain shower, a rainbow greeted them, and fair skies accompanied them to their hotel. Róisín had insisted that they stay at the Manor House where she and Lucky had spent their honeymoon.

"Only a few plants in the gardens will be in bloom," she'd said, "but the rooms are lovely, and the food is grand. It's as romantically magical a spot as you'll find, and you'll be needing a bit of help from the fairies to get you through your tests. In fact, your being there in December is already a miracle. They're not usually open this time of year."

Indeed, Róisín was right. The impeccably restored Georgian property and grounds were stunning. Their lovely room in the main house—complete with four-poster bed and view of the entire walled garden, down the main lawns, and on to the tropical garden beyond—felt every bit the honeymoon suite their friend had promised.

Delicate twinkle lights and other tasteful holiday decorations graced the common areas. The aroma of cinnamon and spice wafted from the kitchen. The scent of pine permeated the entryway where fresh boughs twined around the grand staircase. An elegant Christmas tree and crackling fire invited a leisurely rest in the parlor.

"I could stay here for weeks," exclaimed Sarah.

"We'll come back again, when we can do just that," promised Kevin. "I definitely sense some fairy magic at work."

When they inquired about gaining access to the area around the Great Island Power Station, they were met with a surprisingly positive response.

"Oh, sure, you'll be wantin' to see the old caretaker at Dunbrody," said Bríd, a very helpful concierge. Her flame-red hair and clear green eyes reminded Sarah of her mother, Eileen. Her family seemed so far away right now. She dared not think she might never see them again.

Kevin noticed her mind wandering and nudged her to pay attention. They both needed to have Bríd's suggestions well in mind.

"The abbey's not been a religious focus for decades, but Brother Milligan knows all about the place. I've heard tell he can get you onto private land that folks say still has traces of an old forest.

"They say there's some trails that nobody's walked for years. If you can talk Brother Milligan into helpin', you may find what you're lookin' for. Don't count on it, though. He's a right crusty old fella. You'll want to catch him in a good mood."

"Then we'll ask your namesake, Saint Brigid, for her help." Kevin winked at the teen-aged concierge and said, *"Go raibh maith agat,* Bríd," as easily as if he always offered a thank you in Irish.

Before they strolled back to their room, Sarah had a suggestion.

"Let's go for a walk around the grounds before dinner. They have a tropical garden, and the camellias are supposed to be in bloom. Who would have thought, at this time of year?"

Although spring blossoms were months away, the gardens were far from dormant. Exotic trees from all over the world grew tall and stately. Palms and ferns created a lush atmosphere. Immaculately sculpted box trees invited wandering through a mini-maze.

Sarah walked slightly ahead of Kevin, taking in the fine silhouettes of deciduous trees and vegetable beds tucked up for winter. All around her the earthy aroma of soil beckoned to her soul that here was a place like Alana's home—the seat of druidic mastery she hoped to regain.

She stopped on the path, her eyes seeking into the distance. Kevin came up behind her and put his arms around her waist.

"Cad a fheiceann tú, a ghrá?" he asked her.

Sarah leaned back against him and answered in English, as if she'd understood his wanting to know what her eyes were telling her.

"I'm seeing the garden that was Dearbhla's—where Alana found peace and healing. And where she met her panther spirit guide."

"Feicim é freisin," agreed Kevin.

"I'm so glad you can see it, *a ghrá*," said Sarah. She breathed in the fragrant air of her recollection. Then spun around to face her husband.

"Wait a minute! Kevin! When did you learn to speak Gaelic? And when did I learn to understand it?"

"I didn't, and you don't."

"No, but Ah-Lahn and Alana did, and probably still do."

A realization settled over them both.

"Sarah, do you feel what I feel?"

"The merging is happening already, isn't it, *mo chroí*, my heart. See, I can't help myself. The Irish words are on the tip of my tongue."

"Tell me you love me," said Kevin eagerly.

"*Tá grá agam duit,*" said Sarah without hesitation.

"And I, you, *a ghrá.*" He gave her a powerful hug. "Let's find out if dinner is being served. Then I'm ready for a cozy night in our honeymoon suite."

As they strolled arm-in-arm back to the main house, they did not notice the pair of emerald-green eyes watching them from the shrubbery.

Alana's panther guide, Sprid, was on duty—ready to guide and protect her mistress and her soul's twin throughout the adventure they would begin in earnest on the morrow.

Thirty-Eight

Breakfast in the garden cafe was a delight and a blessed oasis for the two travelers. Situated in the sparkling daylight of the Manor House conservatory, every white-clothed table offered an enticing view of the walled garden.

Even in the relative barrenness of winter's subdued greys, beiges, and dark green pines, Sarah thought she had never gazed upon a more restful scene. White-trimmed window panes framed postcard images of spreading oak and yew trees. Love seats tucked into secluded niches spoke of romantic trysts. The dry-stone wall whispered of secrets told in centuries past, just waiting to be rediscovered.

The organic breakfast foods were bountiful and demanded one's full attention, which husband and wife were happy to provide. Other than the occasional shared "yum," conversation lagged as they savored warm scones, fresh creamery butter, homemade jam, crisp sausages, organic eggs, the side dishes Kevin especially loved about Irish breakfasts, and cups of hot tea that tasted this good only in Ireland.

Finally tearing themselves away from the main house, where everything was polished to immaculate gleaming, they got into their rented car and drove less than ten minutes to Dunbrody Abbey.

After a few inquiries at the visitor center, they found the caretaker, Brother Milligan, in the Tea Room. He was clearly reticent to admit to any knowledge of the trails they mentioned.

"Please, excuse me for a moment," said Sarah, patting Kevin on the arm. "Call of nature. I'll be right back."

She quickly walked to the women's restroom and entered a stall. Under her breath she whispered emphatically, "Saint Germain, we need access to those trails. Please inspire Brother Milligan to help us."

When she returned to the Tea Room, she could see that her husband and the caretaker were now in deep conversation.

Kevin smiled knowingly. "Brother Milligan tells me that ours is an unusual request—all the more remarkable because the name of his friend who works at the power station where the woods and trails are located is MacCauley. What are the odds? Anyway, he's happy to contact Mr. MacCauley for us."

"Thank you, Brother Milligan," said Sarah sincerely. "You have no idea what this means to us. We have a very special family tie to that land that goes way back in time."

"Sure, don't you worry, lass," said the elderly monk. "I'll ask my friend to accommodate you. I'll send him a message and join you back here till we get your answer. Then I'll tell you some stories about the old abbey and what really went on here. I know you Irish-Americans are mad for your history."

While they waited to hear back from Mr. MacCauley at the power station, Sarah and Kevin listened eagerly as Brother Milligan expounded on details of the abbey's beginnings in the twelfth century as a small Cistercian monastery.

Along with the surrounding Anglo-Norman colony, the abbey had thrived and grown in the boom times of the thirteenth century, but then declined over the next several hundred years.

"Of course, that rascal, Oliver Cromwell, had to cause a pack of trouble in the seventeenth century," said Brother Milligan.

Sarah couldn't help marveling at the description as a "rascal" of the genocidal fanatic who had perpetrated murder and mayhem all over Ireland, giving no quarter to innocents in his path.

To contact the vibration of such vicious destruction was to touch the mind of evil. Sarah and Kevin both saw and felt the akashic record and grew dizzy in a wave of nausea that passed through them as the old monk concluded his recitation of the abbey's history.

"The private owners who took over in the nineteenth century let the buildings fall into the ruins we see today. Still, we love our old abbey and do our best to preserve her so folks like you can visit."

Finally, an assistant brought Brother Milligan a message. "Ah, grand. My friend says you're most welcome to wander his trails, as long as you don't approach the power station or cross any barriers or fences marked *Private*."

He handed Kevin a scrap of paper on which was scrawled the name MacCauley and a phone number. "Here's the information for the guard at the gate. He'll have a map for you and can direct you away from where you shouldn't go.

"Enjoy your visit, but do be careful. I've heard stories of a ruined stone circle in the midst of the woods. The locals never went near the place, even when it was open to the public. Maybe you'll find what you're lookin' for. Maybe it will find you. You never know. Ah, well, may the Blessed Virgin guide you on your way."

Making the briefest sign of the cross, the elderly brother shuffled off, leaving the couple standing in the Tea Room, wondering what else he hadn't told them. Time was slipping away, but with limited daylight remaining this afternoon, there was nothing they could do until tomorrow. Next steps would simply have to wait.

Neither Sarah nor Kevin slept well that night. Despite the beautiful accommodations and a delicious evening meal in the manor's formal dining room, they were restless and perhaps a little afraid, although neither would admit it.

The sky was still dark when they arose. They weren't particularly hungry, so they settled for a continental breakfast. They would leave at first light, around 8:30 a.m. here in winter's short days.

The only concession they made to a meal was to take a thermos of coffee, some sandwiches they had ordered the night before, and a bottle of water each. Otherwise, they were dressed for moderate hiking with only small backpacks.

When they arrived at the entrance to the power station, the sky was overcast, the breeze off the River Barrow damp and chilly. They encountered no resistance from the guard who had been expecting them. He gave them a map and directed them to a side road where they could park their car.

Yes, there was a trail, though it was poorly marked once it entered the woods. However, if they could find the path, it would take them to the river's edge and the remains of a forest which had been cleared to accommodate the power plant buildings, tanks, and electrical towers.

"Do you feel anything?" Sarah asked as they made their way into the small forest.

Neither of them had expected to notice any unusual energy while they skirted the perimeter of the industrial property. However, now that they were away from the power plant, they were hopeful of some sign that the grove they sought was near.

"Nothing yet." Kevin was searching the ground for any markings that might indicate a path between the trees and bracken that lay before them.

"Got it!" he exclaimed at last. "See how the bushes are not quite so dense there to the left? I think that's our way through."

"Doesn't that take us away from the river?" asked Sarah.

"Yes, but think about it. The grove was hidden. You couldn't see it from the river. The oak trees grew around it in dense rings. Of course, they were ancient even then. If the stones remain, the trees are probably thinned out by now. Let's go through that little clearing, if you can call it that, and see what we find."

"Okay. I can't believe how dead it feels in here. I realize it's December and most of the trees are bare, but there's something else. Almost like the life has been sucked out of the land. Listen, do you hear that?"

"Sounds from the power plant. Nothing else, though."

"Exactly. No birds. No little animals scurrying into the bracken. Kevin, I don't like this."

"Neither do I, but we've got a job to do."

He paused, then said more to himself than as an audible prayer,

"Saint Germain, help us."

However, as soon as the words escaped his mouth, he was inspired to walk between a group of gnarled oak trees. He found himself standing in an open space filled with what appeared to be a pile of stony rubble.

"Oh, no!" cried Sarah. She rushed past him and fell to her knees beside the rocks. "Oh, no!" she cried again and burst into tears.

"What have they done to you, my precious stones? Kevin, we're here. This is the grove. But the stones have decayed, or somebody has chiseled away at them. I know we're nearly two thousand years later, but this is so much worse than I expected."

Kevin stood at her side, unable to speak. Ah-Lahn had spent hundreds of hours here in the company of his beloved Uncle Óengus, head of all the Brigantes druids and his personal mentor.

Here he had learned the deep occult knowledge of a master druid and here he had guided Alana in reviewing the past lives they had shared. To see the neglect and possible desecration of this holy place was a knife in his heart.

Sarah looked up from where she was kneeling and into the despair on her husband's face. She dried her eyes on her sleeve and rose to her feet. She put her arms around his waist and embraced him with all her strength until she felt him return to himself.

"Come, *mo chroí*," she said, "we have work to do. Let's see if the old stones still have any life in them. We are where we're supposed to be, you and I. These stones have given us miracles in the past. Now, perhaps, we can return the favor."

"You're right, *a ghrá*. The first thing we need is a hearth and a fire. I don't think we should separate, even for a minute. There are plenty of stones around here, and these poor trees have dropped enough branches for a blaze that's not too big. We don't want to burn down what's left of a druid sanctuary."

Like mourners tending the grave of a departed loved one, Kevin and Sarah gathered small stones and built a circular hearth in the center of what remained of the ancient grove. Every once in a while, they looked up from their work at the ragged trees surrounding them.

"I think they're watching us, don't you?" remarked Sarah with a wan smile. "The old druids, I mean. Remember how the trees had faces that looked like our predecessors? I can almost feel them, ever so slightly, waking from a long, long sleep. We're here for you, *a chairde*, dear friends. Oh, help us if you can. We miss you so much."

Her eyes misted over again as she stood gazing into a distance that was not physical.

"I feel them, too," said Kevin wistfully. He kindled the fire and stepped back. "It's time to begin."

Now that cheerful flames were warming the atmosphere in the grove, the couple stood in front of the center stone and tentatively placed their hands on the weathered limestone mass.

As druids, they would not have dared touch it. Getting within even three feet of the megalith had sent sparks of blue fire shooting out at whoever had the temerity to approach.

Today there was no response.

On and off throughout the day Kevin and Sarah stood across from each other with their palms on opposite sides of the massive rock to create a figure-eight flow of energy between them and then triangulate it into the limestone.

They chanted the OM and visualized a huge sphere of violet flame surrounding the entire grove. They focused on maintaining a powerful concentration of energy between them. As they did so, every once in a while, they each could see another presence hovering around their partner.

Were the spirits of their druid selves participating? They dared not utter that hope aloud lest they break the flow of their invocations.

As the afternoon light began to fade and the chill increased in the breeze that swept up from the River Barrow, they nodded to each other and closed the ritual.

Sarah stepped back and sat on a small, flat stone close to the hearth where the fire had burned down to embers. "I did feel a tiny flicker of recognition, but nothing else. Certainly nothing like the power the stones produced when we were here centuries ago."

Her eyes grew misty as she cast her mind back into ancient times. Here was a song not sung for nearly two thousand years, she mused. The voice of wisdom these once-proud stones contained had receded deep into the silent interior of ordinary limestone.

"We will come back tomorrow." Kevin spoke a promise to the grove. He carefully extinguished the remaining embers of the fire he had kindled, and offered an invocation to Saint Germain and spirits of the ancient druids of Ireland, asking them to seal and protect the fledgling forcefield of energy they had begun to create.

Without another word, he and Sarah returned to their car for the short drive back to the peaceful beauty of their hotel accommodations.

Thirty-Nine

Winter's watery sunlight was just easing over the horizon when Sarah and Kevin awoke the next morning. Instead of arising refreshed, they felt as if they'd been fighting a battle all night long. Indeed, they had. For they had stirred more than a fragment of recognition from ancient stones in a deserted druid grove.

When that tiny spark ignited deep within the limestone megaliths, a signal had gone forth that Divine Light was generating where it had long been dormant. And not only the Great White Brotherhood felt it.

The brothers of shadow also received an alert that servants of *An Síoraí*, the Eternal One, were quickening a vibration of light energy that could undo their dark deeds. This they could not tolerate.

So, as was their unrelenting pattern, they sent forth demonic forces, such as have opposed the Divine for eons, to attack the pair who were not fully cognizant of their mission's gravity. After last night, they were more than aware.

In their dreams, Kevin and Sarah had seen themselves, no longer as druid priests, but as soldiers. They wore white metallic armor that shimmered with invisible power. They wielded swords of the same substance.

They stood shoulder-to-shoulder with legions of angels, masters, and other pairs of twin flames against hordes of darkness that came in waves, rising up out of the astral plane like red and black ants, warring amongst themselves, and pitting their murderous intent against the sons and daughters of *An Síoraí*, the Eternal One.

Time after time, the evil forces were repulsed by the power of Divine Love wielded by the Brotherhood's legions until the darkness was purged from the scene.

As morning dawned, the vast plain on which the battle had raged was swept clean by magnificent angelic and elemental beings whose brilliant auras bathed the field in great swirling spirals of violet flame.

Sarah and Kevin and their compatriots stood in reverent attention as the night's victory was proclaimed—and a warning given that another battle was already gathering as storm clouds on the horizon. A fresh confrontation must be won each twenty-four hours, and every member of the Great White Brotherhood must perform his or her best work—step by step, day by day, love by love.

So it was that husband and wife arose in the safety of a beautiful hotel room, humbled and awake to a somber realization that they were part of a great conflagration whose purposes had been going on for millennia. More determined than ever, they made ready for the day and gladly took upon themselves the burden of their assignment.

Despite suffering the very real effects of battle fatigue, in order to have a full day in the grove, Sarah and Kevin set out soon after dawn.

Aware that their mission required more protection than they had previously imagined, to begin their ritual this morning, they chanted prayers to Archangel Michael for protection and visualized a golden ring the color and vibrancy of the sun around the grove.

Within that circle they invoked concentric rings of blue, green, ruby, purple, and white light so that nothing untoward could interrupt their work.

"What else can we do?" Sarah asked as Kevin kindled the fire in the hearth they had built yesterday. She knew they both had been masters of ritual on Atlantis. Was that attainment available to them now? Saint Germain had said their former mastery was sealed like a bank deposit in their causal bodies. Would the necessity of the moment give them access to the spiritual treasures they had laid up in etheric octaves?

Kevin turned his attention deep into his heart where a focus of the Divine was always present. Sarah felt his communion and followed his lead into her own heart where she rested for several minutes.

"Táimid ag éirí níos láidre!" they declared together and laughed that they had spontaneously spoken in Gaelic.

"Yes, we are growing stronger," reiterated Kevin as they took their places by the primary stone—now with increased determination.

Today the fervor of their invocations reverberated throughout the grove as had not been heard in this place for centuries. They gave the very fullness of their devotion in their chants. They poured love, love, love into the central stone as if resuscitating a living being who had slipped into a coma.

Hours later they felt little more than a slight resonance tremble the stone. Nevertheless, their intuition told them they were making progress. *Faint not,* they heard the voice of inner wisdom encourage them as they extinguished the flame in the center of the grove. They prayed for angels to protect what had been gained and returned to their hotel for a welcome meal and rest.

Despite the previous night's dream of pitched battle, this evening they were spared from service at the front. In fact, they slept long and hard, awakening refreshed when the sun rose on the day that would change them forever—one way or another.

"Day Three." Kevin spoke solemnly during the hearty breakfast they agreed they needed to sustain them for today's rituals. "Are you ready?"

"I am," said Sarah. "In fact, I'm surprised at how ready I feel. But we're nearly out of time. If we don't connect with Alana and Ah-Lahn today, I don't know what we'll do. Yet somehow, I'm not worried."

"Neither am I," said Kevin. "I don't remember our being with Saint Germain last night, but I almost feel like we were—as if he gave us an extra boost while we slept. At least I feel stronger today, more able to give another full round of chants and invocations, whatever it takes."

At the power station they saluted the guard, who waved them through the gate as they made their way to the grove. The grove felt lighter this morning, telling them that the forcefield they had created was intact. That was good news. They would build on their momentum from the previous two days.

However, by the afternoon, they had nearly given up hope. Every so often the central stone would shudder as if it were trying to shake off a burden. But then it would grow still again, somehow lacking the strength they were trying to help it summon.

Completely exhausted, Sarah knelt down on the ground and leaned her forehead upon the stone. She could not stop the tears that seeped into her eyes and trickled down her face.

She wept for herself, for Kevin, for their druid selves, for all the pairs of twin flames she could feel depending on their success. And most of all, she wept for their Master who had taken upon himself a portion of their karma so they might fulfill their commission.

At her wit's end, she prayed:

Beloved Saint Germain, you know we would not willingly disappoint or fail you, but we have done all we know to do. We have spent our last drop of energy and still the stones do not awake. Beloved Master, we of ourselves cannot work this miracle. Help us, Saint Germain. Help us and show us the way to overcoming.

Kevin walked around the stone and laid his hand on Sarah's head. He did not try to stop her tears. He felt her weeping for both of them. All he could do was stand with her. He was empty—completely spent.

Then he heard it—they both did. The voice of inner wisdom speaking so loudly that it echoed around the grove.

If you love enough, you can do anything! it boomed. Just like their old mentor, Uncle Óengus, had admonished them in their studies with him. "If you love enough you can do anything!" he had thundered at their recalcitrance when faced with difficult initiations.

They could hear him now. "Do you love enough to change these leaden stones into golden tones?"

Sarah lifted her head. "I do," she said. "I love enough."

"And I," said Kevin. "Whatever it takes, we begin again."

Without warning, Sarah shot to her feet, flinging herself and Kevin away from where she had been kneeling. The central stone suddenly began to vibrate and hum. The other stones, although reduced to little more than a pile of rubble, took up the vibration until the entire grove was alive with vibrant energy.

Saint Germain had prepared them for such an eventuality.

They turned toward the fire that now burned brightly, shooting up brilliant sparks of rainbow-colored flames. Through his blessing the Master had imparted to them ancient prayers that Óengus had taught Ah-Lahn, and that Alana had subsequently learned from the old druid.

Saint Germain had not spoken the words. Rather he had quickened the knowledge from their causal bodies so that now, in this moment, they began to repeat words that had been handed down through lineages of the Great White Brotherhood since the days of Atlantis and before.

With their backs to the stones, whose vibration and audible humming was increasing, Sarah and Kevin raised their arms with hands outstretched, and visualized a cloud of milky white radiance forming a translucent sphere within their combined auras. Gradually, they intensified the energy, visualizing it expanding to encompass the entire grove in the *féath fíadh* mist known in druid lore.

Steadily, they held their arms at shoulder height, focusing with all their might on the millions of light points that were coalescing from the atmosphere to intensify the milky white radiance around them. The mist was swirling, increasing its vibration, though not its density. It remained transparent, yet immensely powerful.

Sarah's arms were beginning to ache, but she dared not speak or entertain doubt. She could only pray that she would be able to hold the intense focus for as long as was necessary.

When she felt herself nearly on the verge of collapse, she momentarily turned her head to the left and saw them! Ever so faintly, now shimmering into view, two figures began to take shape before her. Could it be?

She turned her body and lowered her arms, catching Kevin's attention. Seeing her riveted in place, he moved to her left and followed her gaze. Their hearts leapt in unison. The figures were real!

Standing side by side at the far distant edge of the grove and within the *féath fíadh* mist were the resplendent forms of Ah-Lahn and Alana— he on her right, male and female smiling across at their counterparts.

They were clothed in their finest druid robes, crowned with circlets of oak leaves. A shimmering gold and amethyst medallion hung around each one's neck, the disc forming a base upon which burned tripartite flames of pink and blue with gold between them.

Equal flames burst forth within Sarah's and Kevin's heart chakras as countless light points whirled faster and faster within the mist. In that instant, a crystalline bridge appeared, and they were drawn across to meet Ah-Lahn and Alana, who were likewise approaching the center.

When the two couples were about three feet apart, they halted and focused their full attention on each other, gazing deeply into their counterpart's eyes, as if through will and purest love their very hearts would merge.

As the four stood immersed in the sight of one another, the ineffable sweetness of roses began to permeate the atmosphere. In that moment Kevin watched as Ah-Lahn's right hand moved from his side and pointed to the medallion he wore. *Come closer and observe,* he seemed to say.

Without a word, the two couples came nearer to each other. In that moment, to Kevin's astonishment, he saw that the designs carved on the medallions the druids wore were those of the twin pillars that supported the temple roof in Saint Germain's Cave of Symbols. He clearly detected tall, straight columns on his left and swirling spirals on his right.

Kevin suddenly realized he was standing in the wrong place. Carefully he moved to Sarah's right. As soon as he changed position, silver filigree cords spun out across the diagonal from Sarah's heart to Alana's and from Kevin's heart to Ah-Lahn's—and all went still within the mist.

The two couples were now within arm's length of each other. The filigree cords wafted gracefully up and down as if a gentle, cosmic breeze blew around them, intensifying the ineffable sweetness of roses.

Without hesitation, Kevin and Sarah were inspired to utter the words of ancient connection they had used in lifetimes past. "I am here," they spoke together. Kevin took Sarah's right hand. Ah-Lahn took Alana's, as they answered, "And I."

As naturally as if they had always known how the link that must be made, Sarah extended her left hand to Ah-Lahn and Kevin extended his right hand to Alana, joining palms to palms, creating an unbroken circle, like a golden wedding band, joining past and present in a sensation of unspeakable joy.

The silver cords linking their hearts briefly vibrated together, then dissolved in a shower of tiny crystals as Alana stepped across the circle and vanished into Sarah's heart.

Ah-Lahn fixed Kevin with an expression of profound gratitude and, likewise, crossed over to merge with his counterpart in a vortex of fiery energy that shot up to the heavens and back down to the earth, illuminating the grove with new life as it had not seen in nearly a millennium.

Husband and wife turned to each other in utter amazement and lost consciousness.

Forty

Daylight was fading when Kevin and Sarah came back to themselves. They were sitting on the ground, leaning against the central stone, which was now silent. The fire on the hearth had gone out, and they shivered in the damp air that was growing cold. Both gripped a circular object in their right hand.

"Kevin, what are you holding?" asked Sarah, turning her hand over, palm up. They opened their fingers together to reveal golden chains on which hung medallions made of amethyst and gold, each one uniquely engraved with the image of a magnificent pillar.

"I think we should wear them," they said together and laughed as they slipped the pendants over their heads. The medallions felt warm against their hearts, almost like a personal presence.

Another phenomenon caught Kevin's attention. "Sarah, look at me," he said. "What color are my eyes?"

"Violet. They're violet like Saint Germain's and F. M.'s."

"So are yours. Another sign that we succeeded?"

"I hope so. We won't know for certain until the Master tells us, but I have to believe we did. I feel her here." Her hand went to her heart, her eyes filled with tears. "Alana and Sarah together. As if the rent in my soul is healing."

"I feel the same," said Kevin simply. Emotion robbed him of words.

Although evening was fast approaching, both Sarah and Kevin basked in the inner glow that warmed them heart and soul. They were eager to return to their hotel, enjoy a gourmet dinner and a good night's sleep. Perhaps they would take a dip in the heated swimming pool or relax in the sauna before retiring.

They knew their commission required another step before completion on solstice morning at Newgrange. But, tonight, they would meditate upon the extraordinary experience they had shared in the ancient grove of Uncle Óengus.

They were all smiles as they quickly disassembled the little hearth they had built and chanted a closing invocation to return the light they had invoked to the realms of Spirit—never to be misqualified by anyone's human consciousness.

They had gathered up their belongings and were gazing lovingly around the grove when Sarah turned abruptly.

"What was that? Did you hear something? I thought I heard footsteps. Who would be here at this hour?"

"Hold my hand, Sarah," said Kevin. "We'll check together."

Carefully, yet not carefully enough—so enthralled were they by the vibrant energy that still pulsated within them—they stepped out of the grove and into the thin woods that showed no sign of the miraculous events that had recently occurred mere inches away.

Shocked beyond words, Kevin halted and tensed, quickly sweeping Sarah behind him.

Standing arrogantly in front of them, feet planted and arms akimbo, was Arán Bán, robed in the full regalia of a chief druid and smirking haughtily. He spoke to them in accents of their shared lifetime from two thousand years in the past.

"Ha! Did you think I could not have you followed?" he sneered. "Of course, I did not have to wonder where to find you. I knew you would eventually bumble your way to the site of your former power. And mine. For did I not also use this grove when I held the position of *ceann-druí*, before you stole it from me, Ah-Lahn.

"So, you've managed to merge with your pitiful former selves. Well, this insignificant transformation will do you little good. I am still stronger than the two of you and, believe me, I have plans.

"Indeed, I have plans, and this is a warning. Desist cavorting with Saint Germain, and you will not be harmed. Continue to wield whatever power you may think you have gained, and I cannot be responsible for what happens to you, your friends, or to those twins you're so fond of."

He laughed menacingly at Sarah's gasp.

"Oh, yes, I know all about you. Think on that while you remember my promise, Alana. You will come to me again, without this one around to protect you."

Sarah thought she saw a dagger flash in Kevin's direction, but then she was blinded by the cloud of sulfurous smoke into which Arán Bán vanished. She and Kevin were left shaking in the harsh, cold wind and driving rain that now slanted up from the river below them.

They were both trembling as they stumbled back to their car, though not entirely from the cold and wet. Kevin had gone deathly pale and was leaning heavily against the driver's side door. He groaned and gripped his side.

"Kevin, what is it? What's wrong?"

Sarah pulled his hand away. A growing stain of blood was oozing through his shirt.

"Oh, my God, you're hurt! What happened?"

"I don't know," he said weakly. "There was a flash of grim light from Arán Bán and I felt something stick me in the gut. I don't think it's too bad or I couldn't have walked here, but I need a doctor.

"See if you can wrap something around my middle, Hon, and put me in the passenger seat. You're going to have to drive."

Sarah willed her hands to stop shaking as she eased Kevin into their rental car. Then a light dawned.

"Róisín's kit!" she cried.

"What?" asked Kevin feebly.

"Róisín gave me an emergency kit before we left. Now, where is it? I know I put it in my pack." She opened the car's back door and began feverishly yanking things out of her day pack. Of course, the kit was in the bottom, but she had it!

She unzipped the pouch and pulled out the vial. "Here, Hon, drink this down while I bandage you."

"It tastes like violets and roses." He smiled weakly.

"Oh, good. Can you hold up your shirt?"

Trying not to fumble, Sarah placed a sterile pad on the gash in Kevin's side. She was about to start winding a length of gauze around his middle to hold it in place when she spied a short length of wood that was gnarled and blackened with age. It was also scored with dozens of rune-like marks she recognized from druid lore.

Here was the length of hazel wand Róisín's note had said she was to bind onto an injury. How had her friend known? Was this event ordained—or was it merely likely to occur, given the players in this cosmic drama?

Regardless, there was no time to lose. Sarah placed the ancient piece of wood next to Kevin's skin and wound the gauze around him, then covered him with a blanket she found in the back seat.

"I love enough, I love enough, I love enough," she repeated aloud as she rushed around the car and situated herself behind the wheel.

She stuck the key in the ignition and thanked God when the engine turned over. She stepped on the gas and sent the vehicle hurtling away from the forest, past the power station, and out onto the road that would take them to the safety of their hotel.

Sarah drove as fast as their little car would bump along the narrow country road until she reached the Manor. She leapt out of the car and ran to the front desk.

"Help! My husband has been stabbed! He needs a doctor," she cried to the teen-aged boy who was on duty.

"Oh, ma'am, there's no doctor here. You'll have to go to Campile. They've a fine clinic there. It's only seven miles. You'd best drive on."

"I can drive. I can drive. Archangel Michael, help me drive," Sarah repeated the words like a chant as she eased the vehicle onto the road to Campile. Kevin was dozing now, his breathing easier than it had been.

"Don't worry, Hon, we can do this," she reassured him and herself, though she knew he wasn't hearing her.

"Saint Germain! Help me find a doctor! Help me save my husband! Help us do our work for you!" she cried aloud to their Master.

She squinted her eyes in the dark. The sun had completely disappeared behind dense clouds, hastening a moonless night. The road, though paved, was barely visible—each twist and turn hidden by grotesque silhouettes of thick hedges that scraped the car when Sarah veered too far to the left.

Then, suddenly, running in front of the car, illumined by the headlights, just far enough ahead for Sarah to follow—there was Sprid, Alana's panther guide. There were no other cars on the road, so within minutes, Sprid guided Sarah right up to the small infirmary in Campile.

"Help! My husband's been stabbed!" she cried to the two men who were having a smoke outside the building. Quick as lightning, they got a wheel chair and gently pulled Kevin from the car.

"Don't worry, ma'am. Doc O'Brien is on call. He'll get your man fixed up. Go on to the chapel, if you want to pray. The doc will know where to find you."

Sarah did as they suggested and fell to her knees at the altar to pray.

Beloved Saint Germain, Lady Master Nada, Archangel Michael and all the angels, be with us this day. Cast out the darkness that opposes our work for you. We would be your hands and feet, dear Masters. Please guide us in the way you would have us go.

With the intuition of her druid self, Sarah knew her prayer had been answered. She felt a remarkable peace settle into her heart. She sat back on her heels, but she did not move from the altar.

After a while, she rose and lit a candle for Kevin, then lit a second one for all the unknown souls who were depending on them. The simple ritual made her feel as if she were making contact with the many twin flames whom she and Kevin were meant to serve—when he recovered.

"Please God, help him recover," she breathed one last prayer.

She took a seat in the front pew and closed her eyes, resting in the inner knowledge that the masters had heard her.

"Don't worry, lass, your man will be fine."

Sarah's head jerked up. Was this the doctor already? She turned to her right to see an old woman sitting at the end of the pew. Her head was covered with a dark blue shawl, her dress an indistinct homespun that could have been worn a century earlier.

"We won't let anything happen to Ah-Lahn this time. He's too important, and so are you. The two of you together have great work ahead of you. And now you know the battle lines have been drawn. Arán Bán was not supposed to have spilled blood. He has violated the Brotherhood's terms of engagement and will face the consequences.

"Never fear, brave Alana. You possess the means to complete your commission in this life. But you must be very careful to invoke the protection of your masters every step of the way.

"Now, see, here's your doctor with good news."

Sarah turned to see Dr. O'Brien coming toward her. She looked back to thank the old woman, but there was no one else in the pew.

"Mrs. MacCauley? Your husband's a lucky man, though I am puzzled by his injury. It appears to have been made by a stone blade of some kind. Can you account for that? The blade had been tipped with a substance I swear was poison, but that couldn't be or your man would have died on the way here. Never seen anything like it. The *garda* will want a report. Can you identify his assailant?"

Yes, I can, thought Sarah, shivering in the realization that Arán Bán had tried to repeat his deadly assault from centuries before. Attempting to explain that mystery to local police would prompt more questions than she was prepared to answer.

"No, doctor, I don't know who attacked us. We were out hiking, perhaps a little too late in the afternoon, and someone jumped us. I thought it was a robbery, but nothing was taken. We didn't even know my husband was injured until we got to our car."

"Aye, very strange. Well, you brought him here in plenty of time and I've stitched him up. Fortunately, the wound wasn't deep. I am curious, though, about the little stick that was tucked into the bandage you put on him. Do you want it back?"

"I do, yes. Uh, just some folk medicine that came in handy," said Sarah casually. The doctor handed her a plastic baggie with the piece of hazel wand, which she carefully stowed in her pocket.

"Here you are, then. We'll keep your husband overnight, and you can be on your way in the morning."

"Thank you. We're due at Newgrange on the twenty-first. We really need to be at our hotel in Drogheda by tomorrow afternoon."

"Going to the sunrise, are you? Quite the sight. I've been there a couple of times, myself. Even won the lottery one year. Can't say I understand what those ancients were all about, but they surely did build an impressive place for mere farmers—if anybody really believes that's who made a structure that's stayed dry for five thousand years. Wish my own roof was half that tight.

"Now, you go see your man. My wife, Siobhan, is the nurse tonight. She'll get you some blankets and a cot so you can stay with him. The kettle's on if you'd like a cup of tea, and there's a nice bowl of soup ready for whenever you want it. We've a single private room here in the clinic. You'll find your man in there.

"Oh, a lad from the Manor brought your belongings so you won't have to backtrack in the morning. He said to tell you his sister, Bríd, packed up your hotel room—'real careful-like,' he said—so you needn't worry about your things."

Forty-One

Sarah found her way to Kevin's room in the clinic and carefully opened the door—not sure what she would find. To her delight, he was sitting up in bed with a wide, though pale, smile on his face.

"*A ghrá.*" He stretched out his right arm and motioned for her to sit next to him on the hospital bed. As soon as she felt the warmth of his body, her shoulders began to shake with sobs as the build-up of nerves and worry finally got the better of her. Tears spilled down her cheeks onto the thin cotton hospital gown he wore.

"I'm sorry, Hon. I don't mean to go all weepy on you. I promised myself I wouldn't. It's just that . . . I was so afraid." She leaned down and buried her face in his chest.

"I know. I know." He stroked her mass of auburn curls. Had she ever been so dear to him?

"I'm okay, Hon. I'm here. I didn't die this time. I thought I might, but I didn't. Whatever you did was enough. You saved me, Sarah."

She raised her head and looked into his eyes. "I think Róisín is the one who saved you. Don't you remember? Before we left home, when we were packing, Debbie gave me that emergency kit that Róisín had prepared. It contained the tincture you drank and everything I needed to stop the bleeding. I just drove like a madwoman and prayed all the way."

"Well, the two of you make a great EMT squad, that's all I say."

"I couldn't help wondering—as I was trying not to panic—if this whole thing was ordained. I mean, who knew that Arán Bán was going show up and stab you, or that Róisín would have given me an emergency medical kit, complete with a piece of old hazel wand—just in case of an injury? Too many coincidences."

"A piece of hazel wand?" asked Kevin.

"Yes, look." Sarah drew the baggie out of her pocket.

"We've seen this before," said Kevin. "When Ah-Lahn saved Alana from a witch's poison."

"You're right," said Sarah. She thought for a minute. "I think this was part of a record we had to go through—and survive this time. When I was in the chapel, while the doctor was taking care of you, an old woman appeared next to where I was sitting and praying.

"She spoke to me and told me not to worry. 'We won't let anything happen to Ah-Lahn this time,' she said."

"Really?"

"Yes. She said we were too important because we have work to do and the battle lines have been drawn. There was more—I'll remember later. The odd thing was, she looked like a young person in disguise. There was something in her eyes. They didn't look old. They glowed with the vitality of someone full of life and spirit . . . someone like Lady Master Nada. I wonder."

Sarah could see that Kevin was drifting off to sleep. She called the nurse to help settle him for the night and gratefully accepted the cot and blankets next to his bed. Tomorrow was another day. Thanks to their many helpers, seen and unseen, they were both alive to enjoy it.

After surviving being threatened and stabbed by his ancient nemesis, Arán Bán, Kevin was relishing the bus ride to Newgrange. He was looking forward to an experience today that would build on merging with his druid self rather than escaping from the brothers of shadow.

Sarah was also ruminating on the past two days. Only a true master like Saint Germain could have precipitated so many miracles.

She could not quite believe that Kevin had recovered well enough during the night to leave the clinic yesterday, that she had managed to drive (on the left!) the two-and-a-half hours from Campile to Drogheda, and that they were in their seats on the tour bus to Newgrange in time for solstice sunrise. The whole thing was a blur.

She was just grateful they had made it and that Kevin was able to engage in the final ritual they were to complete at Newgrange.

Another miracle had facilitated their presence at the Neolithic structure. Only sixty guests with tickets were allowed inside for the solstice ritual. Outside hundreds of people were gathered to catch whatever glimpse they could of the phenomenon that had fascinated pagans and non-pagans for thousands of years.

Due to Kevin's injury—he was still under doctor's orders to be careful—he and Sarah had been seated at the front of the tour bus and were being ushered to the start of the line so they would be the first visitors to traverse the megalith-lined passage that soon would be the sun's pathway.

Sixty people were almost more than the interior could accommodate. As a result, Sarah and Kevin were squashed, shoulder-to-shoulder with the other visitors who lined the perimeter of the interior so as not to block the rays of the sun.

As if their Master had made the arrangements, the right side of Sarah's body was in full contact with the central altar. Because her consciousness and Kevin's had been so thoroughly charged with light by their initiation in the grove, they were highly attuned to the subtle vibrations emanating from the stones.

Minutes before sunrise, Sarah felt a quivering, a sort of rippling anticipation coming from the altar—a decidedly feminine presence, eager as a new bride awaiting the arrival of her bridegroom.

She was completely lost in thought. And then it began.

"Sarah, look," whispered Kevin. He was standing slightly behind her where he could feel her body opening to the vibrations that started to hum through the structure's interior at the moment when Helios began his astonishing rise over the eastern hills.

As the first rays penetrated the stone light box atop the entrance, the visitors gasped as a single voice. Slowly, inexorably, the golden beam moved toward its goal to deliver its promise of abundance to the earth for another year.

Sarah was riveted in place as she beheld the single golden ray approaching her—as if she herself were the sun's destination. When the enormous ray filled the entire passageway and landed full force on the altar where she stood, she merged with the Earth. She was the Divine Feminine, and the Divine Masculine had come upon her for the conception of the Holy Child that she would bear.

She remained transfixed for the duration of the sun's transit and then leaned back against Kevin, her knees weak, heart pounding at the powerful gnosis that was now lodged in her body as a divine presence.

Man and wife held each other until the other guests preceded them back out the entrance. They quickly found a place to sit away from the crowds which were already dispersing. Their bus would be one of the last to depart, so they had some time to collect themselves.

"Kevin . . . I . . . I . . .," Sarah stammered.

"I know," he said. "Something extraordinary happened in there. You're glowing like a sunbeam, *mo chroí*, and your eyes are violet again."

"So are yours. My God, I've never felt anything so incredibly physical and yet so profoundly spiritual at the same time. I was the Earth . . ."

"And I was the Sun." Kevin completed her thought. "I was moving as if in a solemn procession to meet my bride. There you were and here you are in the fullness of your being, my darling Sarah. My beloved Alana."

"Oh, Kevin, my Ah-Lahn. Do you remember I told you the twins said I would be able to get pregnant again? I'm no longer afraid, *mo chroí*. If you feel well enough after your injury, I'd like to try while we are here in Ireland."

"What injury? I feel like I suffered only a mild scratch. Sarah, I love you with my whole heart. If you're ready, I'm ready. We have today and tomorrow before we fly home. Let's rest and meditate and figure out who we are now as our merged selves.

"I have a feeling that *An Síoraí*, the Eternal One, may have another miracle in store for us. I cannot imagine a more wonderful Christmas gift than to conceive a child—or two."

Forty-Two

Debbie's heart was filled with the spirit of Christmas as she drove across Long Island to meet Kevin and Sarah at JFK airport. Seeing her friends safely home was the gift that mattered most to her right now.

"Are you eager to see them?" she asked Hero and Sprite, who were riding in the back seat of her SUV.

She had not meant to bring the MacCauleys' pets. However, as many domestic animals will do, they had known that she was going some place exciting.

As she'd started out the door, Hero had planted himself in front of her, and Sprite had curled around her feet with some very insistent "meows." They'd given her no choice but to load the dog into the back seat and secure the cat in her travel crate.

"I suppose they'll be very tired after enduring the challenges that greeted them in Ireland." Debbie continued her conversation with the animals. She actually was glad they were with her. Having two sentient beings to talk to helped calm her nerves.

"No one has heard if they were successful in completing Saint Germain's commission. However, Sarah did sound upbeat when she texted four days ago that they had reached their lodging in Drogheda in time to join the tour to Newgrange on solstice morning.

"This morning she sent me only their flight number and arrival time at JFK. I didn't expect any more info than that, but still . . ."

Her voice trailed off and she remained silent until she parked the SUV at the airport. The animals had kept their own counsel regarding their humans' condition and appeared content to wait in the car while their friend retrieved their people from the terminal.

Debbie had disciplined her mind not to conjure either positive or negative images of how Kevin and Sarah might appear as they exited customs. That was just as well, for she could not have imagined the scene that met her astonished eyes when she saw them.

The vision lasted only an instant, but Debbie knew she would never forget it. For there—in the midst of travelers of every age, shape, and size—were two radiant beings. They were dressed in long white robes and were wearing intricately carved medallions that hung from gold chains around their necks.

Here before her were Ah-Lahn and Alana as she had known them in ages long past—their faces beaming the brightest of smiles at her, their violet eyes a-glow with soul-fire. Her dearest fellow pilgrims on the path to eternity had returned to her at last.

She blinked, and the image vanished as quickly as it had appeared. She blinked again, and there were Kevin and Sarah, pushing their luggage carts through the crowd.

"Debbie!" cried Sarah as soon as they reached her. The two women hugged each other, emotion flooding them both.

"I didn't mean to go weepy, but I'm so relieved to see you in the flesh," said Debbie. "I did my best to hold positive thoughts, but there was a part of me that was afraid I'd never see you again."

"We know, *a chara*," agreed Kevin. He hugged her and rested a hand on her shoulder. "There were moments when we had our doubts."

"But you succeeded, didn't you?" she said softly.

"We did," he nodded.

"And we're eager to tell you about the amazing things that happened to us," added Sarah. "However, . . ."

"However, you need to speak with the Master first," said Debbie. "Of course, I understand, and I won't ask until you're ready."

"Thanks," said Kevin. "There are things we encountered that we don't really understand. So we'll all wait until Saint Germain gives us permission. But we do know that we accomplished at least part of what he sent us to do."

"I can attest to that," said Debbie. And then she told them what she had seen.

"That gives me hope," said Sarah with a deep sigh. "And now that we're back on U. S. soil, I'm suddenly very tired."

"Then let's get you home to rest so you can enjoy Christmas dinner tomorrow. Lucky and Róisín said not to worry about bringing anything other than yourselves. We're only five for dinner, so it's an easy meal to prepare. We just want you with us."

"How are the fur kids?" asked Kevin as they walked to the car.

"You're about to find out," laughed Debbie. "They couldn't wait to see you. You'd better hold onto the door while I let them out. I don't think Hero is going to be able to control himself. Nor will Sprite for that matter," she added as Sarah's kitty leapt into her mistress's arms. "Merry Christmas!"

They all laughed together and were glad to be distracted by the animals, so Sarah and Kevin were not tempted to reveal details of their adventures that were not theirs to disclose.

Neither the Callahans nor the MacCauleys had expected Sarah and Kevin to return from Ireland in time for Christmas, so the couple was free to enjoy the intimate celebration that Lucky and Róisín had invited them to attend along with Debbie.

No other friends from the Fibonacci community were coming for this gathering. F. M. had let it be known that he would stop by after dinner for a private conversation with the travelers.

"Being at Fibonacci's today with all of you is the perfect Christmas," said Sarah as she sipped one of Róisín's calming tea blends. She was contentedly nibbling the last bite of pie that Debbie had whipped up.

"Thank you for understanding that we can't share any specifics right now."

"We do understand," agreed Lucky, "and we won't pressure you for details." Then he added with a wink, "Are you sure there's nothing you can share without giving away too much?"

"We learned some sobering lessons," said Sarah, and Kevin nodded.

"First, evil never sleeps," he said, "which means we must be far more vigilant and consistent in our prayers than we'd ever imagined."

"And second," added Sarah, "even though we may tap into our former attainment and merge with aspects of our ancient wisdom, the commission for this life is in the present. We clear the vessels of mind and heart for better perception of what has come before, and then we take action here and now for the love of today and all that may follow."

"Well said, my daughter," declared F. M. Bellamarre from the archway to the bookstore. The store was closed for Christmas, but a locked door had never proved an obstacle to the Master who appeared and disappeared as easily as the *féath fíadh* mist Sarah was certain he invoked regularly.

"Please, excuse us," the Master said graciously to Lucky, Róisín, and Debbie. "Sarah and Kevin, will you join me in the loft alcove next door? We will be more comfortable there."

Forty-Three

As soon as they were settled upstairs in the alcove, which seemed to be much more spacious than Kevin remembered, F. M. focused his radiant smile on the couple he knowingly had sent into danger and who had returned with considerable merit.

"Tell me, my son and daughter, in what way do you experience yourselves differently after your transformation in the druid's grove?"

Kevin closed his eyes briefly and took a deep breath.

"There is a knowing, a peace, a feeling of completeness, of confidence, yet a profound humility that we still have much to accomplish on our path to unity with *An Síoraí,* the Eternal One."

F. M. nodded and turned to Sarah with a twinkle in his violet eyes. "If I read your countenance correctly, my dear, you are transformed as only a woman can be. Am I right?"

"You are, Sir—at least I believe I am. Already I feel the whirling of new life within me. How can that be after only a couple of days?"

"You are more sensitive than you can fathom in this moment. Of course, you would feel the presence of the one—or ones—who will stay with you for the full term of your pregnancy. Never fear, Sarah. You will be successful in this sublime act of co-creation with the Divine. You are worthy, as your husband is worthy, and the Brotherhood thanks you for your courage."

"Master, I have a question that has troubled me since it happened. In truth, I have several questions," said Kevin.

"Proceed, my son."

"How was Arán Bán able to find us? Why did he apparently have to wait outside the grove to confront us? Why was he able to stab me after we had only just merged with our druid selves? And why did I not die if, as the doctor said, the dagger had been treated with some kind of poison—exactly the scenario when Arán Bán killed Ah-Lahn? I hope you don't think me ungrateful to be so curious."

"Not at all," answered F. M. "These points are critical to your understanding of how you must proceed in your ongoing mission for the Brotherhood. Remember, you are striving for the union of other twin souls, as well as your own. Let me respond to your queries in order."

F. M. closed his eyes briefly and breathed in deeply. As he exhaled, Kevin and Sarah felt a wave of relaxation and peace come over them, and they also closed their eyes. The fatigue that had blanketed them since their arrival home seemed to dissolve in the presence of this amazing Master of Change—as he had introduced himself to Sarah only weeks earlier.

When they opened their eyes, they were not surprised to find themselves in the presence of the Ascended Master Saint Germain. They opened their minds and hearts to receive his instruction and vowed never to take this blessing for granted. He smiled at them and began.

I have told you that the brothers of shadow—individuals who once had great attainment, yet have chosen the left-handed path—have been able to wrest from the hand of the Almighty energy and mastery that made them powerful and ingenious foes of our Brotherhood.

Because they have been of the Light, they are able to perceive and track the presence of that Light in our best servants.

You radiate, my dears, like fireflies on a summer's eve. Anyone with the perception of a Lucifer can follow your path and predict your movements with a fair amount of accuracy— unless and until you learn to guard that luminance with the assistance of the protection the Brotherhood can provide you when you call upon us.

Sarah felt the Master answer her unspoken question. Words were no longer necessary for profound communion to occur between them.

The call for our assistance is absolutely necessary. Free will reigns supreme in our Universe. Before we can intercede on your behalf, we must have your consent, your request. This is the law that not even *An Síoraí*, the Eternal One, can break. In the future, you will remember.

Yes, I will, Sarah agreed in her heart. The Master's countenance glowed as he continued.

To your next question, Kevin. Arán Bán could not enter the grove because, by your invocations to Archangel Michael and others, you had placed a ring of protection around that forcefield. He could not penetrate the power you sealed there.

However, when you stepped outside the grove, forgetting in your ecstasy to protect the merging you had only just achieved, you were vulnerable to his murderous intent.

Kevin looked down, feeling himself admonished. He had been so caught up in the merged presence of Ah-Lahn that he was careless at a critical moment. He took a deep breath and bravely raised his eyes. He was grateful to perceive the Master's loving expression.

Do not condemn yourself, my son. Next time you will not be careless. There are often multiple reasons for certain events and multiple opportunities to make the right decision.

In this case, your being stabbed was the last vestige of a particular karma that required transmutation before your initiation could take place at Newgrange.

You did not die because your beloved twin prayed fervently and unselfishly for your healing—not only for yourselves but also for the service you two are destined to perform.

The presence of your attainment as Alana and Ah-Lahn and Sarah's timely application of Róisín's emergency kit neutralized the poison on contact.

"Thank God for Róisín," said Sarah earnestly.

"She is one of my best alchemy students." Saint Germain nodded, assuming a more conversational tone. "I encourage you to spend time with her, Sarah. She has much to teach you that will assist you in your new role as co-creator with the Divine."

The Master paused and tenderly focused his deep violet eyes on the two bright beings seated before him. Here was the final step of their initiation.

"We have some time before your next assignment begins. And you, young mother, must take care to nourish your body and keep your mind free of fear or doubt or any other negative feelings that may arise. You are under my protection as long as you invoke it and do your part in the physical.

"Before I send you off to rest, I have a question for you both."

"What would ask us, Sir?" said Kevin.

"You will recall that you were sent to retrieve the treasure that Alana and Ah-Lahn left in the druid's grove. Did you succeed?"

Kevin's face fell. He looked at Sarah in disbelief. After everything they had been through, had they failed at their most basic assignment?

Sharing his distress, she offered a suggestion, "We found their medallions in our hands after the merging and they have remained with us. As you see, we are wearing them."

"Well done, yet that is not the treasure. What else might it be?" The room was silent as the Master waited for their response.

Sarah searched her soul. Yes, there was a treasure lodged in her heart that had not been there until she and Alana had merged. But what was it?

After a full minute, she exclaimed: "Their love! They left the treasure of their love, our love. We found the completion of our union when we joined our hands with theirs in the *féath fíadh* mist. Is that it?"

Saint Germain nodded. "The love you have possessed, lifetime after lifetime, is a portion of the treasure we sent you to find, though not all. What else did you discover?"

Kevin closed his eyes and drew his attention into his heart and remembered. Ah-Lahn had given him an answer before they merged.

"The treasure could be the pillars that I observed in our first meeting in the Cave of Symbols, that are etched on our medallions and now in our hearts. Here are the symbols of masculine and feminine, of Alpha and Omega—the essence of our original twin flames."

"I feel them, too," said Sarah quietly, "as source and goal of all our strivings, now and in the future."

The Master waited, his expression enigmatic.

Kevin also paused until he felt a deeper knowing than he had had before descend upon him from the heart of *An Síoraí*, the Eternal One.

"We already knew that Alana and Ah-Lahn were fragments of our souls that split off from the totality of our beings in the trauma of Arán Bán's murderous act two thousand years ago.

"And I see now that other twin flames have suffered the same fragmentation. They have been separated from themselves as well as from each other. I believe that helping these couples to retrieve their scattered soul parts is the work we are now charged to perform."

"You have the right of it," said Saint Germain with a solemn nod. Once more he assumed the role of illuminator—the better to infuse their souls with an understanding so necessary for their future work together.

> In the moment of that terrible separation, those pieces of your souls fled to the grove where they remained trapped until you released them, still wearing the ancient emblems of your True Self.
>
> I can tell you now that Ah-Lahn and Alana were meant to act as bulwarks against the malintent of Arán Bán, which had begun eons before the final days of the Atlantean civilization. That commission was thwarted, burdening your souls until the present lifetime—which may well be your last opportunity, as well as ours of the Great White Brotherhood, to right the wrongs perpetrated by this individual and his consort.
>
> With your victorious retrieval of your soul fragments, each of you has become an inner pillar, a support in the temple of twin flames, a treasure that only you could find.

The Master gestured for Kevin and Sarah to stand with him. In an act of unspeakable kindness, he opened his arms, beaming the light of his heart to the man and woman who had become as precious to him as if he had sired them himself.

Lest he overwhelm them with the intensity of his radiant presence, he quickly tucked in his aura and spoke a parting comfort.

Be at peace, beloved ones. We will soon convene again. The reward for service is always more service, and you have much to complete as twin flames before your race is run.

Until then, may you carry with you this inspiration from *An Síoraí*, the Eternal One.

Love is stronger than death.
Love is stronger
than loss of any kind.

Love is stronger than the pettiness
of human discord or desire
or the mundane questions
that will fill up your days
if you allow.

Love is the bridge
between the unseen and seen.

Love is the way through
the veil between worlds,
and the foundation
of every good and perfect work.

Love is both source and goal,
the beginning and the ending
of all the Brotherhood's purposes.

Love is the vessel
that holds us all together,
and the means for dividing
what is real from the unreal.

So powerful is Love
that all men's doubts
can be swallowed up
in a child's innocent faith
that all will be well in Love.

For Love is the essence,
the ineffable, the eternal glory of life,
and the reason for your striving.

You are meant to be Love.
All else is illusion.

Epilogue

Meanwhile, in his luxurious penthouse office, located high atop the Manhattan skyscraper he had recently acquired in a conveniently arranged foreclosure, A. B. Ryan was moving ahead with his own plans for the new year.

"Tony, get that kid, Rudy, on the phone. I want to find out what he knows about the bookstore and coffee shop business that's holding up my land deal on Long Island. The whole block should be knocked down. I don't know why they won't sell. Probably hoping for a better price—which they won't get."

He laughed sardonically.

"Dig into it. If they won't sign a contract, I'll have the place condemned. Might do that anyway. The price'll be cheaper. Go ahead and schedule the demo for next summer. It'll take that long for all the city councilmen to be convinced."

"Right away, A. B.," said Tony, whisking a stack of papers off the boss's desk. "Happy New Year, by the way."

"Huh! Maybe it will be. Maybe it won't. Depends on who you are, doesn't it, Tony?"

With a dismissive flick of his hand, Arán Bán turned away from the man he knew he must tolerate for a while longer, and let his midnight blue eyes gaze out at his growing empire. He licked his lips lasciviously.

"Oh, yes, Ah-Lahn—next year's happiness depends entirely on who you are."

Read the story that sparked the
Twin Flames of Éire Trilogy,
and learn where the path of reunion began
for Sarah and Kevin and their Friends of Ancient Wisdom.

Sometimes to move forward
you have to go back...

Sarah and Kevin recognized their connection as twin flames within minutes of meeting at a party that neither had wanted to attend.

They soon vowed to stay together forever. Yet, seven years later they are on the verge of losing each other—and not for the first time. For as they discover through dreams and visions, their shared embodiments were often scarred by painful separations.

Will Sarah and Kevin find a way to reconcile past and present to escape a future neither of them wants?

Only going back in time will tell.

Don't miss these exciting sequels to *The Weaving* in the *Twin Flames of Éire Trilogy*

The Ancients and The Call - Sarah and Kevin believe they resolved all of their differences last summer in the luminous atmosphere of Éire. But that experience was only the beginning of their mission on behalf of twin flames. Now they know that love can be lost unless they return to Ireland and merge with their ancient druid selves, Alana and Ah-Lahn.

The Water and The Flame - Broadway actress Glenna and Irish monk Rory are worlds apart. The chances of their meeting and realizing they are twin flames are slim. Until the magic of Éire and the support of their Friends of Ancient Wisdom sends them on a voyage of self-discovery and overcoming malevolent forces they never could have imagined.

The Mystics and The Mystery - The path of reunion for twin flames has never been more perilous than for seers Debbie and Jeremy. Must she surrender her visions of the love they shared in the past for the sake of his soul? Or will he summon his inner strength to join her and other mystics to combat the ancient forces that have opposed them?

Turn the page for a preview of Glenna and Rory's story in The Water and The Flame

The sold-out audience clapped and cheered, hooted, stomped and whistled in the loudest, longest standing ovation Glenna Morrissey and her company had ever received. Closing nights were always exciting. This one was spectacular.

Tonight's performance had been one of those shows that every actor lives for. When you can do no wrong. When every member of the cast has brought their A-game to the stage. When every joke gets a laugh, every sad song evokes tears, and every big chorus number is a show-stopper.

The glory of success whooshed up Glenna's spine and out the top of her head like fireworks. Looking left and right at her fellow actors as they stood hand-in-hand across the stage receiving the applause they had earned, she knew her blue eyes flashed with the same joy, her face registered the same wide grin as theirs.

However fleeting those emotions might be when the applause stopped and they all transformed back into every-day mortals, this was a great night.

The year-long run had been a blessing of steady work. Glenna had even received a Tony Award nomination for her role as the leading lady's best friend.

Winning would have been the cherry on top of this sundae of a show. She almost didn't mind losing to her friend Cassie, who had always been favored to win for Supporting Actress in her own musical that was still playing across the street in Manhattan's theatre district.

Almost.

Glenna had tried to be gracious, but even now, as the magnificent, gold velvet stage curtain descended and the house lights came up, she had to admit she was bitter about the loss. And more than a little worried about her future.

What if tonight is as good at it gets? she thought as she changed into street clothes and brushed her dark blonde hair into long, casual waves. Had she already peaked at the age of twenty-six? Would she ever get such a terrific part again?

Competition was fierce in New York, and hopeful ingenues were moving to the city from every corner of the world. Being cast was more difficult than ever, in part because so many Hollywood celebrities were now taking their turn on the stage. That didn't seem fair to Glenna, but there was nothing she could do about it.

Worse still, an actor with principles was likely to be overlooked in favor of one who would do anything to land a part. To a certain extent, show business had always been that way. But Glenna and her friends agreed that, these days, they had to be more wary of the unscrupulous.

Fortunately, her hard work at regular dance classes, acting workshops, and voice lessons had payed off. Her notices were the best of her career, and her agent, Mel, was busy lining up a score of auditions for the coming season. Only last week he had looked her straight in the eye and made her promise to stay positive.

"Mel says I should be encouraged, so I will be," she declared to her image in the dressing room mirror.

"C'mon, Glenna, the party's starting!" called her co-star, Patsy, urging her to the bar down the street where actors had gathered for decades to celebrate their successes and commiserate over their status as newly unemployed.

Patsy had been Tony-nominated for her sparkling portrayal of their show's leading lady. She had lost out to Lenore, Cassie's co-star, who won her second Tony in as many years. Glenna was astounded that Patsy seemed honestly not to care.

"I don't do this for the awards," she had answered Glenna's undisguised amazement at her nonchalance. "Just being on that stage night after night is reward enough for me, don't you agree?"

Glenna didn't agree, though she wouldn't say so.

She'd been aiming for a Tony since she was five years old. She remembered the day well. She'd been tap dancing on the tile floor in her parents' kitchen. "I'm going to be a famous actress!" she had declared to her mother—and she had never given up on that dream.

But was that dream giving up on her? She dared not consider the possibility. Not when a cast party beckoned.

For a few hours she would celebrate with her fellow players. After tonight they would all be going their separate ways.

The laughter and the tears would be genuine, as they always were. Impermanence was simply part of the deal of living the actor's life. Many of her friends thrived on the uncertainty.

She could only wish that she did.

Libations were flowing freely by the time Glenna walked through the bar's heavy oak doors. At least for tonight, all the cast and crew were friends again, and the inevitable backstage squabbles that made a company operate like a typically human family were forgotten.

She sang heartfelt songs of farewell with her pals. As more than a few of them were Irish, "The Parting Glass" rang out from full throats and teary eyes. You had to have a heart of stone not to feel the emotional tug of that melody and those words, thought Glenna as she joined in.

> But since it falls unto my lot
> That I should rise and you should not,
> I'll gently rise and I'll softly call
> Good night and joy be to you all,
> Good night and joy be to you all.

The singers were gearing up for another round of boisterous tunes when who should stride in, but the famous theatrical producer, Roland Newhouse. Heads turned and conversation hushed.

Excitement and speculation about who might be getting good news rippled through the company. However, when Newhouse approached

Glenna, her pals turned back with a shrug and conversation resumed. Tonight the luck was hers, not theirs.

Newhouse was dressed in a thousand-dollar cashmere overcoat. Nothing unusual there. What was different (he was notoriously wary of being upstaged) was that he was accompanied by an even more expensively dressed man whose tall stature and full head of silver hair gave him an air of powerful self-importance.

Glenna did not know this second person, although there was something oddly familiar and troubling about his expression. His midnight blue eyes seemed to flash at her with a jolt of surprise. However, he quickly changed his demeanor to one of intense interest, as if he knew something about her that he would exploit if given a chance.

Newhouse spoke first. "Good evening, Ms. Morrissey. May we have a word?"

"Of course. How nice to see you, Mr. Newhouse. I didn't think you frequented noisy cast parties."

"I usually don't, but I was told you would be here. I wanted to be the first in what I'm sure will be a long line of producers and directors vying for your considerable talents in their next shows. Right, A. B.?"

The man only raised his eyebrows and nodded.

"Let me present A. B. Ryan, my partner in an exciting new theatrical venture. I've told him that securing you as our leading lady guarantees the show's success."

In the space of an in-breath Glenna felt herself start to extend her hand to A. B. and then draw back from touching him. Instead, she returned his nod and addressed Newhouse, "You flatter me, sir."

"No, indeed," he enthused. "Not after reading reviews like this." He pulled a clipping from his jacket pocket, puffed out his chest, and read aloud with stentorian emphasis:

Ms. Morrissey's performance is no mere revival. There is a freshness to her talent we have not seen in the parade of ingenues that have graced our Broadway stages of late. She sings like a nightingale and dances like a fiery gypsy. *Brava!* Ms. Morrissey.

With the assertiveness of a skilled salesman, Newhouse carried on. "I have it on good authority that your agent is already fielding a number of inquiries about your availability. I want to be your first consideration. Our new show is a guaranteed Tony for you, my girl. It's got everything. Great songs, dancing, drama, comedy. Hollywood people are already asking about the rights to produce the movie.

Gesturing to A. B., whose face was enigmatic, he declared, "My colleague is ready to fund the production. Are you interested?"

"Obviously, yes," answered Glenna. Any wariness about A. B. Ryan evaporated in Newhouse's enthusiasm. "To tell you the truth, after not winning the Tony I wasn't sure that my career hadn't already peaked."

"Nonsense, my girl. You're just getting started. Stick with us and we'll make you a star the likes of which you've never imagined. I'm off to Boston tomorrow, but I'd like to see you in my office next Friday. Shall we say 11:00 a.m.?"

"Thank you, yes, that will be wonderful." Glenna tried not to gush. "I look forward to our discussion, Mr. Newhouse."

He ostentatiously kissed her hand and breezed out, obsequiously ushering A. B. Ryan through the doorway before him. That imposing personage had not said a word to Glenna, only nodding once more as if his acknowledgment were sufficient to seal the deal.

Her friend Patsy thought Roland Newhouse looked like the cat who'd just swallowed the canary. But who, she wondered, was the bird?

"What did they want?" she demanded of Glenna, whose clear blue eyes followed the producers out the door.

"To make me a star," she said dreamily.

"Well, be careful what that stardom might cost you," Patsy warned. "You know what they say about the Newhouse casting couch."

"I'm not worried," said Glenna. "I know he's got a reputation, but isn't that with the newbies? I'm an established actress, and Mel will look out for me."

"I hope so," said Patsy. "I'd hate for you to be taken advantage of by him or his partner. Are you sure his show is the real deal?"

Suddenly feeling annoyed that her friend would question her good luck, Glenna shrugged and answered brusquely. "Guess we'll find out, won't we? Anyway, I'm going home now. See you later."

Gathering up her coat and bag, she quickly made the rounds of good-bye hugs and air kisses with her fellow actors and hurried across the street to catch the subway to her tiny apartment in Brooklyn.

Once Glenna got home, she fell quickly into bed where she dreamed of glowing reviews from all the New York papers, bouquets of scarlet roses, multiple curtain calls, and the well-deserved Tony Award, which, of course, she would graciously accept with all due humility and poise.

She watched as her image was projected onto enormous movie screens around the world in the film version of the role that, naturally, would be hers. Surely an Oscar would follow.

The dream's only puzzling image, which she completely forgot upon waking, was of A. B. Ryan standing like a spectre with his face obscured in an odd sort of fog or mist.

Glossary & Pronunciation Guide

Note: Names with * are the author's invention.
(W) following the meaning denotes names that are Welsh in origin.
Letters ch (written phonetically as chk) are pronounced as in loch

Names	**Pronunciation**	**Meaning**
Ah-Lahn*	ah-LAHN	*Var.* Alan, noble, rock
Alana	ah-LAN-ah	Dear child
Arán Bán*	rahn BAHN	White bread
Bleddyn	BLEHTH-in	Wolf (W)
Bríd	BREED	*Var.* Brigid
Brigantes	bre-GAN-tez	Pre-Roman Celtic tribe
Carwyn	KAHR-oo-in	Fair, blessed (W)
Cróga	KRO-guh	Brave, hardy
Dearbhla	DAR-vla	Daughter of the poet
Nhada-lihn*	nah-dah-LIN	*Var.* Nada
Óengus	O-en-gus	Singular strength
Riordan	REER-duhn	Royal poet
Róisín	roh-SHEEN	Little Rose
Siobhan	shiv-AWN	God is gracious
Tadhgan	TIE-guhn	*Var.* Tadhg, bard, poet

Place Names	**Pronunciation**	**Meaning**
Cois Abhann	cush OW-enn	Riverside (village)
Éire	AY-(rhe)	Ireland
Tearmann	TAR-a-mun	Place of refuge (village)
Tír na n'Og	TEER-na-nog	Land of the Ever-Living
Ynys Môn	en-nis MOHN	Anglesey Island (Wales)

Endearments	**Pronunciation**	**Meaning**
A chara, mo chara	a-CHKAR-uh	O friend, my friend
A chairde	a-CHKAR-dyeh	My friends
A ghrá	a-GHRAH	My love
A iníon mo chroí	a-IN-een mu-CHKREE	My darling daughter
Mo chroí	mu-CHKREE	My heart

Terms	Pronunciation	Meaning
An Síoraí	un SHEE-uh-ree	The Eternal One
Bandruí	bahn-DREE	Druidess
Beannachtaí	BAN-achk-tee	Blessings
Ceann-druí	KYAHN-dree	Chief Druid
Druí	DREE	Druid
Féath Fíadha	fay FEE-a-duh	Mists of invisibility
Garda	GAHR-deh	Police
Seanchaí	SHAN-uh-chkee	Storyteller
Taoiseach	TEE-shuchk	Chieftain

Phrases with Pronunciation and Translation

Beannachtaí duit   BAN-achk-tee-duhyt
Blessings to you

Céad míle fáilte   cayd-MEE-luh-FAL-tyuh
A hundred thousand welcomes

Cad a fheiceann tú...   CEH(r)-duh-EK-ehn-too, a-GHRAH?
What do you see, my love?

Feicim é freisin   FEH-kim-ay-FRESH-un
I see it, too

Go raibh maith agat   GUH-ruh-MAH-haht
Thank you

Slán abhaile   SLAHN-a-WILE-eh
May you go safely home

Tá grá agam duit   tah-GHRAH-ahm-duhyt
I love you

Táimid ag éirí níos láidre   TAH-mid-ag-AY-ree-nees-LAH-(dhr)
We are growing stronger

About the Ancients

Many spiritual traditions have their own words and definitions for the manifestations of the Divine that mystics have been observing and experiencing for centuries. The following denote specific aspects of divinity as they are understood by the characters in the *Twin Flames of Éire Trilogy*.

An Síoraí, the Eternal One

> Higher Self, I AM Presence, The Magic Presence
> Individualized manifestation of the I AM THAT I AM
> Soul's unique God-identity, God Self, Divine Monad
> The soul's spiritual origin, source of one's divine plan
> Spiritual Home to which the soul longs to return

Because *An Síoraí*, the Eternal One, abides in Spirit, the human mind requires a mediator to bridge the communication gap between Spirit and Matter. This "translator" is referred to as the True Self.

True Self

> Higher Mind, Christ Self, Buddha Self, Real Self
> Source of intuition, the still small voice
> Inner guide, voice of inner wisdom

The True Self can be thought of as a personal, inner counselor who operates through the Higher Mind and communicates with both the Higher Self in Spirit and the human mind, which functions through the brain and does not have direct access to the I AM Presence.

In order to commune with *An Síoraí*, the Eternal One, the soul strives to become one with the True Self through various disciplines and practices designed to increase awareness of the Divine and dissolve limits of human consciousness.

Goddesses & Gods

> Cosmic beings who can hold the consciousness of a certain divine quality, such as God of Freedom, God Harmony, Goddess of Liberty, Goddess of Light, or God of Gold.

Adepts, Ascended Masters & the Great White Brotherhood

Adepts are men and women from every culture who have answered the call of *An Síoraí*, the Eternal One, passing many profound initiations, and bonding with their True Self. Some remain in embodiment for a time and others ascend, depending upon their calling.

Ascended masters are adepts who have balanced their karma, fulfilled their divine plan, and reunited with their Higher Self.

The Great White Brotherhood is a universal body of adepts and ascended masters who, like Saint Germain, have dedicated their attainment to the liberation of souls from the bonds of the lesser self.

"White" refers to the pure white light surrounding their forms. Certain devotees of the highest spiritual truth are also members of the Brotherhood, which is very much a Sisterhood.

Ascended Master Saint Germain

After making his ascension in the year 1684, Saint Germain was granted a dispensation by the Great Law to once again take on a physical body so he might guide the monarchies of Europe in their necessary transition to more democratic systems of government.

Widely known as the "Wonderman of Europe," he appeared for decades as a man in his early forties, dazzling those whom he wished to assist with his diplomatic skills, alchemical feats, incomparable wisdom, boundless grace, and loving-kindness.

Despite his monumental efforts, stubborn monarchists failed to heed his warnings, and many fell in the horrific reign of terror during the French Revolution. Finally, after Napoleon's betrayal in the early nineteenth century, Saint Germain declared that he would not be seen for a hundred years.

In the twentieth century, the Master once again contacted embodied individuals, this time empowering them as his hands and feet in the physical, and as his messengers to deliver his spiritual teachings.

The *Twin Flames of Éire Trilogy* novels are the author's musings of what might transpire, should our dear Saint Germain gain a new dispensation to appear in a physical form suitable for face-to-face communion with his friends of ancient wisdom.

Acknowledgements

Every life is a journey through many planes of existence, both seen and unseen. Every person, place, or event we encounter on that journey is a teacher. Their lessons may bring us exquisite joy. Or they may challenge us to the very core of our beliefs about ourselves and others.

All are equally valuable because they form the warp and woof of the tapestry we weave that becomes the fabric of the life we create.

Gratitude for life's ups and downs allows us to observe the threads that belong to our partnership with the spirit of An Síoraí, the Eternal One, that lives in the deepest part of us. And, if we are wise, we will also acknowledge the many threads that others have woven into this miraculous creation we could not have fashioned alone.

I am blessed with colleagues Paula Kennedy Kehoe, James Bennett, and Theresa McNicholas who share my passion for publishing.

Special thanks to my dear friends Dónall Ó Héalaí and his father, Dr. Pádraig Ó Héalaí, for their priceless assistance with the Gaelic terms that speak to the beauty of the ancient Irish culture that inspired *The Twin Flames of Éire Trilogy.*

I have done my best to make faithful use of their suggestions. Any errors in spelling, usage, or pronunciation are mine alone.

These novels reach far back in time and point to a future that is still unfolding, which gives me the opportunity to gather several millennia of thanks and send them out to countless teachers and mentors for all the lessons, including more than a few dark nights.

The story of twin flames belongs to all of us. Thank you, Mother, for letting me tell one small part of it. And to my beloved Stephen, whether together or apart, I live in you as you live in me. Thank you for helping me finally understand what that means.

Cheryl Lafferty Eckl has played many roles since she began her career as a singer/actress in musical theatre. Award-winning author, mystical poet, professional development trainer, life coach, inspirational speaker, and retreat facilitator.

These days, her favorite role is *seanchaí*—Irish for storyteller.

If you ask, she'll tell you that it's her love of Ireland—its people, language, land, and culture—that continues to inspire characters and stories in thrilling novels that follow the trials and triumphs of twin flames who sometimes struggle and very often succeed in unlocking Love's mystery.

Learn more about Cheryl's books, videos and audios
at www.CherylEckl.com.